Running Through Deserts

by

Jill Thornton

To Rebecca
God bless!
Jill Thornton

PUBLISH AMERICA

PublishAmerica
Baltimore

ISBN: 1-4137-6620-X
PUBLISHED BY PUBLISHAMERICA, LLLP
www.publishamerica.com
Baltimore

Printed in the United States of America

Dedication

To all the missionaries, at home and abroad, who dedicate their lives to the spread of the Gospel.

Prologue

The jungle was silent except for the wind in the trees and the crackling fire in the settlements beneath them. The fire in a small pit cast dim, orange shadows on the shrubbery that was beside it, failing to penetrate the darkness of the forest beyond. The jungle birds had long ago ceased to cry out as did usually happen when the sun went down.

Small huts with walls made of palm leaves and grass roofs stood still in a clearing. Even with the fire dancing on the outer walls, the bright, clear sky gently outlined the huts with a silver varnish. The wall of the great jungle was a blue tint at the edge of the fields beyond the settlements, with only an occasional jungle cry reaching out from the mysterious abyss beyond. The wall was beautiful at night, but forbidden, as the members of the village knew well.

Suddenly, emerging from a hut on the edge of the village, a tall, graceful figure hurried through one of the fields toward the fire. It was a woman, about thirty years old, but she was not from the village. She wore modern clothes, and her long, blonde hair was easily noticeable in the darkness, despite the playful shadows that danced around her as she entered the area where the fire quietly blazed.

As she approached the fire, she found three figures sitting nearby. They were all men, taking in the night's beauties with humility. Their presence appeared ominous, but the way she watched them revealed how harmless they were.

One man was gently strumming a nameless tune on a guitar. He was a black man with bushy hair. He wore green cargo pants to deflect the night's chill, but the bow and arrow that sat on the log next to him were characteristic of his indigenous blood.

Another dark man stared effortlessly into the burning wood pile. His eyes were growing heavy, and every time he closed them to feel the fire's warmth on his face, his head bobbed and he tried to wake up.

The third was standing, and appeared to be waiting patiently for the woman. This man's skin was not dark like the other two, though. He was very tall and he, too, was blonde. His big, muscular form suggested that he had played football in high school, and that he was probably voted most valuable player. But the way he looked at the sky and breathed the jungle air into his lungs, it was obvious that he believed true value was in everything except himself.

The tall, blonde man stepped away from the wall he was leaning on as the woman came into view from the moonlit field. She paused briefly when she knew he saw her, but immediately began to move toward the hut again. Finally, the silence of the night air was broken, and she spoke to the white man.

"Is he asleep?" she said softly, in unaccented English.

"Just barely," the man replied. "He'll be awake once you go in there, though."

They stood there a moment, an uncomfortable silence between them. Neither one moved or spoke for what seemed like an eternity.

Finally, he said, "Are you gonna go in?"

"Yes, once you move away from the door."

It was a cold response, but he should have seen it coming and he absently stepped away from the entrance to the dark hut. He should have known she wouldn't go in until he had moved, but he was still adjusting to her peculiar mannerisms she seemed to have whenever he was around.

She avoided eye contact with him as she was engulfed in the blackness of the hut. She took a quick stride over to the lantern that hung from the fragile ceiling and slowly lit it, allowing only the smallest amount of light to brighten the room.

The room was lived in. It contained a desk that had been brought in from the outside world, as well as a couple of chairs randomly placed in different regions of the floor. Books were piled on the desk next to an old typewriter that looked like it had survived every major disaster known to man. Next to the chairs on the floor were old dishes that had been left for the ants to conquer. Overall, it wasn't homey, but then again, who said life in the jungle was comfortable?

The woman glanced at the room with a guilty grin. How could she leave it like this? At a time when showing organization and responsibility was vital to gain respect from the villagers, she was leaving a messy hut for three weeks.

She shrugged her shoulders and decided the time set aside for cleaning had been spent wisely. She had just returned from a dinner with the chief of the village. This was always a priceless time because it enabled her to continue planting roots in his circle. Slowly, throughout the years, she had convinced him that she meant no harm to his people. In fact, she was here to save their lives, but he always changed the conversation at that point. Just as well, she thought. God would open his heart some day.

The woman looked to the corner of the room where one of two hammocks was gently rocking back and forth. A small child slept soundly within the warm space, and she almost felt tempted to let him sleep. But this, she knew, would be a mistake.

If he woke up the next morning realizing that she had gone without saying their special prayer, then her absence would be more difficult over the next few weeks.

His little, dark body was squeezed into a ball and his arms were pressed snuggly under his chin. He was not snoring, but a slight wheezing steadily pulsated out of his nostrils. She frowned and reached down to stroke his cheek.

So precious and so fragile, all at the same time, she thought.

The boy's eyes slowly opened and he turned his head to stare at the person that had interrupted his dreamless sleep. He saw her, and slowly opened his mouth with a wide smile, revealing a large gap in his teeth where he had lost some only days before. She returned the warm smile as she remembered the days when she lost her baby teeth, some 24 years in the past.

He took her hand in his and waited to hear their prayer. She pulled her hair back with her hand and leaned over to his ear. She whispered with the volume of a hushed breeze, and said in his native language, "When the Lord shows me the stars, I will remember your sparkling eyes. And when He shows me the sun, I will remember your bright smile."

And she gave him a little kiss on the cheek and rose above him again. He gave a little nod, and drifted back into the sleep that she had drawn him from.

She turned to find that the tall man was standing in the doorway, his silhouette shading her from the orange glow beyond. She began to move around the room, tidying up a bit before her night departure. Papers were stuffed into the small, make-do night stand on the floor. The dishes were placed in an empty basin used for cleaning, and all the while she was whispering instructions to the man.

"I won't go unless I know that you'll always be watching him," she said firmly.

She seemed to be cleaning the room with the mere purpose of avoiding a face-to-face conversation with the man.

"He requires constant attention, especially with his asthma."

He nodded his head as though he had heard the speech a thousand times before. He knew she didn't want to leave, but he also knew that she preferred that he watch over the boy while she was gone. He was almost glad to see that she needed him, even if it was just for a baby-sitting job.

"He likes me. Everything will be fine," he told her gently, from across the room. "I'll have him push the heavy wheel barrows at the site."

She stopped abruptly and shot him a glance.

"That's not funny," she said.

"I know, I know. It was just a joke—"

He was interrupted by the man that had been playing the guitar by the fire. He was much shorter than the white man as he almost fit under the arm that the other was holding up while he leaned on the door frame. Despite the easy fit under, the taller man humbly removed his arm so that the other could enter. Now two silhouettes filled the doorway, and the dark man spoke in his native language.

"Excuse me, but we really must be going. The truck will be at the road in only an hour. We must give ourselves enough time to go on the trail."

"I'm ready," she replied, half-heartedly. She didn't want to go, but she picked up her enormous back-pack anyway, and walked out into the crisp night air that the confinement of the hut had averted.

The woman and the two native men began to make their way toward the field when the white man said, "Have a good trip."

She gave him a little wave as she continued on, into the darkness.

"And, Kathleen," he said. "You know that I'll take good care of him."

Her brisk walk stopped, and she turned to face him. They were several yards away, but he could see her relaxed face give only a slight grin.

She replied, "I know," and continued her journey.

The man watched as the three figures crossed the moonlit field and entered the jungle through a barely distinguishable opening in the silver wall of trees.

And they disappeared, immersed in the inky blackness, and the man said a prayer for the group as he walked inside the hut to watch over the child.

Los Angeles, California

Ella Levene stared blankly out the window of the office she stood in, her eyes looking beyond the crowds of people scurrying along the street below. Some of them raced their electric carts through groups of pedestrians that were hurrying to destinations of their own. Others were dressed in fanciful costumes: two men were wearing cowboy outfits while they talked on their cell phones. A woman dressed like a nun smoked a cigarette on the sidewalk before a man came out of the nearest building and motioned for her to return inside.

The overcast sky made the scene look somber and shallow, like watching a movie that had recorded a minute by minute account of the lives of Hollywood actors as they went from their trailers to the set. It was a whirlwind of talent, vanity, and creativity below her, but she paid no attention. She listened while the man behind her spoke in a wannabe-professional tone.

"Ella, do you hear what I'm telling you?" Ira Manning, the head of the studio, asked. "We can't continue this project until we either get a new director or find someone who will be able to handle your attitude. I think we may go with the first option."

The British beauty standing in his office was a director for one of his movies that was in pre-production. The film had not started yet because they couldn't find a lead actor to work with Ella Levene. Manning hated to tell her this, but the woman's temper was out of control and everyone she worked with was offended by it.

She continued to stare at nothing while she listened to the news that she was being fired. It was something that she had been expecting, but never really wanted to have happen. The last movie she'd directed had no feel, no bite. It had a script that covered every aspect of the human condition and she had turned it into her own private film. She had all but openly insulted the actors that were being paid top dollar to star in it, and this tore away at her soul as she knew that she would have quit show business altogether had it not been for the merciful directors she'd worked with in her acting days. Those directors had caused her to make the shift from an onscreen role to a directorial one.

Now, here she was, standing at the window of Manning's office while her plug was being pulled. She blinked for the first time in what seemed like years as she began to play with the thought of how she would go home and tell her family. Her husband, John, she knew, would be undoubtedly hardened by the fact that his wife had blown it.

Manning continued to ramble on about her future.

"Maybe if you just take a few months off. Take the kids on a relaxing vacation and drink some daiquiris by the pool. Work on anything but your job. I've seen plenty of talented actors and directors go through dry spells. Even if you produced an Oscar winner tomorrow, the chip you carry on your shoulder would still be there, and I can't afford for you to keep it. You've lost your edge, you're not the same ball of energy you were three years ago..."

And he rambled on. Ella wanted to cry, but her head was devoid of all tears. Her piercing green eyes looked at emptiness, and it was all she could do to keep from collapsing to the floor with exhaustion.

Finally, she spoke, her strong British voice betraying her disappointment.

"What if I just take a smaller script? I know I can do better. I just need a lighter storyline, and then we'll get back on track with—"

"No, Ella, you need a break. When was the last time you spent more than a week with your kids?"

This was true. Every time Ella had been with the children, she was surprised at how much they knew, how much smarter they were getting, and how perceptive they were. Freddy, her eight year old son, had been especially cold about her absence the last few months...

"Is it my problem people don't have tough skin?" she asked him. "I'm Mary Poppins compared to so many people in this business—"

"Ella, it's time to throw in the towel and take a break. I'm giving it to you as a gift, not a punishment."

"I won't give up," she told Ira. "I'll go on this damned break and then, when I return, I'll give you the best movie you've seen this decade."

She stormed towards the door, and as she opened it to leave, she turned back to Ira and said, "I'll be back in four months, a changed person. I'm thirty-five years old. My career is far from over."

"I hope you're right, and I wish the best for you, Ella," he replied. "But mark my words: if you come back, and you still have a short fuse and emotional baggage, I guarantee that your career will be over. The saddest part, though, is that you're the only one who is ruining it."

At that, she gave a slight nod and left the room.

Ella walked down the corridor of the studio, bewildered. She felt flustered and unable to grasp what was happening. How could they be so blunt about it? She had given her heart and soul to this business since she was eighteen years old, after she came to Hollywood from London. She had been the most beautiful actress to ever grace the silver screen, and she knew it. She never asked for more money than what was expected of her, and she got along beautifully with her co-workers. That was a time when movies and acting were everything to her.

She met her husband on the set of her third major movie, where he, too, was a hot commodity in the acting world at the time. They were going to be Hollywood's upcoming romantic couple, perfect in every way. They began to show up at premiers and other events together, were openly dating a month later, and within a year, John Tucker was down on one knee at the world premiere of their movie that would make them big. It was a time that meant big money, even bigger fame, and a promising future for both.

Ella Levene and John Tucker: "America's Sweethearts."

But that was ten years ago, and John had given up show business after that. As it turned out, he was painfully shy, and it was his entourage that had insisted on the red carpet proposal. In the end, they won, he gave a public proposal to Ella, and after their private-made-public wedding, he quit acting and turned to being a full-time husband and father, with a writing career in between.

This left the burden of the business on Ella's shoulders. She continued to make some movies, she won a few awards, and somewhere buried in all the chaos, she had two children. It was on her thirty-second birthday that she told John she was tired of being America's "sweetheart" and would try her luck at directing, and it was then that her soul began to slowly diminish, and she was gradually eaten alive by writers, producers, and even the actors themselves.

Ella grew a hard outer shell, and her demeanor changed when she entered a set. She boomed orders out to people she didn't even know, and had the dreaded director's days when she would spend twelve hours on a scene that she insisted was being done wrong.

The daily cigarette turned into the hourly cigarette, and cocktail hour was transformed into one perpetual drink that she found everywhere—a glass on the night stand, a flask in the drawer, a beer after shooting a scene. It had been three years since she had felt alive, and now all she felt in her was dead skin. It was like her organs had rotted away and all that remained were stunningly beautiful looks and the name she had made for herself. This break, in the end, would mean nothing to her.

Nothing.

She got into the backseat of a black sedan and looked absently out the window. The driver waited for directions, but she was silent. She was deep in thought, thinking of what to do for the next four months. Spending those months with her family was not Ella's idea of a vacation, especially since she barely knew them. If anything, she wanted to be somewhere to think, a place where she could be by herself and without interruption.

Living in Hollywood, and constantly being around people all day, made it difficult to comprehend that any place in the world existed where a person could merely sit in silence for an hour without being bothered. Especially since most of the world knew who she was, the possibility of getting away was almost non-existent.

"Where to ma'am?" the driver finally asked.

Ella hesitated for a moment, and watched as a crowd dressed for some sort of native movie walked by the car. They were all laughing, and she didn't recognize them, but something made her watch as the indigenous actors walked by the car. She suddenly remembered a movie she had done ten years before when the producers were trying to research Indian culture and history. They had gone to an agency somewhere in Darwin, Australia. The filming in Darwin itself had been the reason she'd insisted on buying a home there.

Maybe she could visit an Indian tribe or something. They were out in the middle of nowhere, and probably didn't have any electricity, so they wouldn't recognize her and she could at least be outside. She had heard of actors and actresses doing work with elephants or chimpanzees, or going to Africa to work with AIDS children. This could be her claim to fame, that she had spent time in a tribe with head hunters. Or whatever.

"Ma'am?"

"Take me home," she quickly replied. Of course! This would be her ticket to enlightenment. Her mind worked rapidly, and as the car drove away from the studio, she picked up her cell phone and started dialing. The person on the other end answered, and she spoke with a new found passion.

"Daryll, I'm off the movie, but listen. I'm going out of the country for a while and I need you to cancel everything on my calendar for the next couple of months. Make arrangements for a flight to Australia for me, John, and the kids. Yes, that's right, we're going to the Darwin Estate." A pause. "Apparently I need a break, and I think I know where to take one. The only problem will be to convince a Missions agency to let me go."

Darwin, Australia

"The life of a Christian is undeniably the most spiritually rigorous, exhausting, confusing, and strengthening way of living," Kathleen Newman said. Her young audience was watching her with big eyes. "But it is the most glorious and fulfilling experience a person can ever go through. A lot of times, it hurts to follow a path you're not comfortable with, and it hurts even more to gain wisdom. We see what we want in life, we move towards it, and we are constantly yanked back to what seems like the beginning. It seems like justification when we tell God what our plans are. I may have all the best motives for doing something, but in the end, it's what God wants me to do that takes me somewhere. And it's always somewhere different than what I had originally anticipated."

The small room of college-aged students stared at her blankly. She could tell they were completely lost after her opening remarks. The basis of their curriculum for the next two weeks had just been outlined in about five sentences and encompassed several themes of the Bible.

Too bad, she thought. *I'm still going for it.*

Kathleen glanced at the ceiling as though she were looking for an answer, and then focused her attention on the group again with a small grin. "The movie, *The Matrix*. How many of you have seen it?"

All hands went up.

"Okay, Neo wants to know what the matrix is, but in order to do so, he must choose to give up a life that he is familiar and comfortable with to embark on a journey that will answer all of life's questions. If he takes a blue pill, he can continue to live a life within his comfort zone. The option of taking a red pill will lead to something that is not easy, is not comfortable, and is not easily grasped by the human psyche, but is he willing to take that chance?

"He, of course, chooses the second pill because he has devoted his life to searching for the matrix. The pill takes him into a world that is painfully real. He's reborn, and while this life has wonderful privilege and wisdom, it brings the stunning realization that the life he lived before had been radically veiled. The life he knew is actually the matrix, and the life he has now chosen opens his eyes to what reality is: a dying breed of people caught up in a world of jobs, cars, money, food, fashion—anything that keeps them from seeing or wanting to believe the truth."

Kathleen said a prayer and asked God to give her the words.

"After I became a Christian, I saw things about the world that I didn't want to see. The children of God are living in a matrix. They live in a world that is real unto themselves, but in reality, I saw that we all live in a massive grid of spiritual warfare that will decide our fate. I saw people being weakened by alcohol and drugs, their lives being decided by the evil hand that works on them. The worst part about it is that they don't even know that they are pawns in a game whose sole purpose is to separate the good from the bad."

The students in the room seemed convicted, especially since most of them were here because they had recently seen the errors of their ways and knew exactly what she was talking about. Kathleen could tell they didn't want to hear it, but they needed to. It was nothing they didn't know, but they had to understand.

"You're all here because you want to help people to see Jesus," she continued. "You want to go out into the world and make a difference. You are all vehicles for the Lord's use; you just have to let Him take the controls. I know you've heard it before, but you must step aside to let His plan flow through you. In order to do that, you need to understand and respect the difference between believers and non-believers, the matrix and reality.

"Non-believers are consumed by anything and everything. They submerse themselves in anything to take their minds off of that red pill, that leap of faith, that plunge into a new, unfamiliar life. Got a problem, have a drink. Make a mistake, blame someone else. Everyday eats away at their souls, and every morning they feel a bigger void. They can't pinpoint it, because then it would be just that easy to remedy it. Some people live each day by a thread, and while others do a good job hanging on, they know that deep down, they don't know anything at all. The non-believers run, but don't know where they are going.

"The believers, on the other hand, are quite the opposite. We go through some hard times. Actually, hard times is an understatement—seemingly unbearable times is more like it, but that's because we know what we're up against. We gain wisdom through life's hard earned lessons, but don't realize it until we are out of those hard times. Evil lies to us, tells us we are alone, and tries its tenacious tricks on us like it does to the rest of the world. But, like it says in Corinthians, we are wasting away on the outside, but on the inside we are being replenished and renewed, every day.

"We don't need to run anymore. The search is over, we have found the remedy to our pain, and it is the cross. Always remember that our reality is different than a non-believer's, but always be willing to reach out to them using the pain and knowledge that you have had to endure using only the strength of God. Be weak in order to be strong, and don't ever think that you know what will happen."

Kathleen sat down in the nearest seat as the worship leader stepped up to the front of the room and began to play a song about Jesus' death on the cross. Her heart was pounding. She was pretty sure she was unable to remember anything she had just told the group, due partially to the adrenaline rush.

Doubts started running through her mind. Sometimes she had to remind herself of the things that she told other people. She had a deep fear of misleading people, and she was always a little uneasy about telling these younger groups about hard elements of the Christian faith, such as listening to God's plan and stepping outside of the comfort zone that every person has marked around them. But she relaxed again as she faced the fact that God had been with her through the entire speech. The doubts slowly dissolved to nothing as she focused on the students' worship time.

The music was playing loud now, and all the kids were standing and raising their hands with praise towards Heaven. She closed her eyes and started to sing as she remembered the day she had been called to the tiny country of Vanuatu. She had been in a room within this very building that rested on the outskirts of Darwin, Australia. Her prayers had gone on for days when she finally looked down at her piece of paper and found that she was writing "Vanuatu" on the line that asked what country the applicant was being called to go to.

Kathleen had heard of the small island nation through the organization that she was working for called Tribal Missions. Apparently, the South Pacific country had once been a group of islands that missionaries boldly approached in the nineteenth century, only to find themselves being eaten for dinner. This, obviously, was not why Kathleen chose to go there.

Kathleen Newman had come to Tribal Missions seven years

previous as an intern. After graduating with an anthropology degree from Oregon State, she decided to enter the Missions field and reach the unreached people groups of the world. So few within the American population knew of the many indigenous tribes throughout the world, but Kathleen knew about them, and more importantly, so did God.

At the age of twenty-two, Kathleen flew to Darwin and joined the South Pacific Branch of Tribal Missions, where she took classes and training in linguistics for one year. The primary goal would be to enter a tribe, learn its language, teach its inhabitants how to read, and many years down the line a written Gospel could be translated into the tribal language.

When Kathleen came to the tribe at the young age of twenty-three, the book of Galatians had already been published into Tanna North, the language of the people group she was living with. The only problem was that among the North Tannese population, literacy was at one percent, so an entire book from the Bible had been published, but none of its speakers could use it. That was what Kathleen was working on now, some six years later. The North Tannese that had become Christians were open to literacy, and knew how to read and write some words, but until the chief of the village approved classes, Kathleen would spend most of her days translating books and preparing curriculums for classes that didn't exist yet.

Her heart was heavy for warm cultures that had been corrupted by the modern, Western world. When she was still living in America, she cringed when she saw her college friends going to wild parties. She watched television, and felt the burden that pressed on her heart as she saw sex, alcohol, and pure vanity control the lives of the millions of spectators that viewed the magic box.

The ni-Vanuatu, which is what the island inhabitants called themselves, had been on their islands for hundreds of years, and yet the Western world had found its way to their gullible doorstep. During World War II, the American

soldiers came with their radios and other more technologi-
cally advanced items that the ni-Vanuatu saw and
immediately desired.

Kathleen's heart had dropped with shame and sadness when
she learned that the society she had grown up in had already
made its way to the unknowing souls of the South Pacific. The
Lord told her their name, and she listened, even though her
mind occasionally glanced back at the stories of former
missionaries ending up in a large soup bowl. Still, she knew she
could do anything with the strength of the Lord, even if it meant
sleeping in a jungle with a previously hostile people group.

The village had become her home, and now she smiled as a
single tear rolled down her face while she worshipped. It
delighted her heart to think that she was only just a visitor in this
room, with new loved ones waiting for her back in the tribe. The
Lord was so wonderful for giving her a beautiful people to share
His love with, and while there were still countless barriers to
overcome, she raised her hands higher as she sang to the God
that would eventually open the hearts of a ni-Vanuatu tribe by
speaking in Tanna North.

Alice Walker opened the sliding glass door of her office and
stepped out to make her way across the courtyard. This garden
was the outdoor heart of the Tribal Missions headquarters,
South Pacific Branch, located in Darwin. She was headed for
another room on the opposite end of the courtyard that was
covered by a large banyan tree which shaded the ground with
its outstretched limbs. It was the perfect climbing tree with its
vines dangling throughout the space beneath its gigantic
branches. On the ground underneath the leafy ceiling were
stone paths that ran throughout different parts of the courtyard,
leading in all directions. Some paths lead to solitary benches that
were hidden from view by thick, green ferns and lush bushes
that had pink and orange flowers growing off of them.

The building itself had been constructed around the big tree. All of the classrooms for teaching had a sliding glass door that walked into the courtyard. Most of the offices for staff members were on the second floor, and they had a direct view into the grand tree's maze of branches and vines. The dormitories were in a separate building where one could look out their window and see the view of the main building: a two story structure with a gigantic tree rising from the center.

Alice continued down the path toward the main conference room at the west end of the courtyard. Her heels made a tapping sound on the hard surface, breaking the silence of the serene feeling that was resting upon the garden. She could hear talking as she approached the room, and when she arrived, she saw that the large group had broken into small groups. She stared through the screen door, looking for Kathleen Newman.

Everyone was bowing their heads with their eyes closed while one person per group was praying out loud. With all the people praying, she was unable to figure out what the main prayer request was, but since Kathleen had been the speaker for the day, she assumed the prayer was probably for people groups that had not heard the Gospel yet.

Finally, Alice saw her sitting in a group very near to the door. Her head was bowed, but her eyes were not closed. On a normal occasion, Alice would have waited until the prayer time was over, but her news was too exciting and urgent, so she gently tapped on the door pane of the frame.

Most of the people in the room were too involved in their prayer, but some looked up at the door, including Kathleen. Alice smiled and waved for her to come outside. Her silver-gray hair was shining in the partial sunlight that was breaking through the banyan tree, revealing her fifty-five years of age. Her clenched teeth as she smiled, and the way she motioned for Kathleen to come over, showed that she had a young and vibrant spirit.

Kathleen rose from her chair and quietly made her way to the door, stepping out into the afternoon heat. Alice was already walking down the path towards her office as Kathleen quickened her pace to catch up and walk along side her friend and mentor. The two walked silently through the courtyard, trying not to disturb the people who were sitting quietly on the concealed benches.

The courtyard was a wonderful place to meditate and pray, especially on such a warm afternoon like this one, but since the majority of the people casually walking through it were usually eighteen or nineteen years old, the solitary benches heard a lot of background noise from excited teenagers.

The women walked into the air conditioned office, silently sliding the door closed to keep the heat out. Kathleen looked around the room and saw that the desk was engulfed in a sea of books and papers. The walls were decorated with indigenous art. Bows, arrows, and paintings lined the largest wall, and a huge map of the South Pacific was posted in the space behind the desk. There were small markings on the map, every other one being a different color. Kathleen had seen the map a dozen times and she still couldn't figure out what the color coding system indicated.

This was the office of Alice Walker, head of Tribal Missions' South Pacific Branch. On a global level, Tribal Missions was an international organization that committed its money and its participants to bringing the news of Jesus to indigenous peoples around the world. There were headquarters all over the globe in Western China, the Middle East, Central Africa, Brazil, Hong Kong, and Nicaragua.

The Darwin office was in charge of overseeing the missionaries that resided in the South Pacific and Australia. There were hundreds of indigenous tribes throughout the islands in the South Pacific, and Vanuatu alone was home to a population of tribes with more than a hundred different indigenous languages. To have Kathleen living with one of those tribes was priceless, as all the missionaries who dedicated their lives to God were.

Kathleen sat on the couch in the room while her boss sat

nervously in the rolling chair behind her desk. She noticed how Alice was fidgeting with her hands as she usually did when she didn't want to say something, so Kathleen tried to lighten the mood by talking about the class.

"They get younger every year, don't they?"

"Who?" asked Alice.

"The students. I mean, they're all so bright-eyed and bushy-tailed, aren't they? They're ready to go out and save the world from evil. It's refreshing, but I still feel older every time I come to speak at these things."

Alice gave a nervous laugh and continued rubbing her palms together.

"Kathleen, I just had a rather remarkable meeting with someone. I've been praying for something like this to happen for a long time now, and my heart just really tells me that you are the one that is going to be an instrument."

"Alice, what are you talking about?"

Alice finally stopped wringing her hands together. "Do you know Ella Levene?"

What does anything have to do with Ella Levene? Kathleen thought.

"Well not personally," Kathleen laughed, "but I was a big fan before I started living away from movie theatres."

The last time she had even heard the name was about six years ago. The actress had been the most famous star of Kathleen's time, but once she had moved to the jungle, she had not thought much about rich movie stars and Hollywood actors.

"Well, Ella Levene was just in this office, asking if there was any way she could spend time in a tribe," Alice responded.

Kathleen frowned and said, "Okay…"

"Do you know what she told me?"

"I can't even begin to imagine."

"She is working on a movie about missionaries. Her studio has sent her here to do some research about missionary life. She wants to portray missionary life on the big screen!"

"Don't you mean expose?" Kathleen said, glumly. She knew what the next question was, so she immediately shut the door on it. Her face got red as she erupted into a flow of rejection.

"No. Uh-uh. Do you know how many people will follow her onto that island? We'll have paparazzi clicking away from within the jungle, helicopters swooping over the village with video cameras. Not to mention the publicity the tribe would receive. This is no way to 'portray' missionary life. The chief will ban us from the village. For good!"

Alice quietly sat at her desk while she gave Kathleen a moment for the initial shock to subside. Kathleen closed her eyes and shook her head as she walked to the sliding door and looked out at the serene courtyard. Suddenly, the tree-covered garden seemed more like an escape route than a place for meditating. Alice's voice eventually broke the silence, and the words of wisdom from this respected woman made their way to Kathleen's ears.

"I know you want the best for the tribe, but you have to trust me on this. I turned her down the moment she asked me if I could help her, but she seems to understand our hesitations and has promised that no one will be following her. She hasn't been in front of the camera in years, so the public has not seen her face in quite a while."

Kathleen gave a side glance in surprise as Alice continued.

"That's right. She's a director now. And if anyone can show her what a missionary does, it's you. You're out there, Kathleen. You have assimilated into the culture, and you have already been a tool in converting several ni-Vanuatu to Christ. You set the boundaries with everyone you meet, and the village is far enough away that no one would find you, assuming they even tried. I want you to pray about this. I won't make you, but this could be a great opportunity to get the Gospel planted in the entertainment industry, and I can't imagine a better person than you to get the famous Ella Levene to see the light and get the Word out."

Kathleen was convicted now.

Man she's good, she thought.

Alice always knew how to calm a rash temper. Ever since she had known her, Kathleen respected Alice and always wanted to make her proud. In the earlier years, Alice had taken Kathleen under her wing when cultural adjustment and life away from civilization would wear down on the young missionary. Being a woman was hard, but being a woman in a tribe in the jungle was even harder.

Kathleen kept her gaze on the garden and sighed.

"Let me pray about it, please?"

"Take your time," Alice said. "You've got until Ms. Levene's return."

"When is that?"

"About an hour."

The Friday sun made its way toward the horizon. It gave the sandy beach an orange glow, but the people on it were not affected by the hint of its descent into the west. The water lapped lazily on the sand as though it was bored and couldn't think of anything better to do. Some children were playing with their sand buckets and shovels, trying desperately to keep their castle alive by building a moat as the water flowed in and out of the kingdom they had so intricately designed. Many people were simply lying on their towels or talking to the friends that had accompanied them to the beach.

It was this active and lively place where Kathleen Newman sat, crunched into a ball with her knees up to her chest. She held them with her arms, and her head rested on top. Her body faced the bay, but her head was looking south, down the beach, at all of the families that had come for a quick rest-and-relaxation time before they had to hurry home and prepare for weekend events.

She slowly closed her eyes and listened to the laughing children as they jumped on their giant castle in defeat. Pretty soon, she heard playful shouts that prompted her to open her eyes, discovering that the once beautiful castle had now been transformed into weapons used for a sand fight. The children picked up fistfuls of sand and chased each other in and out of the water while valiantly throwing the clumps of dirt.

God, what should I do? she prayed. *I can't jeopardize the lives of the tribe, but Alice is right. This opportunity is once in a lifetime. It's just that, it could go very good, or it could go just as bad. I guess it's up to You. This is a leap of faith for me. You know whether or not the tribe will be exposed, because You have already been there. So, I give the decision to You. I know You will reveal the answer in Your time.*

She suddenly glanced at her watch, the one that she only wore when on the mainland, and rose from her place on the beach. She walked back to the main street as she took one last glance at the children. They were digging deep holes in the ground now, most likely for burying each other. She smiled at them and turned to head back to the missionary base where Alice Walker was waiting for an answer.

Headquarters

Ella Levene and her two children walked into the main office of the Darwin base. It was getting to be later in the afternoon and the building seemed surprisingly quiet compared to the busy place it was a few hours earlier. There was no one in the main lobby so she took each child by the hand and walked towards the door that had taken her to Alice Walker's office before.

"Mommy, I'm hungry," said Sara Tucker. She was six, and at the perfect age to be too young and too smart all at the same time. She walked by her movie star mother without a care in the world, pulling Ella's arm back and forth as they made their way across the lobby.

"What did I tell you before we came?" Ella asked with traces of agitation in her voice.

Freddy Tucker, Sara's eight year-old brother, replied, "If we whine or complain at any time during this trip, you'll never take us anywhere ever again."

"That's right. And what else? Sara?"

Sara crinkled her nose at her mother. "If we tell anyone who we are or who our mom and dad are, you're gonna have a nervous breakdown and ship us away to Chuck and Stu's."

"That's Timbuktu. And I'm serious, you guys had better behave if you ever want to go anywhere with your mum again. So be good!"

She proceeded to drag them through a set of double doors and down the hall when Alice Walker emerged from an office in front of them. She smiled widely and said, "Hello there! Welcome back! And who are these beautiful children you brought?"

Ella replied, indifferently, "Freddy and Sara. Did she say yes?" She was referring to Kathleen, who at the moment was still absent.

Alice kept her grand smile and said, "Why don't we wait in the lounge while she gets back. There were some slight reservations that she had, so we can wait for her. Then you can plead your case."

Ella ran her fingers through her rich, dark brown hair as she subtly rolled her eyes.

What is the problem? she thought.

It would only be for a week or two, and since her most recent movies had barely made it on to the screen, the media had all but dismissed her off the face of the planet. Paparazzi shouldn't even be a concern, but then again, maybe the jungle woman thought Ella was still one of the most successful celebrities in Hollywood.

The four of them stepped into the empty lounge and had a seat. Freddy looked around, taking it all in. It was a big room with several heavily padded couches and a table at the front. There was a coffee pot sitting by a sliding glass door that seemed to open up into a jungle. He let go of his mother's hand to move closer and get a better view.

"Freddy, please stay on the couch by me," she said. She didn't sound very authoritative, but rather like she was trying to show that she was a mother. It was a half-hearted remark, so he continued toward the door.

"Freddy—"

Alice intervened. "It's a closed off garden if he wants to explore a little bit. Also, most of the students have left for the evening to go to dinner in the downtown area."

"I don't think that is such a great idea," Ella replied as she watched her oldest son head for the door. She looked at Alice and whispered, "He finds trouble."

"He's a boy. I'm sure he'll be fine. Do you want to go with him Sara?"

Sara was sitting cozily on the couch, running her fingers over Ella's hand. "That's okay. I want to stay with mommy." And she continued observing the lines in her mother's soft palms.

Ella shifted uncomfortably in her seat. It didn't feel right bringing her private life into this woman's lounge. But Alice was a Christian, and they all seemed like good people, so what was the harm?

"They never get to see me, so my hands are a fascination when I'm around," Ella said, trying to make light of her poor parental skills. Alice gave a hearty laugh, and Ella turned to her distracted son who was still standing in front of the door and said, "Freddy-love, you may go out there for five minutes. Don't get into any trouble!"

The boy walked out into the mesmerizing jungle and shut the door behind him.

There was still a good amount of light seeping in through the branches as Freddy walked down the narrow path. He looked way up into the trees only to find that it wasn't a forest at all. It was one huge tree, growing right out the middle of the building.

Cool, he thought.

He continued to walk down the path as he watched the thick branches hold against the soft breeze that made all the other plants come to life. He imagined himself climbing along the big limbs like a monkey and sitting up there all by himself. It would be the perfect place to hide and watch people.

The idea was tempting and he was immediately devising his plan on how to get to the top of the tree. He made his way through a maze of stone paths until he reached the center of the courtyard. He found the tree trunk and walked around it. It was so big! He looked for a branch to hold on to, but found that the lowest branches were still very far above his head.

If I were a grown-up, I could climb this thing in two seconds, he thought.

His eyes drifted up toward the entanglement of branches and his stare stopped at an open window on the second floor. It led directly into the tree!

Freddy glanced back in the direction of the lounge and listened for his mother. The conversation they were having was barely audible through the closed door and cluster of bushes, so he turned to his right and headed for the other side of the courtyard. He made his way down a wider path and swerved in and out of turns and curves that took him to another sliding door. He pulled on the handle and it opened easily.

Yes!

He entered a room that seemed to be some sort of classroom. Freddy was home-schooled, so he had never actually been inside a classroom, causing him to take a brief moment to observe. He then darted between the desks and chairs, and walked through another door that led into a hallway.

The hallway had posters with writing, crosses, and pretty sunset pictures on the walls. He looked to the left and headed to the door marked "Stairs." This was going to be a piece of cake. He would get into the tree, and when his mom would come out looking for him, he could watch her and have a little giggle. He would reveal himself once she started to cry.

Freddy headed up the dark stairwell and entered the second floor hallway. The long, darkening hall was eerily quiet, and the boy began to have second thoughts when suddenly, he saw another open door. He walked over to it and glanced inside. It was the room with the open window!

Jeez, he thought. *Aren't these people scared someone will steal something if they keep they're doors unlocked?*

He didn't care, as long as he could get into that tree. He walked into the room hesitantly. His heart was pounding so hard that he felt like everyone in the world could hear it. It was darker than the lounge because the sunlight was behind this side of the building, so he had to squint at the contents of the office. There was a big map of the world on the wall, and a desk with a computer near the window. There was another picture of a sunset, this time with a cross in the same photo.

What is it with these people and their sunset posters?

Freddy looked at the open window skeptically and finally decided he wanted to go for it, so he briskly walked behind the desk and stared out into the courtyard. The branches were further away then he had thought, but there was a vine only a foot away. He could be like Tarzan and swing to the branch!

As Freddy stepped up on the desk chair and put his other knee on the window sill, he reached for the vine. Got it! He had both knees up on the window sill now and held on to the vine with two hands. The branch he wanted to sit on was a little far out, but he figured he could do it. Boy, would his mom be surprised when she found him way up in this tree.

He held his breath and pushed himself far out into the air, his feet dangling in space. He held onto the vine with all of his strength and headed straight for the big branch he was aiming for. But he floated back to the window, so he pushed off the building wall with his feet and swung toward the branch again. He was going really fast, and he was almost there when—

The vine broke.

Freddy flew into the branch and hit it just well enough so that he could clutch it with his arms. He hit the thick limb with his chest and he could feel all the air get knocked out of him. It was so thick and he couldn't hold on for very long. Somewhere below his furiously kicking feet, he found another branch, and he was able to hoist himself up onto the branch that he had collided with. His heart was pounding hard now, and he hugged the branch with all his might.

He started to cry.

"So there's no electricity?" Ella asked. She had just listened to Alice explain the basic ways of living in the Vanuatu tribe that she would most likely be visiting.

"Well, there is a small maintenance building with a generator that lights up the room for the man that uses it now. He needs the light after the sun goes down for the project he is working on, and Kathleen has found it useful for when she has a lot of work to do after dark."

Ella looked at Alice like she had just told her something very obvious.

Of course electricity is useful. Maybe that's why the rest of the world has it, she said to herself.

Ella looked down at Sara, who was slumping on the couch. Her daughter was obviously bored now and had started to fidget with a loose thread in the seat cushion. Ella was also getting tired of being in this place.

"When is she going to be here?" Ella asked with a whining tone.

Alice shrugged. "Kathleen only wears a watch when she comes to the mainland, so she could have forgotten that she has it. She doesn't need one in the jungle. Time just isn't important there."

"Good god, why?" Ella said. Suddenly, she opened her eyes very wide and put her hand over her mouth.

She had used the Lord's name in vain.

Embarrassed, she waved her other hand at Alice, waiting for a ruler to be slapped down on the back of it. "I'm so sorry—"

Alice smiled, and said, "Its okay, it happens all the time. No one's perfect. Besides, we get college-aged students coming through here all the time. It takes some of these kids months to break bad habits involving their language."

Ella suddenly remembered Freddy and looked out the door, into the courtyard. The light was going fast now and it had been nearly fifteen minutes since he had left the room.

"Sara, will you go fetch your brother for me?" Ella said.

The little girl jumped to her feet excitedly and ran for the door.

"I'll bring him back, Mommy, don't worry," Sara said while she opened the glass door. As she shut it, she yelled at the top of her lungs, "Alfred Tucker!"

Ella squinted her deep eyes in embarrassment and glanced at the hall door with impatience. She needed a cigarette and she wasn't sure how much longer she could wait for the missionary. This was beginning to be a project that was not worth the time. Alice started talking about the food and the bugs, all the problems missionaries were struck with when they first entered a tribe. Ella nodded with indifference and pointed to the coffee pot.

"Is there any left in that thing?"

Kathleen came into a dark, deserted room through the back door. Her face was dry from the salty air at the beach and her hair was crawling down her neck. She felt horrible, partially because she still didn't know what to do about a movie star coming with her to the tribe, and also because she knew she looked awful and she was about to meet one of the most beautiful women in the world.

She shrugged her shoulders and decided she didn't care. Life was not about looks, anyway, so who was she to worry about what her hair was doing? She walked into the hallway that wrapped around the building and noticed that one of the classroom doors was open.

That was odd.

All the staff and students should be having dinner. Kathleen walked into the room where all the desks were and saw that the sliding glass door was wide open, too. Her heart skipped a beat as she began to think of who might be in the building. Suddenly, she heard a little girl shouting in the courtyard.

Kathleen stepped into the twilight heat and shaded courtyard, listening in the direction the voice was coming from.

"Alfred!" the girl shouted.

It seemed to be in the direction of the center of the yard, but Kathleen couldn't be sure. She made her way down a windy path until she reached the banyan tree's trunk, and it was there that she saw the little girl looking up into the tree. The girl was about five or six years old and had on a little blue dress. She turned to the tall woman that approached her and gave a big smile.

"Hello," Kathleen said with a curious grin on her face.

"Hello. What is your job?"

Kathleen knelt down at eye level with the little girl, and replied, "I'm a missionary in the jungle. I help people."

"Neat! Then you can help my brother."

Kathleen tilted her head to the side in surprise, and said, "Okay, what's wrong with him?"

"He's caught in the tree."

The little girl pointed to the tree's branches and Kathleen let her eyes follow the finger. Sure enough, there was a little boy hugging a big branch, about thirty feet up and another twenty feet away from the main trunk. He seemed to be frozen to the limb and he had his eyes closed tightly.

Kathleen immediately went into action. She tied her long, blonde hair back in a ponytail while she spoke rapidly to the little girl.

"What is your name?" she asked.

"Sara."

"Okay, Sara, are your parents around here?"

"Yes."

"Why don't you go run and get them. Right now, got it?"

"Okay," Sara said happily, and skipped down the path to the lounge.

Kathleen rubbed her hands together while she looked at the lowest branch of the tree about four feet above her head. She stepped back and then forward again, jumping upward. As she kicked her leg off the trunk of the tree, she lunged for the thick limb with two hands. While pulling herself up onto the first limb, she was already preparing to lunge for another, gracefully repeating the process. She was trying to talk to the boy as she climbed.

"Are you hurt? Can you talk to me?"

Silence.

"Don't worry, I'll get you down."

Kathleen finally made it to the branch that the little boy was hugging. She slowed her movements down significantly and began to make her way across the limb to the child.

Sara burst through the doors excitedly, startling both Ella and Alice. She ran over to her mother and pulled furiously at her arm, trying to get her to follow.

"It's Freddy!" Sara yelled, out of breath.

Ella jumped up quickly. "What happened? Where is he?"

Sara was giggling. "He's stuck in the tree!"

"What?!"

Ella bolted out the door and down the path with Alice and Sara hot on her heels. She was running down the curving path when she realized she didn't know where she was going. Suddenly, Sara ran past her, grabbing her hand on the way. The small girl led her mother through a maze of bushes and ferns when they burst into an open area.

It was the middle of the courtyard, and a giant tree was growing out of its center. Up above, Ella saw her son grasping a limb while a woman shimmied across to him. They were so high up!

"Who is up there with him?" Ella asked in a panic.

"Don't worry," Sara told her mother. "She helps people in the jungle. She's a monkey-lady."

Kathleen was close to the boy now, her body only two feet from where his head was resting on the branch. The whole limb was surprisingly firm, and Kathleen momentarily thought that perhaps she could walk across the sturdy branch if she wanted to. She decided that could wait for another time.

"Are you okay?" she said in a quiet voice.

"No," the boy answered. He gave a little sniffle, indicating that he'd been crying.

"Are you hurt?"

"No."

"Then why aren't you okay?"

"Cause I can't move. I'm scared." He began to whimper.

Kathleen sat on the branch for a moment and let him cry a little bit. She couldn't see his face since his cheek was resting against the branch, but she could tell he was eight or nine years old. He had on a white tee-shirt with dinosaurs on the back of it. She moved a little closer and finally decided that she couldn't wait for his tears to stop. It would be dark soon, making an easy descent more difficult.

She calmly said, "I'm Kathleen. What's your name?"

There was no answer. From down on the ground, she heard a woman with a British accent yell, "Freddy?"

"Freddy. Is that your name?"

The boy nodded his head, but still faced away from his rescuer.

"So, Freddy, you like dinosaurs? The velociraptor is my favorite dinosaur. What's yours?"

Freddy sniffled a little and finally turned his head toward Kathleen.

"T-Rex."

His face was smeared with gray streaks from the tears running down his dirty face. He looked at this stranger for the first time and became immediately relaxed. She was smiling at him as she held her hand out. She didn't seem to be scared at all, and this made him comfortable. He looked down at the ground and then back at her again, slowly extending his hand.

Kathleen took it and said, "The T-rex is a really cool dinosaur, but do you know why I like raptors?" Freddy shook his head, and Kathleen continued. "Because some people think that they were able to climb trees, and I love anything that climbs trees."

"What about people who get stuck in them?"

"They're even better, because then *I* get to climb trees and rescue them. Now, I want you to follow me back along this branch, okay?"

Freddy nodded, and they slowly made their way back to the trunk.

She continued with her story. "My son gets stuck in trees all the time, and I always have to go and get him, so I'm an expert at getting little boys out of trees."

They were now at the trunk and Kathleen pulled Freddy very close to her. The yard was getting darker and more difficult to see, but she was sure that she could do it.

She looked him in the eyes, and said, "This is where I need you to be very strong and very brave. I'm going to turn around, and I want you to wrap your arms around my neck really tightly. I'll take us both down, but you have to hold on with all your might, got it?"

Freddy frowned, but nodded anyway. Kathleen gracefully turned around for him to hold on to her. When she could tell he had a good grip, she said a prayer and began to make her way down the tree.

He was heavy, but she was strong and used every branch she could for footholds, especially since her upper body had lots of extra weight on it. Freddy was holding on firmly and breathing heavily. Kathleen's muscles burned as she made her way down the banyan tree. She tried to think about something other than the pain.

"Freddy, how'd you get in the tree?"

"I swung out the window with a vine and it broke. Then I tried to crawl to the middle and I almost fell, so I didn't move for a really long time. Then you came."

"Just do me a favor. The next time you want to play George of the Jungle, pick a tree with a ladder, okay?"

Ella watched the entire scene in horror. It was painful to be at the bottom and not able to help, but she was sure that she wouldn't have been able to do what the "monkey-lady" was doing now. She had not the strength nor the grace to descend a tree with a small person on her back.

"Don't worry, Ms. Levene," Alice Walker was saying, "Kathleen is very strong. She has climbed many trees in her day."

Ella was not paying attention, though. She kept waiting for the woman's foot to slip and they both come plummeting to the ground. But that never happened, and at the lowest branch, Freddy got off Kathleen's back, and she lowered him to Ella's opened arms below.

Ella held Freddy in her arms and said, "What were you doing up there?! I told you not to get into any trouble!"

Sara stood by her hysterical mother and said, "Are you gonna ship Freddy to Chuck and Stu's, Mommy?"

"Sara—"

She started to scold her daughter when Freddy's rescuer jumped out of the tree from the limb above. She was tall, blonde, and much more athletic-looking up close rather than in a tree. The woman smiled as though nothing out of the ordinary had happened, and she walked over to where Freddy was clutching his mother as she held him.

"Boys will be boys," the woman said. "It's a good thing it wasn't a palm tree. That would have been a little more difficult."

"Ella Levene, this is Kathleen Newman. Kathleen, I want you to meet Ella Levene," said a relieved Alice. "She has an interest in accompanying you to a Vanuatu tribe."

Kathleen's heart sank and she frowned. She had forgotten about that. A decision was supposed to have been made, but the tree incident had distracted her. She, of course, had recognized Ella Levene, but it didn't click until Alice had spoken.

"Just a small visit," Ella said to Kathleen, noticing the tense look on her face. The missionary and the actress stood face to face like the odd couple. One was strong, ruggedly dressed, and had tanned, rough skin. The other was in a fancy suit with high heels and a fair complexion. Her hair was a silky texture and her face was covered in make-up. Overall, both were beautiful, depending on which option was preferred: durable tomboy or elegant princess.

"I have a few concerns," Kathleen said. "But I leave in two weeks, so you have that much time to get a plane ticket and visa if you decide to come."

Ella nodded and looked at Sara standing next to her. Then she looked at Freddy who she had placed on the ground. They both watched her longingly, not wanting her to go. But she brushed aside their desperate stares and turned back to Kathleen.

"Right, I'll take the kids back to their father and we can meet up for dinner and have a little chat. What do you say?"

The kids whined, and Kathleen looked surprised at Ella's indifference, but she nodded her head in agreement, so they decided on a restaurant. Alice led the way out of the courtyard and they all headed back to the main lobby. It was dark now, and the crickets made a low hum somewhere in the floral walls of the path.

Freddy ran up to hold Ella's hand, and said, "I'm sorry. If I promise to never climb any trees ever again, will you stay with us and Dad?"

Ella ignored the question, but held his hand tighter. They all continued to walk in silence through the building and into the parking lot where a car and driver were waiting for Ella and the kids. They got in the car and made their way home.

Kathleen had heard Freddy's remark and stared in disbelief as the car pulled out of the lot and drove down the street. It turned left at the signal, leaving Alice and Kathleen alone in the parking lot.

Alice looked at Kathleen with a kind face, and said, "It's not my decision. Let me know in the morning." And she, too, got in her car and went home.

Kathleen walked toward the dorms, but decided to sit on the curb and pray instead. She watched as the night came, leaving the orange and yellow sky to fight for life while the midnight blue darkness approached from the east. It was a quiet night, and she saw the first stars making their debut as she began to pray.

Oh God, how can I separate this family? They seem to need their mother more than anything right now. What could taking her away for so long possibly do?

When a person prays to God, there is a great deal of listening involved with the talking. Sometimes one can hear His booming voice while other times a mere breeze can represent His presence.

But Kathleen heard an answer in her heart, and it simply said, *Kid, there's only one way to find out.*

Darwin Estate

John Tucker stood on the balcony that overlooked the beach behind their house. The night had turned cold and the stars shined bright in the clear sky. It was a much clearer night than any found in Beverly Hills. This was his favorite place to smoke a cigarette, and a little ashtray sat on the wrought-iron banister, waiting for the trickle of ash to fall in its place. John inhaled the smoke deeply, then slowly let it out into the crisp, cool air.

He was married to the infamous Ella Levene, and was most known for his successful, but brief, career. He was tall, skinny, had dark hair, and had been a teenage heart-throb a decade before. Unfortunately, all the publicity and media attention had outweighed the optimism of becoming incredibly famous, so after he and Ella were married and had Freddy, he quit acting and decided to test his hidden desire to write.

Through the glass-paned double doors leading out to the balcony, he could hear his wife inside their room. She was getting ready for dinner with the missionary, and John rolled his eyes as he smudged his cigarette into the ashtray. Ella was going to dinner with a woman who worked with naked people. Was a one hour make-up session really that important? He took one last look at the view from the balcony and stepped inside the bedroom, closing the doors behind him.

"You have a commitment to your family," he said out loud while he walked to the closet. "Your kids miss you. Hell, *I* miss you. When are you going to stop turning your back on us when things get rough?"

Ella was sitting in front of a mirror, carefully applying mascara. She was still in her ivory silk robe, and she looked magnificently gorgeous, despite the dirty look she shot at him through the reflection in the mirror. He always did this. She couldn't remember a time when he hadn't been overprotective.

"Whatever, darling," she said condescendingly. "Don't hurt yourself worrying too much, or you might never live to see your grandchildren."

She half meant it to be a joke, but he took it personally, and responded, "If you insist on running away from your personal life, you'll live to see your grandchildren, but they won't know who you are. Same goes for your kids, Ella. Can't you see that they miss you? This long break is a gift, and you want to use the time in a jungle with a total stranger?"

Ella was most known for her short temper, so the remark was enough to make her slam the mascara down on the table and give him a contemptuous look in the mirror.

"I need to get away from everything, John," she proclaimed with her hard, British tone.

"Since when is a vacation from family getting away from everything?!"

"This is my chance to replenish myself and get ready to be in the entertainment industry again. If this doesn't work, we could lose everything. Do you like this room? My work pays for it. Do you like living in the lap of luxury? My movies have gotten us here. I have carried you on my back, and this is the gratitude I get? The kids will not have the same lives they do now if I don't get my name back out there!"

"They don't care about sitting in the lap of luxury," he

argued. "They want a life with you in it. Can't you see that? Don't go tonight. Forget about this excursion."

"Don't be daft," Ella said with a wave of the hand.

"I wish you could see what's happening to you, and realize what your priorities are, Ella," John said with a heavy heart. The cold and careless attitude that seemed to consume so many good people these days had made its way to the woman that had once been his soul-mate. Or so he had thought she was his soul-mate; he was beginning to have his doubts. Her magnificent beauty was now heavily veiled by a grotesque curtain of cruelty.

John walked across the room to stand behind her. She was still breathing heavily from the argument, and she looked at his reflection in the mirror. He was now standing right behind her, and he spoke to her with a hushed voice.

"Do you feel anything anymore? The fame you are so adamantly pursuing is the very thing that is destroying you. What happened to the vibrant spirit I married and had two children with?"

She looked away, focusing all her attention on the glass of scotch that sat on the table.

"If you go on this trip," he continued, "you'll be saying you don't care about your kids. You'll be saying that you don't care about me."

"Maybe I don't," she responded coldly.

He stared at her, stunned. She reached over, took a sip of the scotch, and continued to do her make-up. He shook his head and started to walk out the door.

"You want to go? Fine. But if we aren't here when you get back, I give you my best wishes for you and your damned career!"

He slammed the door, leaving her alone in the room.

Ella stared at herself in the mirror, but had to instantly look away. Her shame was overbearing, and her ear drums burned with anxiety. She felt trapped, alone, and wasted away, so she did the only thing she could think of by finishing off the glass of liquor.

Kathleen entered the darkened cocktail lounge with a weary expression on her face. Had she known this place was a late night quick fix for the socially lonely and depressed, she would have suggested McDonald's as being a better alternative. A waitress motioned for her to sit down anywhere, so she chose a booth in the corner where privacy was most certainly guaranteed.

The place was practically empty with only half a dozen people sporadically seated throughout the lounge. One man sat alone at the bar, watching a soccer game on the muted television screen. He wore a tuxedo, but the bow tie was loosened and dangling around his neck. He occasionally shared a few remarks with the bartender who was cleaning some wine glasses with a fresh towel. The bartender came every few minutes to refill the man's shot glass of whiskey.

In another booth across the room, a couple sat together. They, too, had obviously had a lot to drink. They were giggling and feeding each other the olives from their martini glasses. The woman rose to go to the bathroom, and when the man attempted to follow her, she laughed, pushing him back into the booth. She walked away giggling as the man slouched back in the booth to wait for this week's love to return.

The remaining person in the bar was the old man playing the piano. He was playing a Frank Sinatra song, and looked like a veteran of the Rat Pack days. He looked like he already had one foot in the grave, but the sounds coming from the piano indicated that his fingers still had talent. He turned to look at Kathleen who had been sitting alone for a few minutes now.

"Is he late?" the man said from across the room. He talked while he played the piano.

Kathleen blushed and looked around at the other customers, but they didn't seem to be paying any attention.

"No," she replied.

"He stood you up?"

She laughed. "No."

The waitress came up to her table and asked what she wanted to drink.

"I'd really love a Diet Coke."

"Coming right up," the waitress said. "And watch yourself with Earl. He loves to flirt with the single women."

Kathleen looked at Earl, the piano player, and he gave her a wink and a smile.

She looked back at the waitress and said, "Tempting, but I'll try to control myself."

The two women smiled, and the waitress walked away.

Finally, Ella walked in the lounge. To Kathleen, she seemed overdressed for a ten o'clock drink, but perhaps it was habit to look perfect for every occasion. Ella ignored the waitress and headed straight for the booth that Kathleen was in. She sat down just as the waitress was bringing Kathleen's Diet Coke to the table.

"Can I get you something?"

"Vodka, please," Ella said, agitated. She was busily setting her sweater and purse beside her on the seat, and the waitress raised her eyebrows to Kathleen as though she was saying, *Where did you find her?*

Kathleen smiled and the waitress walked away to fetch the princess her magic fire-water. She watched Ella smooth her sweater out on the booth firmly, and as she rummaged through her handbag, Kathleen finally said, "You seem a little flustered. Is something wrong?"

Ella continued digging around in her purse, looking for her cigarettes. "Everything is wrong."

Okay, Kathleen thought. "So why did you choose this place. It's kind of somber, don't you think?"

Ella stopped and looked around at the setting. She didn't see anything wrong with it. The joint was practically empty, which would allow them to discuss their plans in private. Not to mention, the cocktails were superb.

She looked back at Kathleen and said, "When we're at our estate for the holidays, our friends stay in this hotel. This lounge is just a nice place to be. It's quiet."

The star-struck part of Kathleen couldn't believe she was even in the room with Ella Levene, let alone sharing a booth with her, but the human part of her wondered what the big deal was. The woman seemed to have lost her grasp on life. Then again, that was just the way the world operated these days, and it made Kathleen even more grateful that she would be going back to the jungle in a couple of weeks.

Life was simple there. The villagers, while having been exposed to the Western way of life throughout their culture's history, maintained a relatively similar lifestyle as their ancestors had hundreds of years before. Whatever made this movie star think she could survive in a Stone Age tribe was beyond Kathleen's comprehension, but the more she saw Ella's vanity and materialistic attitude, the more she wanted her to go on this excursion. She also felt like she didn't want Ella to change for a movie production or a great screenplay. She didn't even really want her to change for her kids; Kathleen wanted Ella to change for herself. The rest would come after.

The waitress brought Ella's vodka, and the director quickly began to sip on it. She looked at Kathleen, who had remained silent since her arrival, and asked, "So, you had hesitations? Whatever the problems are, I'm sure they can be fixed."

Kathleen sat quietly for a moment, watching as Ella drank her vodka and stuck a cigarette in her mouth. Finally, the missionary sat back, and said, "Actually, those doubts aren't important anymore. I'm leaving in two weeks if you want to come along."

Ella stopped her lighter in midair and stared at Kathleen. "Are you serious?"

"Sure. But if you want to come, it's two months until I'll be returning to civilization, so you either stay with us for two months, or you don't come at all. And if you decide to come, you have to play by my rules. Vanuatu isn't Beverly Hills, so you'll do what I say, when I say it. If you can do that, you're welcome to come with me."

The actress was shocked. Two months was a lot. And who did this young woman think she was, trying to set restrictions on another person's life? On any other occasion, Ella would have snapped back at her, but there was something different about this girl. With only a few sentences, Ella was getting a very no-nonsense attitude from her, and the fact that she caught the vibe so early on in knowing the missionary told Ella that her future travel partner might actually be trustworthy. So, she finished off her drink, set it down, and looked at Kathleen.

"Fine." And that was it.

"Okay, just go back to the Tribal Missions headquarters and they'll organize travel arrangements. Two weeks from today, at five o'clock in the afternoon, I'll come to your place and pick you up."

"But my driver can just take me to the airpo—"

"No," Kathleen interrupted. "The adventure begins from your house. Just give me the directions and I'll be there at five sharp, got it?"

Ella hesitated a moment, but finally nodded, and scribbled directions on a cocktail napkin.

As she handed the napkin to Kathleen, she stopped and said, "I need to know that you will be the only one that sees these directions. My family and I come to Darwin for privacy."

"I understand."

The napkin was passed between hands. Kathleen carefully folded it and put it in her own purse. She began to rise from the table, but then stopped. Her heart pounded nervously as she settled back in the booth. She looked Ella directly in the eyes, giving a very serious, stone-cold stare.

"What are your motives for doing this?"

"Excuse me?" Ella said, choking on her drink.

"I want to know why you're going on this trip. Because if your solo joy ride turns into a weekend centerfold in all the supermarket tabloids, I'm telling you now—"

"Is this a threat?"

The missionary's face changed, and her features suddenly became very heart-felt.

"No, it's a plea. Can I have your word that my tribe won't be exposed to the public?"

Kathleen extended her hand across the table. Ella stared at it in disbelief. This woman really had been in the jungle a long time, otherwise she would have known about how Ella's name was never seen in the magazines anymore.

"Do I have your word?" Kathleen repeated.

Ella finally took her hand and shook it firmly. "I promise you, I won't be followed. Your village will be fine."

Kathleen nodded. "Thanks."

She got up and started walking away, but Ella felt that the conversation lacked closure, and she found herself shouting a remark to her new associate from across the room.

"Thank you for helping Freddy today. I don't know what would have happened had you not been there."

Kathleen shook her head as though it was nothing and said, "Two weeks. Be ready. Oh, and don't bring anything you don't want to get ruined. The bush is no place for cashmere and cell phones."

Leaving Reality

It was a hot, stuffy day and Ella Levene was running for her life. She ran as fast as she could despite the sweltering heat, her lungs burning as she pumped her arms and legs for her life. She thought her heart was going to burst out of her chest if she kept running, but she could not stop. She had to keep going.

The desert was flat and anonymous, yet Ella had seen it many times. She felt as though she had been running through it her whole life. She could not see where she was going, or what she was running from—she could only see herself. Tears were pouring down her face while she cried in agony. It could have been because of the heat, or maybe it was her internal organs that itched and burned inside her as she ran faster. Perhaps she was crying because of what was chasing her, or of what she herself was chasing but could not catch. Unsure and panicked, all she knew was that her weeping made it harder to run.

Brown, dead shrubs covered the terrain and she darted in and out of them, sometimes leaping right over them. Her muscles ached and she was choking on her own tears. She sobbed out loud, so loud that her ears began to burn, the way they did whenever she felt anxiety. But there was no one around to hear her cries, and there was no one for her to approach. All she could see was her own deteriorating body, running through the bright, dry desert. She wanted desperately to find someone, anyone, to ask them why she was running. Was there something in front of her or was she the one being pursued?

The air grew thicker, and now she could not bellow her cries anymore because she was suffocating, drowning in the great mix of tears and heat. Still, her body kept going, her legs and arms kept moving as fast as they could in this horrid place. She coughed and choked, trying to move the air in and out of her lungs, but the air was too thick, and she was sobbing too much.

And she ran faster, through the desert, toward nothing and away from nothing, just running and burning, with no one nearby to help.

Ella's eyes opened wide as she gasped for air. She was in a darkened room with only a small amount of light. Her eyes were unable to blink for a long time as she regained her bearings, glancing from one end of the room to the other. She was in her bed, staring at the moonlit ceiling that had the curtain's shadows dancing across it from the gentle breeze that entered the room. Her gaze turned to her right, and she saw her husband sleeping soundly next to her.

She slowly sat up in her bed, fully awake now, her breath slowing down as she took in the fresh air. The room was quiet except for the sound of the ocean drifting in through the open window.

My god, I hate that dream, she thought.

It was a constant nightmare she had, and it always seemed to surface when she was going through hard times. Whether it was her way of dealing with things, she wasn't sure, but it plagued her, and she was never sure why it came or what it meant. The feelings in her desert dreams were never the same as they were when she was awake. She never cried, and she was never pursuing anything of such great importance that it ruined her life. Or so she thought.

A glass of leftover vodka was on the lamp stand next to her, and she immediately drank it. There was no harm in having a drink if it could put you back to sleep. After all, she had control over her drinking, unlike almost everyone else she knew that shared the same career. As a matter of fact, half the people she had worked with in her earlier years had already been in and out of detoxification programs.

She was fine.

John rolled over in the bed, and Ella looked at him guiltily. All she could see was his brown hair on the pillow, and although two weeks had already passed since their fight, she suddenly had the daunting urge to wake him and apologize. How could she have told him that she didn't care about him and the kids? That was a mean thing to say, and she had later surprised herself when she ran the conversation through her head again. But, while it was an inconsiderate remark, she really did not care if she missed her children growing up. She was always looking for some sort of compassion within her, but the truth was that she couldn't watch them get more spoiled, start going out on dates, get married...

Ella had seen herself go through all that, and she could not find the energy to see her own children grow up. It was irresponsible, she knew, but no matter how hard she tried, Ella was always finding that she never wanted to be at home.

She rose out of bed and walked into the bathroom. Trying to look at herself in the mirror, the shame became too much and, once again, she turned away. What a hideous monster she had become. No wonder she wanted to go on this jaunt to the jungle—she was running from everything, including herself.

Her stomach turned in knots as she invited the thought into her mind that John was probably right—she was unable to face anything hard and challenging, including her own soul. She walked out of the bathroom, jamming her convictions into the back of her brain where she knew she could never find them again.

The doors opened to the balcony and she walked out into the cool night air. She lit her cigarette and inhaled all of its smoky contents, then let out a long exhale while she listened to a distant boat honking its horn. The moon was slowly making its way downward, and Ella knew that it would be dawn soon.

This was the day of her departure, and she hadn't started packing yet. She would wait another hour before she started to get ready, but for the time being, she would stand sleepily in the night, smoking her cigarette, thinking of a time when her heart's dull pain didn't exist.

An ocean gull squawked loudly as it flew low over the calm, blue-gray water. It glided smoothly along the surface of the sea, announcing the night's end at the Australian coast. Surrounding the bird was a dark sky gradually fighting for the color of day. The sun was returning, and even though the night usually brought its fair share of torment and agony to the Darwin Estate, sunlight would always attempt to reestablish a sense of joy on the house upon its arrival in only an hour or two.

Ella opened her eyes to the semi-dark room, vaguely remembering her return to the warmth of her bed only an hour before. She had taken her time on the balcony with her nicotine friend until the thought of sleep became too much for her, and she came back into the dark confines of the bedroom.

Now, it was dawn, and her arm stretched across the length of the bed, only to find that its second occupant was gone. Ella turned to where John had been and saw that he was already out of bed. The room was silent, and it was apparent that he had prepared himself for the day, but she couldn't be sure if he was up so early to work on the boat, or if he had wanted to avoid her when morning came. Either way, Ella was glad that she didn't need to worry about a grumpy husband getting her in a bad mood before she left for the next two months. She knew she'd been perpetually pissed in recent days, but the burden of divorce threats as she was walking out the door would not help her agitation while she was living in the jungle.

There was a slight knock at the door and she sat up in her bed, rubbing the sleep out of her eyes.

"Come in."

The door slowly opened and two little faces poked their heads into the grand bedroom. Freddy and Sara Tucker tiptoed in the room with their pajamas still on, looking at their mother with sleepy eyes.

"Mommy, can we come lay down with you," Sara said.

"Sara, I have to get up now."

"Please, only for a little while."

Ella looked at the clock and decided she wasn't ready to get up anyway. The bloody sun had not even risen yet.

"Fine, but only for five minutes."

She pulled the covers back for her children to climb under. They ran over and jumped into the bed, giggling. Freddy burrowed his head deep into his father's pillow while Sara nuzzled her little body under Ella's arm. There was an unusual silence that stayed in the room after that, one that does not normally accompany children, but Ella didn't seem to notice while she stared out the window as the day rapidly approached. Finally, Freddy was the first to speak.

"Mom, are you really going to leave?"

"Yes."

"When?"

"This afternoon. Kathleen is coming over."

Ella looked over at her son whose eyes were wet. He was going to cry.

"How long will you be gone?"

She turned her head back to the window and replied, "Two months."

Sara looked at her brother and the two children began to shed their tears in silence, but once again, Ella seemed to pay no attention. But despite their thoughts on her ignorance, she could hear them. The truth was that she sensed their every move—the way the bed seemed to breathe with them, the way Sara dug her face into Ella's ribs while she cried. She sensed everything they were doing, but she could not get herself to react. She simply sat in the bed, watching as the sky developed more color. After a few minutes, a choked up Freddy managed to say, "Do you hate us?"

"No."

"Then why are you leaving us?"

"I need some time for myself."

The comment made Ella want to vomit the moment it came out, but she still held her ground. Freddy just stared at his mother in disbelief while Sara continued to rest under a wing that had suddenly become harsh and cold.

"I hope it works out for you, Ella," Freddy said, emotionless, and walked to the door.

It struck Ella directly in the heart when her own son called her by her first name, and it ripped away at her even more when her daughter kissed her on the cheek and said, "Bye, Mommy. I love you."

Sara walked over to her big brother, took his hand, and the two of them exited the room together while a bewildered Ella remained in bed, staring out the window.

Kathleen pulled up to the gated entrance of the beachfront mansion in her rented car. She leaned out of the window and pressed the button on the intercom. She almost immediately heard a scraggly, "Yes?"

"Um, hi. Kathleen Newman. I'm here to get Ella Levene."

"Come in. You may park at the front door."

"Where else would I park," Kathleen asked herself as she drove through the automatic gate.

Her question was answered when she drove up the driveway and into another world. The road was lined with trees, and there was an occasional separate driveway that broke away from the main road. One road led to tennis courts, and she saw another that led to a pool. She assumed that each site on the property had a path or road that led directly to the house, but as she came up and over a bend, she saw that it was not a house at all.

It was a mansion.

She pulled the car up next to a huge door that she assumed was the front. Memories drifted to the scene from *The Sound of Music* when Julie Andrews saw the Von Trapp mansion for the first time. The driveway was circular with a tall water fountain in the middle, and it reminded Kathleen of the valet entrance to a hotel. The entrance itself was covered by a thick roof, and was held up by Greek pillars that had ivy spiraling around them. Kathleen looked at the ivy and saw that it covered the entire front portion of the mansion, hinting only a small ratio of the house's pink paint color behind the bright green foliage.

She stopped under the awning and got out. Materialism was not something that she strived for, nor wanted to have anything to do with, but she found that she was somewhat intimidated as she stepped up to the door.

A small, black button surrounded by a gold metal cover was in the wall, so she pressed it hard and heard the ringing from inside the house. She quickly pressed her hands against her wrinkly shirt, hoping for a last minute ironing miracle, but the door opened, and it was too late.

An unfamiliar, older woman stood opposite Kathleen, and she appeared to be smiling at the way the new guest was fidgeting with her wilderness clothing.

"Kathleen Newman?"

"Yes."

"Please, come in." The woman stepped to the side and allowed Kathleen to enter. "Ms. Levene had some last minute things to do, but she said to make yourself at home while you wait."

"Great. Where's the kitchen?" Kathleen asked, and laughed as though she had just made the joke of the century. The woman looked at her with a polite, but literal, smile.

Kathleen immediately stopped, and said, "It was a joke."

"Oh," said the woman. "Well, if you want anything, my name is Linda. I'm the housekeeper." And she promptly walked away, leaving Kathleen to explore.

Kathleen stretched her neck muscles, trying to relax.

Tough crowd, she thought.

Her eyes observed the room she was in now for the first time, but she saw that it was not just any room, but rather like a lobby. The entrance where she stood was situated in a standard area with the ceiling only nine or ten feet from the floor, but as she walked forward, the ceiling abruptly stopped, and opened up into a room with vaulted ceilings that were twenty-five feet high. The entire wall in front of her was made of windows, from floor to ceiling, and the view was of the beach below.

Outside, the water sparkled in the afternoon sunlight, and a small boat dock held a beautiful sailboat close to shore. There was a wooden staircase that led down the grassy hill to the dock, and her eyes followed the path all the way down when she noticed that someone was standing on the boat. It seemed to be a man working, but she could not be sure, so she stepped forward into the large room.

As she made her way further into the house, she saw that the big living room went down a small flight of marble stairs, and there were couches at the bottom. Up where she was, the floor was cold and shiny, and a grand piano was placed on a part of the floor that stuck out like a balcony over the area with the chairs and couches. It was obviously a room for entertaining.

Kathleen was starting to walk down the stairs and into the lower-floor area when she heard sniffling. It was coming from under the piano. She slowly crept over to the grand piano, looked down, and saw a shoe coming out from the bottom. She crouched down on one knee, and found little Freddy Tucker sitting under the piano with his knees pulled up to his chest, crying softly.

"Hi, Freddy."

"Hi."

"What are you doing under here?"

"Hiding."

"From what?

"Life."

Wow. Kathleen decided that it was a pretty deep answer for an eight year old, and she wished she had found him playing Pokemon or Mouse Trap instead of "hiding from life." He was so young, and he already had social anxiety. She climbed under the piano with him.

"Can I join you?"

He nodded his head and stared at the floor. She had to crawl on all fours to get under, but she finally cleared the underbelly of the grand piano. Her head was pressing against the ceiling of the little space, and she found it ironic that she was in this big room and her height was still an enemy.

"First trees, and now pianos. How many times do I need to come rescue you?"

Freddy gave a little laugh, but then went back to moping.

"Freddy, what's the matter?"

The boy looked at his new friend with tear-filled eyes. "My mother hates me."

"I'm sure she doesn't hate—"

"No, she does. She's leaving us. Watch, I'll bet she doesn't even give me a hug when you guys leave. Why are you taking her with you?"

Kathleen's heart sank.

Lord, help me to find which words to tell this boy. I don't know the situation, but You do, and You can help.

Now *she* was the one looking at the ground. It was such an elaborate, shiny floor, even here under the piano, but that didn't seem to help a little boy whose mother was closing the door on him.

"I think that your mom is coming with me to learn about other people."

"Can't she learn about people here?"

"Yes. But these people that we're going to visit are very different. Your mom doesn't know it, but I think that when she meets these different people, they are going to help her.

"Help her what?"

Oh boy.

"I think that they are going to help her see who she is. I'm hoping that maybe they will help her see that you and Sara and your dad are all very special."

Freddy looked toward the windows.

"Can't she see that now?"

Kathleen could tell this was a hopeless conversation. No matter what she told this kid, the situation remained: his mom was leaving him for a long time.

She sighed with disappointment, and said, "Your mom is a really talented lady, and she wants to use her talents to give you and your sister really cool things—maybe all the things that she was never able to have. But the people we are going to live with don't have anything that we have. They don't have cars or television, but they are really happy people. I think that if your mom sees how happy these people are with practically nothing, maybe she will understand that the only really physical things she needs in life is you guys. Do you get it?"

Freddy shrugged. Kathleen wasn't even sure that she'd understood herself, but it was just as well. If the kid had low expectations going into this, and Ella returned a changed woman, the results would be miraculous, and all glory be to the God who had made it happen.

They sat under the piano for a while in silence, and Kathleen finally looked out the window to the dock again. This time, there was a figure making its way down the steps and across the wooden platform that buoyed on the water. It was Ella, and she was walking very slowly down the dock. She stopped at the boat where the man was.

The man was, Kathleen assumed, the previously famous John Tucker.

Ella walked slowly down the wooden dock so as not to scare her husband away. Once again, the sun was drifting down into the horizon, making everything orange and warm. John was in the thirty foot sailboat, cleaning the windows with a cloth. He had on old jeans and a tee shirt covered in paint and grease stains. He ignored Ella when she came up to the boat, and continued to do so when she cleared her throat.

"John?"

He kept cleaning.

"Listen, I know you don't feel like talking to me, but I'm sorry about how I've been lately."

Still no comment.

Ella looked out at the deep blue ocean and sighed. She didn't want to leave him like this, not for the next two months. That time period would bring all the same issues when she returned, so she continued to speak, even though he didn't seem to be listening.

"I'll be back by mid-August. I don't know how I'll send word, but I'll do my best to let you know when I come home." And she added, "If I know where you are."

John nodded without looking up from his work, and said, "Have a good trip."

It was such a beautiful day with such foul circumstances eating away at it. The waves of the water shone silver and pink from the late afternoon sun while a cool breeze hit the shore. But the rift between the two people gave the air a sour taste, and Ella wanted to get out of the agony of her goodbye. She started to walk away, but decided to be human for the last minute she was with her husband and come clean with her attitude, so she turned back to him and said, "You know, these past couple of years have been difficult. I can't—"

She hesitated a moment, then continued with a voice that cracked.

"I can't feel anything inside of me. It's just gone. I can't remember emotion ever leaving me and I don't know how to get it back. I wish I could feel the same way about family as you do, but I just can't—"

And that was it. That was all the energy she could squeeze out of the remaining bulk of her soul. So, Ella Levene turned around and walked away. She wanted to tell him what was bothering her. She thought that if she told anyone about her guilt and anguish that lived inside her, it would be better, but she could never get so far as to explain the torment that she dealt with every second of every day. Instead, she gave up trying and walked away, accepting that last statement as her own goodbye to him.

She was only a few feet from the end of the dock when she heard, "Ella?"

Ella turned around and saw that he was out of the boat, standing on the dock. He knew, and understood. His gaze was intimate and it had forgiveness written on it. Ella walked quickly over to him and he wrapped his arms around her.

They stood there, husband and wife, for only a few short moments, but it was the most meaningful of moments that either had had in a while. John slowly swayed back and forth, humming the tune, "As Time Goes By." Soon, they were doing a very slow dance on the dock.

Ella's face was pressed into his shoulder except for her eyes, which peered out along the coast. She was so glad she was forgiven, but dancing with her husband was not enough compensation for the emptiness inside her.

She whispered, "I don't know what to do."

Her eyes closed while he continued to hum and lead her in small, gentle circles on the dock.

Sara dove under the piano at Kathleen.

"HI!" the little girl shouted as she obnoxiously settled her body next to her depressed brother. "This is Freddy's favorite place to think. I like to get in Mommy's big closet behind the shoe rack. Where do you like to think?"

It was an odd question for a six year-old to ask, and while Kathleen figured Sara did not actually *think* in the closet, but instead tried on Mommy's shoes, she politely responded, "In the tribe where I live, there is a big tree that fell down a long time ago. I like to go sit on its trunk."

"That's right, I forgot. You're the monkey lady!" Sara said.

"That's 'missionary,' dodo-brain," Freddy chimed in. The brother and sister began to poke at each other and argue. Kathleen suddenly felt that the floor under the piano was not enough space for three people, so she slid out and rose to her feet. She stretched her cramped muscles and looked out at the water. The sun was going fast, and it hit the water from the side, turning the ocean a magnificent, fire-orange color. She looked down at the dock and saw that there were two black silhouettes against the blazing water, and they appeared to be dancing.

Kathleen looked at the couple hopelessly, and then had an excuse to turn away when Linda, the housekeeper, came into the room from the left.

"Ms. Levene is packed, and ready to go. Would you like me to go tell her that you're here?"

"No, that's okay. It looks like she's making her way up here, now," Kathleen said. The silhouettes had separated, and the smaller one was making its way back up the hill to the main house while the other continued to work on the boat in the late afternoon sun.

Linda had worked for Ella Levene since the start of the actress' big career, in the earlier days when the steady flow of money and fancy things were still abundant. She had kept all of the woman's homes in perfect, stylish condition, and never once questioned the way Ella dealt with her children, her husband, and her travel schedule. Linda had seen the superstar go from an aspiring actress, to a hot Hollywood celebrity, and now, to a struggling director. She had watched Ella bring a man and two children into the homes that Linda had so intricately managed, and had seen the way she left her family there constantly.

The housekeeper thought she'd seen everything—all the parties, all the fights, all the details of a celebrity's life—but never in her life did Linda think she would watch as the famous and beautiful Ella Levene tried to slide into the front seat of a small, cheap Toyota with a giant backpack and safari clothes on. The actress wore a navy blue baseball cap with sunglasses, obviously to disguise her familiar features from the mass crowds that she would be encountering, and she had taken off all her make-up by suggestion of the missionary.

As it pulled out of the driveway, Linda gave the vehicle a little wave and smiled when it drove off into the tree-lined road to the gate. Once the car was out of sight, she turned around and headed back in to the big mansion where Ella's children and husband were avoiding a cold goodbye from the mother that had left them.

Again.

It was odd for Ella to be in the car with a complete stranger. She wasn't sure how trustworthy the woman was, nor was she clear about what the next two months entailed. The two women had talked very little since they had met two weeks before, and Ella was beginning to have her first doubts about the trip as the car pulled out of the driveway and onto the main road.

Sensing her apprehension, Kathleen tried to break the ice. "So, have you ever spent time with cannibals before?"

"What?!" Ella shouted, suddenly terrified.

"Cannibals. You know, people that eat other people? You've been around them before, haven't you?"

"I don't believe you."

Kathleen smiled. "Good girl." After a moment of silence, she continued, "Actually, the country's ancestors were known for eating the missionaries that came to reach out to them, but those days are over. White men still aren't really seen as great, but at least they don't end up in cooking pots anymore."

"If the Indians don't like white men, then how are you able to live there?"

"I came into the tribe as an intern about six years ago when there was a missionary couple already living there. They were good people and the chief trusted them implicitly, so when I showed up, the chief invited me to stay. Then, about a year after I got there, a horrible case of malaria swept through the village, and the wife of the couple got very sick. They had to rush her back to Port Vila, the capital of Vanuatu, and after that she was too weak to ever return.

"When we found out about her health problems, the chief and village elders got together and decided that I could stay, despite the short amount of time that they had known me."

Ella just stared at Kathleen as she drove. What an adventure! "Is malaria still a problem?"

"Not if you're careful in putting on bug spray. The mass outbreak of it was a rare incident that year, and a lot of people died in the village, but that hardly ever happens simply because everyone is very careful." Kathleen turned on the road that marked where the airport was. "I think that was one of the reasons the elders let me stay."

"Because everyone died?"

"No, because I only got a slight fever, and was able to help everyone else. I must have tended to the entire tribe for a week, twenty-four hours a day. The exhaustion alone was the equivalent of being sick. I guess they thought I was strong or something."

Kathleen mumbled the last sentence as though she felt guilty for having survived the tribe's outbreak. She stopped her story, and they drove to the airport in silence the rest of the way. It was awkward for Ella, who was always used to being around noise, so she asked if she could turn on the radio.

"No."

"What?"

"We're here. Buckle your seatbelt, Ms. Levene, because the adventure starts now."

Airplanes

The airplane took off from Darwin's airport at nine o'clock in the evening, and flew gracefully into the dark sky ahead. The lights of the city slowly disappeared and the plane was suddenly flying over nothing as it headed south across the desolate Northern Territory and the outback beyond. In the daytime, it would be a monotonous brown with the occasional green trees and shrubs that covered the dirt, but now, in the dark, Kathleen looked out the window at a seemingly bottomless pit of inky blackness.

She looked over at Ella, who seemed to be unimpressed with the plane's ascent, and Kathleen wondered how many times the woman had been on an airplane. After so many movies on location, and the different homes that she owned, this could have been one of hundreds of flights. She began to think of the tribe who had only seen airplanes fly overhead, and it suddenly became very clear to Kathleen that Ella would be going through a dramatic period of culture shock once they arrived.

The beverage cart made its way to their seat, and Ella habitually said, "Vodka."

Before the stewardess could reach for it, Kathleen leaned over Ella, waving her hand to the server.

"Scratch that, and make it two ginger ales. Thanks."

"But I asked for vodka," Ella said with agitation in her voice

"Sorry, no more alcohol while you're with me."

Ella got red in the face and, without trying to make a scene, whispered forcefully to her new, seemingly fascist, friend.

"You must be shitting me."

"No swearing either. Oh, thank you so much."

Kathleen smiled as she took the two sodas from the flight attendant, and the beverage cart was gone. Ella sat stunned in her seat while Kathleen forced the cup of ginger ale into her shaky hands. This was not happening. Her companion happily drank her soda as though nothing had happened, and said, "Don't you like ginger ale?"

"Maybe with scotch in it. Are you insane? No alcohol?"

Kathleen pointed at her. "Or swearing. You ride with the Christians, you show a Christ-like attitude." And she continued to joyfully drink the ginger ale.

"I'm not a Christian."

"Then you should have called the Peace Corps for help."

"I need alcohol!"

"Are you an alcoholic?"

"No! I'm British. My body is a quarter alcohol, and half nicotine."

"Bummer. Then you only have the last quarter to work with for the next two months, because there's no smoking, either."

Ella's face turned bright red and she clenched her teeth. Kathleen pointed to her soda, and said, "Are you going to drink that, or can I have it?"

The layover in Sydney had been two hours long and the two women had been through the airport without an incident, which is to say that no one seemed to recognize Ella. Kathleen began to have her doubts about Ella's success by the time the plane from Sydney took off at three in the morning. There had not been one photographer or fan seeking an autograph, and to Kathleen, Ella was a big enough star that everyone should have been crowded around them. Then again, when Kathleen had gone into the jungle six years earlier, Ella had been one of the most famous actresses in the business, and it only took one bad movie or a single act of indiscretion to be bumped out of the field and the new upcoming stars take their place.

Kathleen would never admit it to Ella, but she had been one of her favorite actresses in college. Now, after meeting the vain and empty celebrity, Kathleen remembered why she had left the States and come to a place where money and power did not run the lives of society. It was hard for her to be living in a world that revolved around greed, time, and popularity, the very world Ella was living in.

They sat on the darkened plane, and Kathleen looked at Ella while she slept in the seat beside her. She said a little prayer for the burdened woman, and then suddenly remembered that Ella Levene was, after all, a human being. God did not look at a person's job or social status, and He certainly didn't care about their wealth. He looked at their soul and heart, and from what Kathleen could tell so far, Ella had apparently given up on her own soul, succumbing to the work of evil that tore her apart every day. Kathleen had seen it happen before, too many times to count, and despite the conflicting personalities of the women, she found herself saying an intimate prayer about Ella's discovery of the Truth.

The sun was rising in front of the airplane as it landed at Bauerfield International Airport in Vanuatu's capital, Port Vila. Ella looked out the window as the space below the plane went from a brilliant blue to a busy mass of land. The runway was lined with jungle trees that blew crazily in the ocean wind, and when the plane came to a stop, Ella took a deep breath. Her heart was pounding rapidly, and she surprised herself when she noticed how excited she was. She had never even heard of Vanuatu, and here she was, about to be an occupant of the South Pacific country for the next two months.

The passengers rose to exit the plane and Ella whispered into Kathleen's ear as they walked down the aisle.

"How far away is the tribe?"

"We'll get there by this afternoon. It's on a different island."

"How many islands are there in this country?"

"About eighty-three."

"Oh."

They climbed down the steps into the cool morning air and stepped onto the pavement that the plane had parked itself on. Ahead, a large group of people waited behind a fence for the arriving passengers. It was seven-thirty in the morning and the awaiting crowd looked tired from having to get up so early. Despite the melancholy group, there was one man in the back who waved his arm out to Kathleen.

Kathleen waved back with a big smile, and turned to Ella with a whisper.

"From here on out, your fame and fortune don't matter. These people won't care about your movies, and they won't care about *you* unless you treat them as equals, so try to be an Average Joe, okay?"

"You're incredibly rude."

"No, I'm incredibly honest. Now try and be civilized to this man—he's one of our bush pilots for the South Pacific. And remember, you're not a celebrity here."

"Well, if it isn't the famous Ella Levene!" the large man shouted. He was about forty-five years old, balding, and his face was tanned from the sun.

After she gave Kathleen a smirk, Ella grinned nervously while she looked around at all the people who stood close by. No one seemed to care. The big, barrel-chested man took her hand and shook it furiously, speaking with a deep, southern accent.

"My wife and I are your biggest fans. Why, when we were living here in the big city some years ago, we tried to go see every movie of yours that came out. I just can't believe it! The Ella Levene of Hollywood is going to go with our Kathleen into the jungle. How about that!"

Kathleen smiled wide as Ella finally got her hand back from the happy man. She seemed to be in shock after the loud, Texan greeting, but she continued to grin nervously while the big man went over to Kathleen.

He gave her a big hug and said, "How is the greatest little scout in the whole South Pacific Ocean?"

"I'm fine," Kathleen grinned, "and glad to be back. Ella, this is Steve Mackenzie. He's one of six pilots that fly our missionaries in and out of places throughout this branch of Tribal Missions. He's invasive, boisterous, and he tells the tallest tales I've ever heard."

Steve cheerfully slapped Kathleen on the back as though she had just scored the winning touchdown, and said, "You're darn tootin'! But you know, now there are international flights to Tanna Island, but I told Alice, 'No! I want to fly little Kathleen and the beautiful Ella Levene to their island myself!'"

Then, he let out a deep laugh, and said, "Hey! That rhymes! I should give up the pilot's life and be the next Dr. Seuss. Okay, let's go get your bags and then we'll be set."

The three of them walked inside the airport, and Steve picked up their bags while Kathleen and Ella stood in line to get Ella's Visitor's Permit for the country. Kathleen spoke to Ella with a smile.

"I hope you weren't offended by Steve. I knew he'd flip out once he saw you."

"Quite alright. I haven't gotten a greeting like that in a long time."

"Well, either way, he's a character. Just beware: he'll be talking during the entire flight to Tanna."

"Is that the island we're going to?"

"Yup."

"Where are we now?"

"This is Efate, where most of commercial Vanuatu is centered. Tanna is a popular tourist attraction, but the tribe itself is pretty isolated compared to most of the others that are there."

Once they had finished with the permit, they met up with Steve who was sitting patiently with the bags. When he saw them, he stood up while his face broke into another big smile.

"Ms. Levene, this city is a great place to visit, and you'll have to come back sometime. But now, we get to go on my airplane. I hope you like rides, because this will be one you'll never forget!"

Something in Ella didn't doubt him for a second.

The little Cessna soared over the deep, blue ocean. Ella sat in the front with Steve and looked out the window at the beautiful water below. The sun was high in the sky now, and was warming the day as she looked in amazement at the towering thunderheads that dominated the sky to the west. Below them, she saw the colors of the water change with the formations of coral reefs that spread throughout the chain of islands. All around them were little islands sitting peacefully in the ocean, some that she imagined were untouched. Her mind played with the idea of setting foot on an island that had never before seen humans, and the thought made her heart jump.

Steve was busy talking about the country and the people, but Ella could not completely understand him because of the small plane's noise. Then, she looked straight ahead, and when she spotted the big island in front of them, she heard him shout, "That's Erromango, one of the larger islands in the southern part of the chain. Boy, do they know how to party. Why, I might move my wife there just because the people are so nice. And rumor has it that if you go to one of the bays and throw in an American penny—"

Kathleen, who sat behind him, interrupted.

"Steve, you've been on the island once, stopping for fuel. Don't pull Ms. Levene's legs until she's gotten to know you better."

"You know, Scout, I should have left you in Port Vila," Steve shouted while he turned in his seat. "You won't even let me tell one story that makes me sound good?"

Kathleen gave a big smile.

The plane flew along the coast of the island and Ella could see the tree-lined beaches. An occasional lagoon indented the island's shore, creating mystical blue features where random boats could be seen. Divers and snorkelers were just getting out of the water after a morning of exploring the underwater world around the island. Ella decided this was a prime location for vacationers, and already wanted to come back for a diving expedition.

Kathleen leaned to the front to shout in Ella's flustered ears. "There's Tanna!"

She pointed straight ahead as they flew past Erromango and over the open sea again. Ella squinted, and when she saw the little speck, her stomach turned. She could not remember a time when she was more excited. In her life, every day was meeting with the same people, asking for more production money or having lunch with women that were not really her friends. But this place made her feel alive.

As the plane drifted forward, the little speck grew into a large mass that sat in the water. The closer they got, the more visible the island became, and Ella began to see how grand it was. The side of the island that was nearest to them was green and lush with a small mountain coming out of it. Beyond it to the south, a plume of dark smog rose from a brown mountain.

"Is that a fire?" Ella shouted while she watched the smoke cloud rise from the second, larger mountain to the south of the jungle.

"No, that's just Yasur. It's one of the most active volcanoes in the world. It's Tanna's main attraction."

"How close to the volcano are we going to be?" Ella asked with a little nervousness in her voice. She had not signed up for any volcanoes.

"We're on the other side of the island, far to the north," Kathleen said, almost amused by the fear she sensed from her new companion. "Actually, we're going to fly over the tribe. You won't be able to see them because of the jungle, but the low-flying plane should let them know I'm back."

"It doesn't scare them?"

Steve chimed in. "They're used to it by now. Besides, it's not like I've crashed in the jungle. They have no reason to believe that airplanes are dangerous."

He shook his hands, pretending like the plane was plummeting to the ground, and gave another big laugh while Ella looked at him with worried eyes.

"Do many people crash in these planes?" she gulped.

The old Lenakel Airport was eerily quiet and deserted. Ella was holding her backpack on her shoulder and she stared in awe at the ocean to the west. Steve and Kathleen were busy unloading other things from the plane and talking about equipment for the tribe.

"Listen, Scout," Steve said. "We got your list and purchases, and we already sent them into the tribe. Jake got them okay, and he'll be waiting for you on the road when you get there. I guess they told everyone you'd arrive by four."

Kathleen nodded her head with a serious expression on her face. "Did he say how Epi is?"

"Yes, he said he knew you'd ask and to tell you that the kid lost a leg and an arm, but not to worry, Jake sewed them back on for him." Steve smiled at her as she gave him a dirty look.

"The humor everyone shares about the matter is not funny."

"Oh, Kathleen, you worry too much. You've got to learn to trust people. You know Jake loves that kid. I'll bet when you get back, it'll just be an arm and not the leg."

"Okay, okay. You're very funny, Steve," Kathleen said sarcastically, and she walked away. She thought it was poor form for everyone to make her into some overprotective Nazi. Epi was, after all, her lifelong responsibility now.

She walked over to where Ella was staring quietly at the ocean's view.

"Are you ready to go?"

Ella turned to her with a blank face, and cautiously said, "Okay."

"Are you okay? You don't look so good."

"I guess the flight just didn't agree with me," Ella replied. She was lying. While standing on the runway, she felt a wave of anxiety sweep over her. What was she doing here? What on earth did she know about Vanuatu, or Indians, or missionaries?

The last of the three stumped her the most.

Ella did not even believe in God, yet she was here with people who believed God was everything. Hell, they were devoting their lives to Him, and she was standing on this runway expecting to understand? No way. She felt foolish and ready to go home, but Kathleen pulled her back to reality as she shouted, "Come on, the taxi is here. It's going to take us to the base!"

Ella shook her head and tried to relax.

Just relax, this is a tropical vacation.

But something inside her said that this was not a vacation at all, and as she walked to where Kathleen was waiting, Ella got the strange feeling that something big was going to happen in the next two months. For better or worse, her gut told her things would not be the same when she returned.

Steve waved to the two women as they hopped into a taxi that was waiting for customers. He had to refuel for a flight to Espirito Santo, another major island in Vanuatu, and he was disappointed that he could not accompany the women to the base.

"Good bye, Ella Levene! My wife will never believe it!" he shouted.

Ella gave a big wave back, and yelled, "Thank you, Mr. Mackenzie. I hope to see you again in two months!"

Steve smiled wide, then put a serious expression on his face and pointed to Kathleen.

"Scout! The kid is fine. It's okay with God if you trust someone else for a change."

"Thank you, Steve," Kathleen said, rolling her eyes. "Now go home and have Marsha pull out the foot stuck in that big mouth of yours!"

"You got it! I'll send her your love."

Kathleen waved one last goodbye as they got into the taxi. Steve was a good friend, and even though he crossed the line most of the time, she knew he was right. What good were fellow Christians if you couldn't go to them for help and prayer? Kathleen closed her eyes and prayed for Steve's safe travel.

Ella looked over at her and saw that she was praying. Then she slowly looked out the window and asked herself, once more, what the hell she was doing here.

Bobby's Road

The old four-wheel drive jeep bounced along the dirt road, kicking dust high into the midday heat. Bobby, a sixteen year old black native of Tanna Island, was at the wheel, and Ella was holding on for her life. Her previous anxieties had vanished when Bobby hopped into the driver's seat back at the mission base in Lenakel. Ella had watched in horror as the teenager pulled the seat forward to accommodate his short legs.

"Is he old enough to drive?" Ella had asked Kathleen.

"Sure."

That was not the reaction Ella had wanted, but now it was an hour into the trip down the almost deserted road, and the boy seemed to know his way through the landscape very nicely. He turned the wheel and shifted the gears like a professional race car driver, all the while talking to Ella with his Bislamic accent.

"So what is your job, ma'am?" Bobby asked Ella.

"I'm a director," she replied.

"Of what company?"

"I direct movies."

"I don't know about movies. Do you like being a director?"

Ella paused. No one had ever asked her if she liked it; she had always just done it without second thoughts. Her lips slowly

77

broke into a grin as she watched the boy rapidly navigating the hole-infested dirt road. He had no idea what her life was like, and she found that she was a little bit jealous of the simplicity of his. She turned to look at the jungle, still grinning.

"No, as a matter of fact. I hate it."

"Then why do you do it?"

"I don't know."

Kathleen was listening in the backseat, and she shouted over the shifting gears and bumpy jolts.

"You don't like it because you know you're worth more than the job."

Ella didn't understand.

"What?"

"You know you could be doing something better with your life. What does being a director mean in the end, anyway?"

"I don't think that's it."

"I guess only time will tell. Someday you'll know why you stick with being a director, and that will decide whether or not you choose to stay with it afterwards."

"Thanks for the insight," Ella sarcastically replied.

Kathleen smiled, and said to Bobby, "Did you see Epi when you delivered the supplies yesterday?"

"Yes. He looked well. I think he will be at the road today."

Bobby continued to weave around big holes that sat in the middle of the road, and it was beginning to make Ella carsick. She tried to look straight ahead, keeping her eyes focused on one place, but the foliage and landmarks she found were swiftly surpassed by the jeep. She could not imagine what Kathleen must have been feeling in the back seat. Ella turned around to look at the missionary, and her nauseated stare was returned with a wave.

"Are you doing okay?" Kathleen asked with a smile.

"I think I'm going to be sick."

"It's just a little while longer."

"I hope so."

Kathleen continued to grin while she looked out the window to the left. The dirt road ran along the west coast of the island, and it was raised about one hundred feet above sea level, providing a view of the ocean beyond the treetops. To the right of the jeep was jungle with the occasional grassy fields that were all over the island.

She leaned forward to the miserable Ella and said, "You know, Tanna is known for its wild horses. They can usually be found in fields like that one over there." She pointed, and instead of looking to where Kathleen was pointing, Ella just nodded with her eyes closed, trying not to move.

Finally, the jeep slowed down, and the road smoothened out as the dirt turned to green grass. The vehicle drove under a cloud for a few moments, which covered the terrain around them in a dark shadow, and Ella's nausea slowly passed with the coolness of the shade that was over them. She could look around now, and saw how green and lush the view was toward the ocean. The air was cooler, and her body relaxed.

"I feel better," she shared with the other two people. "This place is beautiful. What part of the island are we on?"

"This is the northern side," Bobby said as he slowly made his way around a bend. The road was muddier now- a sure sign that rain had just hit this portion of the island. He carefully made his way up a hill, taking them closer to the interior and further from the windy coast. He loved this drive, but the mud always made it difficult on this part of the road where they went deeper into the bush.

Bobby was the son of a couple that worked and lived at the mission base in Lenakel. His parents had been Christians his whole life, and it wasn't until only three years before that he had accepted Christ. Now, he liked to be as involved in the missionary process as possible while he was still on this tiny island. Being involved with Kathleen's ministry was especially exciting because she was always trying to include Bobby in whatever she was doing while in town.

His parents were running errands all day that day, and Kathleen and Ella would never make it to the tribe unless he drove them. He had driven this particular road three or four times, and he was happy when Kathleen asked him to take them this afternoon before he could volunteer. It told him that she trusted him, and he had jumped into the car before telling her yes.

"Are we almost there?" Ella asked him.

"Yes. It should be just around this corner. Ah, see? There's the welcome party now."

Ella looked ahead and saw a small group of about four people standing at the edge of the road on the jungle side. There were two black men with grass loin covers, one very tall, white man with blonde hair, and a little, black boy wearing yellow shorts. The child was waving his arm furiously at the approaching jeep.

Behind her, Ella heard Kathleen say, "There's my Epi."

Kathleen jumped out of the car as the little boy ran up and leapt into her arms. She began to speak to him in a language that Ella could not understand, and then she put the boy down on the ground. The two of them faced Ella, and Kathleen had her hands on his shoulders. He stood awkwardly looking at the new, white stranger.

"Ella, this is my son, Epi."

Whoa.

Ella stood with her mouth wide open, shocked.

"He's your son? How'd that happen?"

"Long story. I'll explain later."

The three men slowly approached, the two black men stepping up to Kathleen first with big smiles.

"Ket-si!" they were both saying as they laughed.

"Who's 'Ket-si?'" Ella asked.

"It's how they say 'Kathleen,'" she replied, and she moved forward and spoke to them rapidly in an alien language. Ella stood there in awe, watching as Kathleen laughed and spoke to the nearly naked men with a little boy holding her hand the entire time. While the three of them talked and shared news, the tall, white man came over to Ella with a big smile.

He looked like he was probably thirty, but had the charisma of a young boy.

The man showed his straight, white teeth, and said, "So, the rumors are true. The famous Ella Levene, on our little island. How do you do? I'm Jacob Willis."

He shot his arm forward and gave her a friendly hand shake. He was warm and friendly, and despite his recognizing Ella, he didn't appear to be star struck by any means. She liked him immediately.

Jacob did not look like a man who lived in the jungle with natives. His clothes were dirty and terribly worn, but the rest of his appearance was surprisingly clean-cut. The most amusing part of the whole scenario was that Kathleen was ignoring the handsome gentleman entirely, and Ella was dumbstruck at the thought of these two people living in a jungle together with a tribe of Indians.

Without knowing otherwise, Ella asked, "Are you Kathleen's husband?"

Before Jacob could get any sound out of his mouth, Kathleen shot her head around and said, "No!"

The man raised an eyebrow at Ella as Kathleen darted over to where the two of them were talking. Kathleen's entire attitude changed when she came over, going from giddy to agitated. She stood next to Ella and motioned to Jacob.

"Ella, this is Jake. He is the *temporary* engineer for the tribe and is currently working on a sanitary water system for everybody."

Jake brushed away the negative tone, and kept his warm smile.

"Temporary can mean so many different things in this world." He spoke to Ella, but motioned to Kathleen. "In her world, it means I should already be gone, but in everyone else's, I'm here until the job is done."

Then, he looked at Kathleen and said, "How was the trip, Scout?"

"It was fine. Are we ready to unload the jeep? We still have a hike before dark."

She walked away, leaving Ella and Jake in an uncomfortable silence.

Jake shrugged his shoulders to Ella, leaned over, and whispered, "I bet you had a great trip here, didn't you? How are you feeling?"

Ella whispered back, "I'm dirty, carsick, and dreadfully sober. And if I don't get a cigarette soon, I may start cursing just to make her angry."

Jake laughed a little, and said, "When I came here a year ago, she went through all my bags on a substance search. Don't worry, you'll learn to love her."

When he said the last remark, he backed away with a little embarrassment, and suddenly Ella understood.

Wow, this visit is going to be interesting, she thought.

After the jeep was unpacked, they all waved to Bobby as he left, and the party began their ascent up the slightly sloping jungle terrain. Kathleen was holding Epi's hand while she spoke to the two natives. One was limping, and he pointed at his leg while he spoke to Kathleen. Ella watched the conversation go on, wishing she could understand what everyone was saying.

Agmol was the limping man, and he told Kathleen about his injury during her absence. He had been one of the first in the tribe to become a Christian since Kathleen had been there, and he was a loyal friend to her and Jake.

"Ket-si, I was climbing a tree when the ground shook. My branch was not strong and it threw me off. I landed on my foot. Jaap tried to heal it with prayer, but we had to go to Lenakel and get a special shoe. Now, I cannot do hard work."

Kathleen gave a sympathetic grin and said, "It will heal. But you must keep the shoe on. You can help me with teaching if you want to."

He nodded with thanks, then shouted to the other man ahead. "Saki, tell Ket-si about when the ground shook!"

The second man had been leading the group, trying to set a good pace, when he was summoned back. He stepped into sync with the other two, and said, "Ket-si, the ground shook very hard. It is one of the hardest shakes I have known. You were lucky you were not here for it. But it was fine, because Jaap prayed with us and held Epi's hand. He is very special to us."

Kathleen gave a slight nod and turned around to look at Jake. He was telling Ella about the tribe and the island. She watched as he told the newest visitor a story in his own, charismatic way. Kathleen's lips curved into a smile, but she quickly turned away and continued to make her way through the hot, humid jungle.

Ella was busy listening to Jake's tour of the jungle that, to her, just looked like a regular forest seen in some tropical film, but he pointed to this tree and that hunting trail. That was when she noticed how many little trails crept into the bushes from the main one.

"What are all these trails?" she asked.

"They're tracks made by animals, but the villagers use them for hunting."

Suddenly, Kathleen fell back into step with them. She looked at Jake with great seriousness, and he took it as a hint to leave the women alone, so he walked up to where Saki, Agmol, and the boy were.

Ella nudged Kathleen's arm.

"He's cute," Ella snickered.

"I hadn't noticed."

"Are you serious? You live in the jungle with this guy and

you've never noticed that he's cute?"

"Nope. And we both live in the tribe, I don't live *with* him. Besides, he's not my type."

"Oh, so your type is boring, mean, and ugly?"

"Never mind."

Then, Kathleen stopped Ella on the trail and said, "I almost forgot. You'll need this."

She took her backpack off of her shoulder and leaned over to look inside. She pulled out a long object covered in a beige cloth and handed it to Ella.

"What is it?" Ella asked, thinking it was for her.

"It's a machete. You're going to give it to the chief when we ask if you can stay in his tribe."

"He doesn't know I'm coming?"

"You asked to come with me two weeks ago and they don't have phones here. The notice was a little short. Besides, he needs to actually meet you first."

"What if he says no."

"Then at least you got to see some of the tribe. Excuse me."

Kathleen ran up to talk to Jake, leaving Ella alone. Meanwhile, Epi had wandered back to where Ella was struggling to keep up with the rest of the group. He was walking next to her, and it was not until she looked down at him that he spoke for the first time since she had been there.

"Hello," he said, in clear English.

"Hello."

"How are you?"

"I'm fine. How are you?"

But he didn't respond, only giggled and ran ahead to his guardian. As Ella watched him scamper away, she noticed how little his body was. His limbs were frail and his stomach was round like a man with a beer belly, but everything from the way he moved to his little giggles suggested that he was a happy, healthy little boy. Epi grabbed Kathleen's hand again, and watched as his white mother spoke very softly to Jake.

"Did you talk to Sowany?" Kathleen asked him. Sowany was the chief of the tribe.

"Yes, and he told me no, but he'll probably say yes if *you* ask," Jake replied.

Kathleen let out a sigh and continued to walk down the trail with the little boy holding her hand. She had wanted Ella entering the tribe to open arms, but now it appeared that there would be gravelling involved for the guest to stay for such an extended period of time. She looked down at Epi and his yellow shorts.

"When did Epi start wearing shorts?" she asked Jake.

"Yesterday, when we got all the supplies you sent. He went through the donation containers that came from the States until he found a pair that fit him."

"What did Sowany say?"

"Not much. A lot of people went through the containers already. The tribe is more clothed than when you left."

"And the earthquake?" Kathleen asked. "Saki and Agmol told me about it."

"Yeah, it was pretty bad. The volcano was going crazy that day."

"And Epi's asthma? Did it flare from the gases?"

"A little, but he was fine."

"Good."

Kathleen waited for Ella, leaving Jake to walk by himself. There was no use in romanticizing Kathleen's return. She had left Jake in charge of Epi, she returned to find the boy in one piece, and now she could keep doing her job in the tribe while he did his. Why waste time on the "I missed you" statements? Kathleen thought, after all, that Jake should have been out of the tribe by now, but the water project had been postponed because of weather, and he would be there for a long time, despite her constant pleas with Alice to get him replaced.

Kathleen could not figure out who, in management, would put a single man in the jungle with a single woman. It was inconceivable for a situation like this to exist, and Kathleen had voiced her disagreement with everyone, even Jake.

"He can't stay here!" she had said to Alice on the phone a year earlier. "Not only is he single, but he knows me. We went to college together. This is wrong and you know it, Alice!"

"Kathleen, you, and the missionaries before you, have been petitioning for this sanitary water system for years. We can finally give it to you, but Jake is the only engineer available right now. And he was so excited when he heard he'd be working with you. I thought you would feel the same way."

"Well, I don't," Kathleen said with a firm tone. "I just don't think it's appropriate for the two of us to be out here alone."

"Listen, it's a year long project. Then he'll be gone. If it is affecting your work, or the tribe's culture or outlook, call me back. But until then, you're stuck with him."

Kathleen had hung up the phone with clenched fists. She knew it was no way for a woman of God to act, but she was furious.

Lord, just don't let him get in my way, she had prayed with anger.

The day Jake arrived in the village was a holiday. The men immediately accepted him in, showing him how to hunt and speak their language. They sat around the fire at night and told stories, the men shouting, "Jaap, tell us about when Ket-si was young!"

Those were the times when Kathleen turned red with anger, listening as her former schoolmate told embarrassing stories about their college days together. After the first week of this routine, Kathleen had approached him about it.

"Don't tell stories about me anymore."

"Why? They just want to know what you were like."

"Fine. Then I'll tell them what you did in college."

It was a veiled threat, and she could see that it had hurt him, but Jake took the hint, and came up with different stories after that. He had become a Christian since college, since he had last seen Kathleen, and he didn't want the villagers to know the facts of his past life. It was a threat Kathleen could pull on him too well, and she felt awful when she used it, but it worked. After that instance, she vowed she would never use past mistakes against anyone. God forgot and forgave sins, so she would have to as well. But it were those past sins, she knew, that kept her heart from letting Jake in, and without them, she was scared to death of what might happen.

Tribe

The jungle grew thicker and hotter with every step, and Ella was fighting for her breath. She decided she would have harsh words with her personal trainer when she got back home; her muscles ached and her back could not carry the bag any more, but she didn't want to complain because everyone else seemed to be in great shape. She stopped for a moment to push the straps further up on her shoulders, taking in the surroundings.

The jungle was dark from the thick trees overhead and the ferns surrounding her. Sunlight was streaming in through scattered branches, but the ambience was not altered by the light. The forest was still dreary, and a light mist was rising from the jungle floor. Now Ella understood what people meant when they said that the air was so humid you could feel it. Her arms felt every ounce of heat that the surrounding foliage secreted, and the more she thought about the stuffiness, the slower her pace was. After a while, the humidity seemed to be adding weight to the load, and her body sank lower to the ground.

She tried to think of something else as she walked, but found there was nothing she could think of to take her attention off of the pain. The group in front of her was steadily making their way up the trail when they suddenly turned and headed into the brush. Ella quickened her pace to see where they went, and as soon as she heard them walking through the thick bushes to her right, she began to run. In doing so, she tripped over an object that was in the middle of the small trail.

Positioned like a baseball player sliding into home plate, she did a nosedive into the dirt, her arms sliding across the ground as the rest of her body followed. The actress could feel the dirt and leaves slide through her shirt from where her neck was, and when she opened her eyes and looked into the surrounding plants, she saw bugs crawling everywhere.

Ella jumped up, threw her backpack off, and started pulling the tucked shirt out of her pants, trying to get the dirt out. Leaves and clumps of dirt flew out of her clothing as she danced around, suppressing a fearful cry that would surely draw an unwanted crowd. But it was too late, and when she was done having her panic attack, she looked up to see that all the members of the hiking party were standing only a few feet ahead, apparently amused by their new visitor.

The black man with the cast whispered something in his language to Kathleen, but she shook her head in agitation and told the group something. They all left, and Kathleen walked to where Ella was standing in the ferns. The dirt-covered woman's arms were hanging idly by her sides and strands of her dark hair were matted to her forehead with sweat. For the first time on this journey, Kathleen almost felt sorry for the superstar, and she approached her cautiously. She leaned over and picked up Ella's backpack for her, sympathetically brushing the debris off the front.

Ella was in hell. She needed a cigarette, a drink, and a shower, all of which, she knew, she would not be getting for a long time. It was the dirtiest, sweatiest, most unattractive moment she had ever experienced, and it had only been thirty minutes since they'd been there.

Thirty minutes, and the desire to leave was consuming her.

Kathleen brought the pack over to the jungle's newest victim and handed it to her. They were alone in the humid forest now, and Kathleen watched as Ella reluctantly put her backpack on.

"I'm sorry. I should have been walking with you," Kathleen finally said.

Ella just stared at the ground where she had been lying only a moment before. It was obvious that she was embarrassed, and Kathleen could feel the tension in the air so she tried to make light of the situation.

"At least there were no paparazzi around."

Ella smiled and looked up. "That horrid scene would have been all over the news by tonight."

The two women stood there with little smiles on their faces, and Kathleen said, "It'll get better, I promise." Ella nodded in response while Kathleen continued. "Let's go. The village is only another ten minutes up this trail."

The mood was lighter, which made Ella more comfortable. They slowly began to make their way up the hill when Ella had a thought. She turned around to where the main trail was and looked for the object that had tripped her. Her eyes did a quick scan of the cluttered area and she finally saw it.

It was a large, black rock, just sitting there. Her eyes gave it a dirty look, and she cursed at it under her breath.

"Damned rock."

Never would there be a more merciless rock.

The trees above her head came alive, and Ella watched them with curiosity as they swayed back and forth, the wind pounding at them. Kathleen pointed to them and said, "That means we're getting close. The village is on a part of the island where the winds are strong."

Ella was suddenly very anxious. In only a matter of minutes, she would be seeing a real Indian village. Her imagination ran wild as she thought about a million things. Would they be naked, would they welcome her, would they eat her—worry and excitement frenzied her, and the very realization that she was excited made her even more happy.

The two women walked along the trail when, suddenly, there was an unexpected gust of cool air, and they burst out of the jungle into open sunlight. The cool breeze dried their sweaty faces almost immediately, and Ella felt she could breathe again. She stopped at the edge of the clearing and squinted with disbelieving eyes as she observed what was ahead.

They were at the edge of a small field, slashed and burned right out of the forest. Dead remnants of trees lay throughout the field, but for the most part, the area was surprisingly tidy. It was undoubtedly used for agriculture, and different crops rose out of the ground from fruit plants to yams.

The open space was full of people working and going about their daily lives which, Ella assumed, did not involve many other activities than this. Women wearing only grass skirts sat in the rows of produce, working furiously. Some of them were picking the local produce for the upcoming dinner while others worked on the continuously growing plant selection of food. A few of the women looked up at the visitor and gave big smiles while others continued to go about their busy gardening chores.

Jake, Epi, and the two natives waited on the other side of the field for the white women while they moved through the muddy rows. Ella stared with wide eyes as they passed through the rows of working women. Was she really here? She could not grasp the situation; it seemed to her like she had been sucked into a National Geographic documentary.

The half-naked women rose from where they were gardening, and all followed the new white visitor with excited giggles. One woman even reached her arm out to touch the fair skin of the curious new stranger. Ella jumped in surprise when she felt the rough hand brush her arm and she looked at Kathleen apprehensively, but the beaming missionary paid no attention. She seemed to be in a world of her own, squinting in the sunlight toward the end of the field where the friends that had welcomed her were now waiting.

Further up the hill, beyond the field, Ella saw the first settlements. They were little huts with grass roofs and palm leaf walls. Smoke rose from within the plazas of the houses, and she saw more smoke rising from the trees beyond. As they got closer, Ella could see that some of the huts were in the open while others were concealed in the jungle. Each hut had its own small circle for fires in front of it, except for the huts that were in the field. These ones were centered around one circle of ash and blackened wood.

Little fenced areas were sporadically positioned throughout the village, and each had pigs and gardens. They looked like pens or the Stone Age version of a front yard for each abode. The fences were old and uneven, simple structures made of wood that had been nailed together for the mere purpose of keeping other things out. Ella saw how the wood shapes were erratic and disproportionate to any other that they were nailed to, but it was obvious that *feng shui* was not a cultural norm here.

Kathleen finally looked at Ella with a big grin, wondering what her guest's first impressions of the village were. Upon her first entrance into the tribe six years earlier, Kathleen had looked at everything in disbelief, praying that she would be accepted. Now that so many years had passed, she was not only accepted into this culture, but she was almost fully assimilated. She even had a son who was full-blooded, indigenous ni-Vanuatu. She could not think of a more hospitable people, or a culture more deserving of God's great love. This was her home, and bringing Ella here provided the overwhelming realization that Kathleen's personal and professional life were now exposed, and the game began right now.

Large crowds of half-naked people gathered around the group that had emerged from the jungle. Familiar faces greeted Kathleen with hugs and handshakes while every body in the village approached Ella. They shook her hand furiously, greeting her with words she did not understand. Hands touched her soft, dark hair and poked at her dirt-stained clothes. She tried to put a smile on her face, but it was obvious that all the physical attention was overwhelming her. Kathleen smiled at her, but it was Jake who finally came to the overwhelmed director's rescue.

"Ms. Levene! Follow me. We'll go see the chief!"

Then he addressed the crowd with a kind voice while he weaved through the people to reach the fascinating new addition to the village, calmly telling them they would be going to see the head of the village. He reached his hand out to Ella, and she grabbed it, promptly being pulled from the crowd by the tall man. The rest of the villagers stayed behind and watched as Kathleen, Ella, and Jake walked to where Sowany's hut was on the other side of the village.

"Thank you. I have a bit of social anxiety when there are large crowds of people," Ella said to Jake.

He gave a big smile, and compassionately said, "Ma'am, you better get over that really quick. If you thought people wanting to get your autograph back home were relentless, then you'll think these people are carnivores. There's no such thing as privacy here, and they'll want to be around you all the time, so keep that social anxiety back in Hollywood."

Kathleen smiled at Ella, who was suddenly white as a ghost. The missionary put her hand on the frightened woman's shoulder, and said, "Don't worry, you'll get used to it. Now, do you have that machete I gave to you?"

Ella nodded.

"Good. Get it out, and put on your most humble of attitudes. Sowany is the chief of the village, and he can sense unwanted pride and arrogance a mile away. Just stand there until I tell you to give him his gift, and then we can go."

The trio approached the hut at the far edge of the settlements, almost completely submerged in the shadows of the palm trees that sat behind it. This hut was one of the settlements that were partially in the jungle. It, too, had a fenced area with pigs, and further into the jungle was a structure high up in the trees with a rickety ladder leading up to a small opening. The structure looked like a tree house that young boys would make, but it was unbelievable to think that it was only used for play and make-believe war games.

"What is that?" Ella asked, pointing to the tree house.

Kathleen looked up and quickly said, "It's for storing food. Are you ready? Okay, here we go." They entered the cool hut that sat in the breezy shade of the trees.

Ella followed her two new friends into the darkened hut and was greeted by the familiar tobacco odor. A small, black man with a grass loin cover was sitting in the room with a hand-rolled cigarette in his mouth. He was older, but not gray-haired, and when the three white people entered his home, he looked up with squinted eyes toward the lighted doorway. He smiled at Jake, but his entire face lit up when he saw Kathleen.

"Ket-si! Tell me about your trip!" he said with a gruffy voice. She stepped toward him with a smile, but when she moved, the man caught his first glimpse of Ella. His face turned serious again, and he looked at Kathleen with raised eyebrows.

"Who is this?"

Kathleen motioned for Ella to stand next to her and proceeded to tell the chief about her new friend.

"Sowany, this is Ella Levene. She has come to learn about your village and all the people. In the big tribe where I come from, she is a woman of great fame. Almost everyone knows of her, and she is very talented."

"What does she do that is so wonderful?" Sowany asked, unimpressed.

"She is a performer. She entertains all the people in my tribe, and she is very good at it. People all over the world wish to meet Ella."

"Do they all know that she is here?"

"No."

Sowany scratched his chin in deep thought. Jake stood tensely by the wall and listened with approval while Kathleen had described Ella. He admired her descriptions, knowing that he could not have worded it better. A performer. It was a good word for a person that was incomprehensible to Sowany. Had Jake been doing the introductions, he would have tried to explain television and movies for half an hour before finally making up an alternate career that the wise old man might understand.

Meanwhile, Ella was standing awkwardly by Kathleen, listening with disbelief as the tall blonde spoke rapidly in the alien language. She held the machete in front of her, waiting for her cue. Kathleen turned to her and motioned to give Sowany his gift. Ella cautiously stepped forward and handed it to him with both hands.

Am I supposed to bow or something? she thought. Before she broke into a sweat on what to do next, Kathleen discreetly pulled her back by her shirt, sensing the brief confusion.

Sowany held the object in his hands, carefully unwrapping it. He nodded with pleasure at the shiny, sharp machete. Gently caressing the metal, he took a long moment to contemplate his decision. He looked over at Jake and said, "Jaap, what are your thoughts on this woman?"

"Sir, I think it is a great honor that she is here."

"And Ket-si? You believe she is trustworthy?"

Kathleen was still trying to run that question through her

head because it was apparent that Ella had, so far, exuded an indifferent attitude about the entire situation. Kathleen wanted to answer truthfully, but her heart told her to just tell him what he wanted to hear. She would tell Ella later about confidentiality in this case, so for the time being, she answered Sowany with an answer that she prayed was true.

"Sowany, I believe that she wishes no harm on your people or your traditions. I think that the Father has brought her here to learn from you and your people. She does not know your language, but she will help me with my work, and I will make sure that everything is as it should be."

Sowany nodded again with approval, then waved his hand to Ella.

"Tell her she is welcome to stay as long as she would like, but you and Jaap must watch her with a close eye."

Kathleen and Jake nodded, and she looked at Ella with a serious expression, and said, "He's letting you stay for as long as you want, but he is basing his decision on the fact that you're trustworthy. Nod your head at him and smile so as to tell him that you won't blow it."

Ella glared at Kathleen for a second, then immediately turned to Sowany with a big smile. She nodded at him, and said in English, "Thank you."

He waved his hand again and the three of them left him to smoke his cigarette.

Kathleen and Ella walked side by side in silence. A big event had just happened, and Kathleen silently thanked God for the doors that were continually being opened. She wondered if Ella was giving thanks in her own heart, but that question was put to rest when the curious actress broke the silence with, "He can smoke and I can't?"

Sowany had been the key to the village all along, and Kathleen was very aware of this. She knew that if anything of great spiritual relevance was going to occur in the tiny village, it would be through the chief. His traditional side kept his people out of modern clothes, but his liberal side allowed Kathleen and Jake to remain in the tribe as missionaries.

Being an island immersed in old-time culture, Tanna was a rare place to find with its indigenous people and seven different languages within a compact space. Almost all of the tribes within the island were concealed from civilization, new religious movements, and practices. The missionaries who came to the island a hundred and fifty years before were greeted with hostility, and although the Message was spread significantly, they were openly shunned in modern times.

Sowany knew the history of missionaries on the island, and he knew about the other religions that the Tannese people practiced. He kept his tribe animistic, but the presence of missionaries had always been fine with him. He had allowed the couple to stay many years before, and he had permitted Kathleen to stay with them when she came. After he saw her trying to nurse the dying people for a week when the malaria had been so bad, his doubts were put to rest, and he knew that she was here to make things better for his people.

Several of the villagers had become Christians in the years since the missionaries came to the tribe, but he was not one of them. Sowany was a chief and a spiritual leader to his people. He would not change his beliefs because of what a white woman said, but he still respected her and allowed the others to practice their new-found religion together.

Kathleen had seen God working in Sowany's heart from day one. He was a tool being used to help his people, and he did not even know it. It was living proof that supported her matrix theory: nonbelievers are pawns in a game that they don't even know exists. She prayed every day that the old man would find Christ, if not to merely realize the important role he held to saving everyone in the village.

Kathleen had not fully understood what a young heart the tribe leader had until Jake had arrived a year earlier. Not wanting the newcomer to stay, she had taken Jake to the hut with the hopes that Sowany would turn the new white man away, saying how inappropriate it was for a single man and woman to be living in his village.

But the outcome had been the very opposite of her hopes. Sowany had clapped his hands with pleasure, saying, "Ket-si, this is wonderful! He can stay and now you can be married. What a wonderful idea!"

Luckily, Jake's language comprehension was poor at that point, so he missed the gleeful remark, but Kathleen set the chief straight on the subject.

"Jake is here for working on water that will not make your people sick anymore. We are not going to be married."

Sowany nodded like he understood, but he kept a mischievous grin on his face.

"He can stay, even if the two of you are not going to get married."

The sly grin never left, so Kathleen had left the hut with a knot in her stomach.

"What did he say?" Jake had asked.

"He said you can stay." She never told Jake about Sowany's match-making comment, and she never would. There was no use for more than one head to get the idea.

Leap of Faith

The sun was getting low in the sky as the afternoon waned on. The days were getting shorter due to the Southern Hemisphere winter, and it was making efficient work more difficult. The villagers were coming in from the fields and forest to their huts to begin their supper, but the children were still out playing. There was a gang of them from ages five to fifteen, the boys wearing their loin covers and the girls wearing grass skirts. It were these items of "clothing" that distinguished which were males and females as all the children had very short, tightly curled hair, and the girls were too young to have developed breasts.

They ran to Kathleen's hut at the edge of all the other homes and peered in through the door at the visitor. Ella, Kathleen, and Epi were inside trying to get settled. Kathleen was stringing up a new hammock across the room, making the area seem even more compact than it had been before. Epi was playing quietly on the floor until he saw the group of children, then he rose to go play with them. He ran up to them thinking they had come to retrieve him, but he soon found out that they had come to spy on the guest. They asked Epi questions about her in hopes he would know since he would be sharing his hut with her, but he could not answer their questions.

Ella was still trying to wipe the dirt and leaves off and out of her shirt from the rock incident. She pulled her hair out of its ponytail to redo it when she heard giggles from the doorway. Her body turned to face the opening that was filled with twenty or so faces. They quickly backed away when she saw them, and she suddenly knew how a zoo animal felt when people watched its every move.

"Kathleen," Ella whispered, "we have visitors."

Kathleen looked at the door and walked over to the group of curious onlookers. She had a big smile on her face, but her hands were on her hips so as to catch them in the act of snooping.

"What are you all doing?" she said with elderly condescension.

The group nudged the oldest boys forward who they knew would be braver in asking their friend about Ella. Three teenage boys were now standing at the front of the group with their heads down in embarrassment. Kathleen, arms crossed, leaned forward to catch their eyes. Finally, the tallest boy looked up.

"Ket-si, we wanted to show Ella the gorge."

She smiled and replied, "We are really tired, but I can ask her for you."

The boy nodded with a grin while Kathleen turned around to Ella. "They want to show you something before it gets dark."

"What is it?" Ella asked. She was whining with the exhaustion from the day's events. In the past twenty-four hours, she had been on four planes, a nauseating jeep ride, and the hike from hell. Her will was not ready for another adventure.

Kathleen sighed, and replied, "It's a place where you can get cleaned up."

Ella stopped moping. "Let's go."

The group of children led the way through the huts and into the jungle beyond. Jake yelled from across the field, "Where's everyone going?"

"To the gorge. They want Ella to do the leap of faith!"

"I'm coming, too," Jake responded, and he ran to catch up with the group as they made their way into the jungle.

"Leap of faith?" Ella asked.

"Just a nickname we use for it," Kathleen responded.

The trail they were following led up a steep embankment, and Ella was trying to remember if she had even seen a hill or mountain when they were flying over the island that could be this high. She looked ahead where all the children were running and laughing with excitement. Epi was running alongside the smaller children when their little group abruptly cut off the trail and headed downhill, on a different path.

"Where is he going?" Ella asked.

"They're going to wait for us at the bottom."

Kathleen was walking a step behind her. Ella could hear Jake talking somewhere in the back of the line, and when she turned around to look, she saw that Agmol and Saki were following the troop, too.

With the sun going lower, it was getting harder to see the trail within the hot jungle, but she just tried to follow the steps of the kids, despite her not knowing where they were leading her. The trail was suddenly transformed into a climbing area, and as Ella looked up, she saw all the children making their way up the muddy path using the roots and vines that stuck out of the moist ground. She turned around to Kathleen in panic.

"I can't climb this."

"It's easier than it looks. Besides, you've come this far."

Ella turned back to watch the children climb up the steep

hillside. The older boy that had asked Kathleen a question back at the house was half way up the escarpment when he looked down at Ella and saw that she had stopped. He made his way back down and began to point to places where she could hold on. She understood, and slowly stepped up to the first root that would be her foothold. The boy slowly moved up the hillside, pointing and climbing, trying to show her where she could hold on. It was like having a twelve year old rock-climbing instructor.

The confidence inside her grew. Kathleen had been right; it was not as hard as it looked. Ella still tried to look at the small guide above her while pushing herself up with the footholds he had pointed at. The last foot of the hill had a slight overhang, but the boy easily pushed himself over the top. He turned around and pointed furiously at all of Ella's options, but she froze when she saw the muddy overhang.

Easier said than done, kid.

But, somehow, she managed to hoist herself over the edge and she rolled away, onto a soft patch of grass.

Kathleen, Jake, and Saki easily lifted themselves over the edge, too, and when Ella turned away from the hill to continue following the group, she froze. The children were gone except for the boy, and beyond him was a drop-off.

The boy ran to the edge and jumped off.

Ella slapped her hand to her mouth in anguish as the little body flew over the side of the ledge.

"Did that child just jump off the cliff?!" she screamed to Kathleen.

"There's another island in Vanuatu where bungee-jumping was invented, but these kids don't use ropes."

"Is there anything at the bottom?" Ella cried, still stunned.

Just as she asked, Kathleen pointed over the ledge and Ella hesitantly took a step forward. They got very close, and when she looked over the side, she saw a crystal-clear pool of water at the bottom, fifty feet below. All of the children were on the rocky edges of the pool, looking up at her with big smiles.

They had jumped!

Ella's jaw dropped.

"Holy shi—"

"Don't even think about finishing that word!" Kathleen said, pointing a finger.

Ella looked down at the boy who had jumped and he looked back up at her with a big smile. He kicked his legs and glided smoothly across the pool to a flat rock where all his friends were waiting to see the newcomer take the leap.

"See, he's fine," Kathleen said. "There's nothing to it."

"You don't actually expect me to jump off this cliff, do you?"

"Why not? We've all done it a dozen times. It's like an initiation. Besides, you think I'd let you jump off a ledge that would hurt you?"

"I don't even know you."

Kathleen shrugged and looked at Jake. The tall man was taking his shirt off, preparing for his leap. He threw it down the hill to where Agmol was standing helplessly in his cast, then ran past the two women in an adrenaline rush. He looked like a giant child who couldn't wait to go swimming.

"See you ladies at the bottom!" he said as he ran to the edge. He leaped off the cliff shouting like a frat boy all the way down. Only Saki, Ella, and Kathleen remained at the top, and it appeared that Ella was not going anywhere. Kathleen leaned over to whisper in Ella's ear.

"You have to try this. These kids brought you here."

"No, I won't do it," Ella said while she gulped. "I'm a rich, stubborn, British celebrity. No one makes me do things I don't want to do. You can't make me jump."

"Ella, your fame means nothing to these people."

"How old are you?"

"What?"

Ella looked at Kathleen condescendingly, so the bewildered blonde answered, "I'll be thirty in September. Why?"

103

"I'm thirty-five years old. Don't think for one moment that you can treat me like a child —"

Kathleen threw her hands up in frustration. Was this conversation even happening?

"If you want to get clean, then you'll jump," the frustrated missionary scolded. "We won't have time to hike down there to get water because the sun is going down. Either jump for respect and a bath, or climb back down that muddy hill and go back with Agmol. It's your choice, but don't think I'm treating you like a child. I'm treating you like a real person. People have been very careful with you your whole life, and now you're thirty-five years old, and still a brat. Don't expect me to play the star-struck game, Ella. I may live in the middle of nowhere, but at least I live in the real world."

Ella sat down on the grass, breathing heavily with anger. Kathleen shook her head, took a few steps back, and started sprinting for the cliff. She flew over the edge without fear, and Ella listened as she heard the splash and the cheers from the children. She closed her eyes with embarrassment, trying to decide whether or not she should jump.

Kathleen's statement angered Ella, but she knew it was true. No one had ever been firm with her, except for her husband on occasion. She had walked right into the trap of bringing her fame into the scenario, and now it seemed that all the money and the movies she had ever made couldn't give her the faith to leap off the cliff that twenty other people had already conquered.

Twenty other *children.*

Saki must have seen the expression of giving up, because he walked to where she was sitting and pointed back to the hill.

"Agmol will wait for you."

She did not understand him, but she knew what he was saying. She nodded with a cold expression, and Saki walked to the edge of the cliff where he simply hopped off, leaving her alone on the top of the gorge.

At the bottom of the gorge, Kathleen swam to the edge of the pool, gasping for breath as she tried to recover from the stinging cold water. The area within the rocky cliffs was submerged in shadow, and little puffs of air could be seen coming from her mouth as she swam briskly to a flat rock that sat by the pool. She was gasping for air and trying not to curse under her breath.

Why did she leave Ella up there? A part of her had been hoping that if she jumped, then Ella would follow, but now she knew that that would not happen. An obstinate character like Ella would have to jump on her own, and an impatient person like Kathleen would have to learn the value of waiting.

Jake reached his hand out to Kathleen and pulled her out of the water with great strength. She was shivering and looking at the top of the ledge where Ella was probably still moping.

Jake looked concerned, and asked, "She's not coming?"

"No."

"Is everything okay?"

Kathleen took a deep breath, trying to recover from the harsh remarks she had just shared above. Now she had to relax so as not to upset a second person in one day. She avoided eye contact with Jake, speaking to him in a slightly agitated tone.

"No, everything's not okay."

She walked away, still talking. Whether it was to herself or God, Jake was not sure, but she was having a heated discussion with some invisible force as she walked across the flat rocks toward the edge of the gorge.

"I knew this would be a bad idea. This woman thinks she can just walk into a tribe and live like a Beverly Hills resident? She comes in here, wanting a smoke and a hot shower. Well, she'll figure it out, sooner or later. She'll learn we aren't the Plaza Hotel, here to serve hot towels and cookies—"

She stopped mid-sentence and saw that all the children were still standing there, waiting for Ella to jump. They stared at Kathleen with big eyes, and she shivered uncontrollably, trying to think of the best excuse for the kids who had taken the journey to see the guest leap off the edge. Kathleen tried to control her shudders, but she was too cold, and she looked at the ground with a heavy heart. These kids didn't have video games or movie theatres, and they didn't have baseball games or Boy Scout meetings. The event of the year was today, and it was obvious they were sorely disappointed that their guest did not want to play with them.

Kathleen opened her mouth to speak, but Epi stepped forward boldly, his little voice cracking with disappointment and nervousness.

"She's not coming, is she?" he whispered. Kathleen shook her head and he nodded. Then he turned around and faced the others.

"Ella told me that she wanted to wait until the water was not so cold," he lied.

The kids all nodded, and one by one, they made their way down the rocks to where the trail formed below the gorge. Kathleen, Epi, Saki, and Jake stood at the edge of the clear pool in silence. Epi turned to his mother and she leaned over to kiss him on the forehead.

Her heart was warmer now, and she asked God for forgiveness. This little boy wanted everyone to have a clean soul, even Ella, and he had covered for her.

"Ella would be really happy to know that you said that to them," she told the little boy.

Epi humbly smiled, and said, "I'm sorry I lied," and scampered off to where his friends were trekking down the rocks. Saki also smiled as he began to go down the rocks, and the trio descended the gorge, reaching the trail back to the village just as darkness was engulfing the forest.

Ella had not moved from her sitting position for a long time, and the sky was turning twilight gray. She stared at the ledge, trying to push herself to leap over it. Sometimes, she would convince herself that she was not afraid, her muscles would relax, and she would move like she was going to jump. Then, the moment her muscles pretended like they could do it, her body settled back down in its original position, frozen with fear. So she sat there, staring emotionlessly at the drop-off, trying to figure out why she could not trust something so easy that ten year old children could do it.

When darkness had finally fallen and it was hard to see anything in front of her, she heard a whistle from the muddy hillside behind her. She crawled to the edge and looked down. Agmol was waiting faithfully at the bottom, waving for her to come down. Ella looked back at the cliff and decided that even if she *did* jump, she wouldn't know where to go, so this gave her an excuse to ignore the idea altogether. It was almost relaxing to know that jumping was not an option anymore, so she dangled her legs off the edge of the dirt overhang and began to climb down the muddy embankment. Her stomach rubbed against the cool ground while her legs hung in space, trying to find a root in the side of the hill. She found one, and slowly made her way back down to where her injured guide was patiently waiting.

The lantern was fully lit and Epi was eating his spaghetti with gusto at the little table in their hut. It wasn't tribal food, but Kathleen got shipments every few months, and it was his favorite dish, so tonight's "Welcome Home" feast would be Italian. She had changed into dry clothes and hung her wet ones on the edge of the table. At the desk, she meticulously organized her books and papers that had been abandoned three weeks before.

Outside, the crickets hummed in the hot night, and mosquitoes flew rapidly in the field. Many bugs came into the hut because they saw the light, but it didn't seem to bother the mother and son. In fact, they were both happy to be with each other again, eating dinner in the tribe the way they did every night.

The fire pit next to the hut was glowing with activity, and a group of the village's Christians were gathered around it, laughing and talking while Saki strummed at his guitar. Saki's wife, Lauriny, sat shyly next to him, giggling at the jokes that the others made. They were scooping fruit and stew into their mouths, taking in the excitement of the day. None of them had had the opportunity to communicate with the newcomer, but they were all anxious to learn about her. The one thing they did know, though, was that Ella was a very different creature than Kathleen.

Upon Kathleen's arrival six years earlier, all the men and women that were now gathered around the fire had been teenagers, and they had taken her to the leap of faith. The event had become a tradition, even an initiation, and Kathleen had passed with flying colors, fearlessly jumping into the bitter cold water below. When Jake had arrived the year before, he couldn't be restrained from leaping over the edge.

But there was something different about Ella. They discussed it during supper, but it never occurred to them that the woman was starving for any type of soul. As a matter of fact, Kathleen was the only one who really understood that Ella had issues that stemmed deep within her, and she even thought that maybe Epi, her observant son, had picked up on it as well. Either way, the cheerful group continued to talk around the fire about the long, dark hair and beautiful green eyes of the visitor.

Kathleen listened to the conversations outside her door while she shuffled through papers and cleaned the typewriter on the desk. When she heard a light tapping at the door, she turned around to see Jake, freshly clothed and waiting for permission to enter. She smiled at him for the first time since she'd arrived that day and waved him in.

Epi saw him and held his fork up, his mouth overflowing with spaghetti. "Jaap!"

"Spaghetti!" Jake said as he shuffled to Epi's side. Then, he walked to where Kathleen was sitting, and said, "What's the occasion, Mom?"

Without looking up from her work, Kathleen replied, "We're celebrating my return. Or didn't you notice that I've been gone."

"Oh, I noticed. The absence of your cold shoulder kept me warm on chilly nights."

Kathleen smiled while she shook her head.

"So, what do you think of our new guest?"

"I'm shocked," Jake said, leaning his hand on the desk. "How'd you meet her, and how'd you get her out here? I've heard of celebrities doing adventure races and things, but Ella Levene has never struck me as the outdoor-type."

"That's because she's not. The closest she's probably ever come to camping was sleeping in her trailer on location for one of her movies. I doubt if *she* even knows why she's here?"

"Yeah, that's so weird. How did she end up in this little Tannese village?" Jake pondered.

"She claims that she's going to do a movie about indigenous people or something. I'm not really sure. The whole thing came about so quickly."

"She's probably trying to replenish her career," he said, half joking.

"What do you mean?" Kathleen asked, turning to face him. "She was the most famous actress in the world when I left the States."

"Well, that was almost seven years ago, and she's not an actress any more. She's a director, and the last thing I knew about her and her husband was that their careers were finished."

This was news for Kathleen, and she sat a moment, absorbing the information. Even though he'd been joking, Jake made a good point. Was this two month visit going to be written into a ground-breaking film? Kathleen immediately dismissed the thought, not wanting to lose what little trust she had with the stranger. Instead, she confessed her own convictions.

"I'm so afraid that I may have brought her here with the wrong intensions."

"How so?" Jake asked, crossing his arms while he leaned on the desk.

"I feel like the Lord wants her to be here, but something else is telling me that I just wanted her to come to see this life out of selfish ambition. I was hoping she would see what we have here and become a believer in an instant. Then, she could go back and ignite the spiritual heartbeat of Hollywood, and I—"

She was unable to finish her remark. She looked down at the ground with guilt while Jake finished her statement for her.

"Then you would have been responsible for the conversion of the famous Ella Levene."

Kathleen nodded, and Jake watched while she put her face in her hand. He looked over at Epi, now watching the conversation with great concern. Jake shrugged at the little guy and turned back to where Kathleen was sitting.

"Those were some pretty big goals in such a small amount of time."

Kathleen nodded, and continued.

"Now that she's here, and I know her, I don't know what to do. She is so lost, so burdened. It's too easy for me to just restrict her vices and put her soul to the ultimate test, but that may end up scaring her away. Besides, I don't even think I like her very much. Does that make sense? A missionary having trouble liking someone?"

"I think you need to ditch the title for a minute and realize that you're human, first and foremost. And you're used to reaching out to people you love, not dislike."

"I just need to pray for wisdom," she said. "God may not use me to get through to her, but something life-changing will happen to her. I can feel it. It could be through anyone."

Just then, Epi leapt out of his chair and ran to the door. The crowd outside began to cheer and the music got louder. Jake and Kathleen went to the door and saw that Ella and Agmol had returned from the jungle safely. Agmol limped over to the group and sat down while Ella stood uncomfortably outside the circle, not knowing what to do.

Jake leaned over to Kathleen and whispered, "Everything happens in God's time, and for His purpose. Believe me, I know. *Your* leap of faith can be to just let Him do His thing."

Then, he clapped his hands together and walked over to Ella with a hospitable smile on his face.

"Hey, Ella, how was the hike back?"

Ella sat at the table where Epi had been eating as she poked at her spaghetti. It was not luxurious by any means, but she had been expecting to eat bugs, so this was one step up. She was in the hut by herself, listening to the singing outside by the fire. The group outside was worshipping God, and she had opted to eat instead, so now she was glumly picking at her cold spaghetti. She had barely eaten in the past day, and even then it had been airplane food. Ella thought she should have been hungry enough to eat anything, but her anxiety was keeping the hunger away, and now it was all she could do not to throw up.

The whole jumping scenario a couple of hours before had pushed her over a different ledge, an emotional ledge. She suddenly became very aware of how strong everyone in this village was, and how happy and warm they all seemed to be. Most of all, she saw that they had nothing compared to what she had, yet it seemed to be enough for them. Her mind drifted in and out of a state that saw the only necessities to life as being food, water, and shelter, and this made her life back home seem so obsolete.

Suddenly, the anxiety hit hard, and she found herself realizing that she was not happy anywhere. She was not happy with a family, beautiful homes, and a career that brought fame and fortune, and she was certainly not happy being by herself in the middle of a Stone Age tribe where a bath required jumping off a fifty foot cliff. Where was her place in this world if not on one extreme end or the other?

Her hands began to tremble with nervousness, and when she heard the music outside stop, she tried to quickly control the shaking. Epi and Kathleen walked in, and Epi hopped into his hammock while Kathleen went to join Ella at the table. She sat down slowly, trying to seem as peaceful as possible. Ella continued to stare at the half-eaten spaghetti while the two of them sat in silence for a moment.

"I had no right to say those things to you at the gorge. I'm sorry," Kathleen finally said.

"Thank you. Apology accepted."

Kathleen looked around the room, feeling the intensity of the moment.

That was easy enough.

Then, she noticed that Ella wasn't eating.

"I thought you'd be starved."

"I guess the day has finally caught up to me. I'm not hungry after all."

"I can give it to Epi if you don't want it—"

"No, I'll finish it."

Ella began to shovel the food into her mouth while Kathleen stared blankly. She was having a really hard time understanding what Ella was thinking about. Not hungry one moment, hungry the next. Cold and heartless ninety-five percent of the time to everyone. Unwilling to participate in any activities with any of the people she had come to learn about. If Kathleen were filling out a report card for Ella to take home to the parents, it would not have looked good.

When Ella was finished, she said, "Thank you," and climbed into her hammock. It took her a few moments to adjust her body in a comfortable position, but she finally came to rest.

Kathleen shrugged, looked up so as to plead with God, and then rose to turn off the lantern. The room was dark now, except for the way the light from the fire outside danced its way through the door.

Kathleen walked over to where Epi was curled in his hammock, and she told him something in his language before she kissed him on the cheek. Ella listened to the hushed remark from within her own hammock, wondering what Kathleen had told her son. But the wonder lasted only a moment because exhaustion hit her, and the last thing she remembered was seeing Kathleen climb into the hammock beside her and settle in for the cool night ahead.

"Good night," Kathleen whispered to Ella. But Ella was unable to respond as the overwhelming feeling of sleep pulled her into its dark dwelling.

Long Night

The light was a magnificent, white glare that blinded her, making her trip and stumble across the dirt. She would give anything for sunglasses as the light struck her fair-skinned face. The sky was so blue, so high, and it seemed like it rose forever, allowing the sun's brilliant light to hit the Earth as if the planet was only a foot away.

Ella ran and ran, crying, trying to breathe, trying to look around for anyone to help her. The ground was no longer firm dirt, but fine-grained sand, and it was harder for her to run. Her feet sank into the ground, and she used all her might to pull them out so that she could keep up the pace.

But what was the pace for?

Running from what or to what, she was so confused. The tears kept running as fast as her feet, and she wiped at her face furiously, trying to dry them.

And the heat.

The heat was unbearable. She felt like she was breathing fire, inhaling the scorching air, and exhaling the remains of her lungs that had been singed by the temperature. But the pain in her lungs and her muscles only made her run faster. Faster and faster, she ran through the desert, that nameless desert that plagued her body like leprosy.

This desert she ran through seemed to run her, control her. Her entire being was to merely survive this desert without falling or stumbling, but she knew she had to stop sometime, and this realization only made her cry more. When would it end? When would this desert end, and when would she find someone to help her? Someone had to be out there, watching her, seeing what she was running from, seeing what she was chasing.

The bright, blue sky suddenly turned dark and the sun grew. It was close now, and all the clouds in the sky rapidly floated away, but the color was still dark. Then the sun's body came within the atmosphere, and Ella ran so fast that her body let off smoke while the radiant heat pressed down on her.

Ella's eyes burst open in panic. She was looking into the side of her brown hammock that gently swayed back and forth in the air. The fire outside was completely out now, and she lifted her head to gaze at the dark room. Everything was quiet except for the chattering bugs outside her mosquito net, and the symphonic crickets in the field beyond.

She looked at Kathleen, who was hidden behind her netting and within the confines of her own hammock. She could hear a soft snoring from where Epi was sleeping near the door, and Ella quietly lowered herself back into her hammock, breathing heavily. The dreams were getting worse, and she didn't know why.

Her wristwatch gave a little beep indicating that it was the top of the hour and she looked down at the lighted screen as she pushed a button. It was only midnight. She must have been sleeping for three hours, and now it seemed like she would never get back to sleep, because every time she tried to close her eyes, she felt the desert's heat and saw the sun grow larger in the sky.

She was tempted to wake Kathleen up, but she decided that

that would do nothing. What could Kathleen do for her? Sing her to sleep? Ella simply laid there, heart still pounding and breath still heavy. She could not think of what to do for the next seven hours before daylight. She finally had the courage to close her eyes, and when she did, she smiled a little, thinking that this meant sleep would return to her.

That was when she heard an animal cry from within the jungle, and her eyes shot open. It had made the crickets and frogs outside stop their music and everything in the tribe was silent. No one else in the room responded to it, and it had only been for a second, but Ella froze her muscles for ten minutes, waiting to hear the animal walk into their hut and eat them all. She kept her eyes on the doorway, expecting to see a black panther walk in and catch her opened eyes with its night vision eyesight. Were there even panthers on these little islands? The things she *didn't* know about the island were what scared her most.

Ella continued to lay in her hammock, tense with fear, until she finally heard the bugs begin their song again, telling her that all was well. She relaxed in her swinging bed and closed her eyes, but her watch beeped again. It was already one in the morning. Where had time gone? She tried to cuddle in a comfortable position.

The chirping crickets stopped again, but this time there was no animal cry.

It could be an animal silently moving into the settlements, looking for a late night snack. Did animals hunt at night? Ella opened her eyes again and stared at the doorway, waiting for something to come in. Or what if it wasn't an animal at all? It could be someone from another village—an enemy village. What if they had heard that a strange, white woman was coming to this one? What if they wanted one of their own? Would Kathleen be enough strength to keep an Indian from kidnapping Ella and taking her back to his village?

Ella shot her eyes to where Kathleen was sleeping, suddenly

realizing that she did not feel safe. Why couldn't Jake or Agmol be in here? She decided Agmol's injured leg would not allow for good defense, but certainly Saki could take on another Indian. Yes, she would go get Saki or Jake to come and sleep in the hut with the women and the boy.

Then, she would be able to sleep.

Her body relaxed at the thought of a strong man coming in the hut for protection, but it tensed up again when she remembered that she didn't know where either man lived. Memories streamed back to two weeks before, when Alice Walker had said something about a maintenance building. Jake was the engineer, so maybe he slept there. But Ella had not seen a building like that so far.

The watch beeped again.

Two in the morning! She couldn't believe she had spent the last two hours thinking about how to protect the hut. And the crickets had not started again, so she knew that the threat could be closer now, maybe even right outside their door. She continued to watch the doorway, waiting for the ravenous cannibal to come in and take her away. But the cannibal never came, and a few minutes later, the crickets finally started chirping again, and they kept going until Ella had finally convinced herself that she was safe.

Once again, she shut her eyes, trying to go back to sleep. She had to sleep, or the first full day in the village would be a waste of time due to the exhaustion. In order to distract herself from worrying about being tired the next day, she mentally recited all the lines from her first major film role some fifteen years before. Unfortunately, once she got past the third scene, when the space crew knows the alien is on board, Ella realized that it was harder for her to go to sleep because she was putting too much effort in remembering the lines.

Bee-Beep. Three o'clock. The air was getting colder, and she could feel a draft rising up from beneath her, making the parts of her body facing the ground colder than others. She shifted in a warmer position and still found that it was cold. Listening to the soft snoring of Epi began to make her jealous of the sound sleep he was getting. Even Kathleen had not moved, and Ella wanted to know what the secret was to sleep around here.

Suddenly, the crickets stopped again, and Ella would have let it slide this time because it had been such a normal occurrence, but then she heard a rustling noise outside. Her eyes opened wide, and she froze for fear that the creature would hear her every move. The rustling sound grew louder, and she could hear that it was right outside the door. Ella remembered that the hut was slightly raised, so whatever was out there, she knew she would hear its entrance by the sound of footsteps on the stairs leading into the room.

The tiny noise stopped for a moment, but then continued, growing louder. Ella slowly lifted her head in a position to where her eyes were only a centimeter above the hammock's edge, trying to see what was outside. It was so difficult to see through the mosquito net, but she didn't dare move it. She wasn't going to make a sound. Her eyes tried their best to adjust to the darkness, and her ears were on full alert, trying to listen over the seemingly loud noise her pounding heart was making.

Once the noise was at its loudest, it stopped, and the grass was still, but it turned into a tapping, and that was when Ella knew it was walking on the steps into the hut. What was she going to do? Her voice was dry and she tried to call for Kathleen, but she couldn't get her vocal cords to work. The tapping continued, but there was something strange about it. It was so light, and constant. A person would have been visible by now.

A shadow caught the corner of her eye, and she shot her head to the floor at the entrance to the hut. The creature was about a foot long, and it crawled past the door, its little toes clicking on the wood. It looked at Ella in the dark and slithered its tongue out at her.

It was an iguana.

Ella let all the air out of her lungs, realizing that she hadn't taken a breath in some time.

"*Son of a bitch,*" she said while the air rushed out of her.

She took deep breaths in relief as she watched the lizard make its way past the door and head back out into the night. She gave it the finger as it walked away, wondering when this island would start giving her a break. So far, a rock, a cliff, and a lizard had been the near causes of death for her, and now sleep deprivation was sure to follow. Ella rolled over in mental exhaustion, trying to close her eyes. She decided that the next time she heard a noise outside, she would let it come and get her, because no creature could be worse than this night.

At four o'clock in the morning, she had started silently singing every show tune she could think of, despite her lack of musical talent. Once she had gone through every song she knew, Ella decided that this place would never provide her with any sleep. She would go to Kathleen that day and force her to send her back to Lenakel for a plane ride home. A couple of glasses of scotch and a cigarette would have cured the sleeplessness so far, but it was clear that she wouldn't be getting those the rest of the trip, so any attempts to sleep at night would fail.

It was almost five in the morning when her mind was completely made up. She would wait until Kathleen woke up, then she would demand a return back to civilization. How could Kathleen keep her here against her own will? It would be kidnapping if that happened. Ella would have to go back.

The sky started to turn a dull gray, and the sun was going to be up in an hour or so. Ella could hear activity around the village. Fires were being started and people were moving about. Morning whispers could be heard in and around the settlements as dawn slowly emerged from the cold night.

She heard footsteps outside the door and looked over to see Jake standing at the entrance. He had sleepy eyes, and was bundled in a hooded sweatshirt and jeans. He did not enter, but he tossed a piece of paper across the wooden floor to where Kathleen was sleeping. He started to walk away, and Ella was going to call out to him, but nausea suddenly swept over her.

She didn't feel too good all of a sudden, and she knew that it was because she had not gotten any sleep the night before. Whenever she didn't sleep, she was sick the next morning. Alcohol and nicotine withdrawals probably had something to do with it, too. She had tried to quit drinking a few years before and had been sick non-stop for two days. When she went back to the booze the next day, she decided that a life with liquor was easier than a life without.

The swaying of the hammock was suddenly exaggerated, and Ella blinked her eyes several times, trying to get her head to feel firm. It was no use. She was going to be sick if she stayed in the hammock. Where could she go, though? There were no bathrooms, and the hole in the ground surrounded by tall bamboo walls was not what she considered a toilet.

Kathleen rose from her hammock and pulled the mosquito net over her head. She looked at Ella when she moved, and Ella rose from the hammock, also pushing the mosquito net aside. She dangled her feet over the edge of the bed and stared at Kathleen with a face as white as a ghost. Kathleen gave a little grin and asked, "Did you sleep okay?"

Ella shook her head, her cheeks starting to puff out a little.

"I've been awake since midnight." Then, suddenly, she jumped out of the hammock and darted for the door. "I'm going to be sick." She bolted out the door with Kathleen running behind her.

Ella stumbled to the back of the hut that faced the open field. There were no houses back there, luckily, and she bent over to vomit. Kathleen ran up behind her to hold her hair back, and Ella threw up. She knelt down to her knees, trying to stop the movement of the hammock, but it was no use, and she continued to be sick while Kathleen held the hair and put her hand on her back.

"Dammit!" Ella shouted, embarrassed that she had gotten sick in front of someone. Even though she wasn't crying, her eyes and nose ran from the gag reflexes, and she tried to wipe her face with the long sleeve of her shirt.

"It's okay," Kathleen said, deciding not to correct Ella's language. She stood over the sick woman, trying to pretend like everything was fine. But things were not fine, and Kathleen shook her head with concern while Ella continued to gag in the tiny ditch.

"It's just the withdrawals," Kathleen said. "I should have known this would happen. I'm sorry."

Ella still hunched forward and, trying not to move, replied, "You know, if you were really sorry, you'd get me a beer."

Kathleen laughed a little, and Ella finally sat up, leaning against the wall of the hut. She looked at Kathleen with dark circles under her eyes and a white face. It reminded her of a ghoul, but she didn't share that with Ella.

The nauseated woman continued. "It's the withdrawals, it's the lack of sleep, it's the stress. It's everything. It's rock-bottom, and you get to witness it."

Kathleen, sitting against the wall next to her, opened her mouth to say something, but could not. Instead, she prayed for the suffering woman. She prayed that some type of peace would come to the rescue, and that God's light would shine on her by any way possible. Her heart was suddenly heavy for Ella, like it was with the villagers, and Kathleen wanted for her to meet the Lord so badly.

The two women sat in silence for a minute while Ella tried to get her breath back. She leaned her head against the wall and stared at the field, which was now fully lit. She could feel her white face absorb the cold air from the early morning, and her head was sweaty while tiny strands of hair were stuck all over her cheeks and forehead. If she'd had a mirror, she knew she'd probably throw up again. Her hot breath hit the crisp air, leaving little puffs of white clouds to float away. She didn't know why, but the moment of physical weakness and vulnerability made her want to share her burdens with Kathleen, so she continued to talk. Her hoarse voice sounded like she was on her deathbed.

"I was thinking about what you said last night, and some of it was true. People *do* treat me differently, and in return, I can't trust anyone. The people I meet day to day are out for themselves, and I'm more guilty of that than anyone. I can't trust them, and I can't trust myself. And the fact that I know that makes me wonder how I've even gotten this far in life."

Ella gave a care-free, little laugh, like it didn't bother her in the least. She continued to wipe her face with her sleeve. Kathleen kept her silence, absorbing Ella's confession. It was her first insight into what this woman's soul was like, and she decided that Ella was in need of a major cleaning.

Finally, Kathleen took a deep breath and said, "What do you say we get off this muddy ground and go inside?"

"All right."

Kathleen stood first and helped Ella to her feet, pulling her up by the forearms. It took Ella a moment to shake off the wobbly legs, but she soon started walking back around the hut. The fire had been started, and Ella paused for a moment before going inside. She looked down at the wristwatch that had plagued her through the tormenting night and decided that time was just another burden out here. Alice Walker had been right—a person didn't need a watch in this tribe. Taking it off her wrist, she sighed and threw it in the fire, watching as the flames engulfed the hands that linked her to time and reality.

She was going to try this jungle thing again.

Nice Gestures

Epi had crawled out of his hammock and sat down at the table by the time Ella and Kathleen entered the hut. Ella was still very nauseated, so she sat at the table, put her head in her hands, and tried to keep her body still. Kathleen had two towels, one wet and the other dry, and she came over to where Ella was fighting for her health at the table. The dry towel was placed on the dirty surface for Ella to rest her head on while the other was used as a cold compress.

"Thank you," Ella said gratefully when the cool cloth was handed to her. She put her head down on the dry cloth and closed her eyes.

"I'm so tired."

She tried to lay the wet towel over the side of her face, but it kept falling over, and when Kathleen saw this, she said something to Epi. The little boy nodded and crawled onto the table, taking the wet cloth out of Ella's hands before he gently dabbed her forehead with it. Ella made no effort to stop him. He was the most sensitive, calm child she had ever seen, and it was almost soothing for someone to be helping her through the upsetting moment, even though he was only a kid.

"He's the best nurse we have in the village," Kathleen said, working on their breakfast with a Coleman stove.

"Does he speak English?"

"He can recognize a few words, but he doesn't put them into sentences. I try to speak Tanna North to him as much as possible."

"Tanna North?"

"That's the name of the language everyone speaks on the north side of the island, where we are."

"I see." Ella's eyes were getting heavy, and her body started to relax more. Not only was she feeling better, but she felt sleep coming.

"I must look dreadful," she said.

"At least there were no paparazzi around," Kathleen said with a grin.

"Are you going to bring that up every time something embarrassing happens to me?"

"Only if I can remember."

Ella gave a hint of a grin and slowly closed her tired eyes. Epi continued to gently dab her face, carefully wiping the loose strands of her dark hair away from the skin. She was so tired, but she wanted to know about the little boy.

"I don't see any family resemblance between the two of you."

"That's because we're not related," Kathleen responded dryly, moving to where she could clean out the typewriter.

Ella ignored the blunt remark and continued her interrogation while she yawned.

"How did he come to be your son?"

"It's a long story."

"I'm not going anywhere."

Kathleen glanced at Ella, and saw that she was near the point of sleep.

"Do you remember what I told you about the outbreak of malaria we had a few years ago?"

Ella nodded.

"Well, Epi had just been born. His parents were only teenagers, which is the normal age to be married, and he was their first child. They had both become Christians when they were children, when the missionary couple was still living here. When I arrived, they opened their arms to me and taught me a lot of the language that I didn't already know. I think they could relate to me more because I was closer to their age than the older couple.

"So, when I got here six years ago, Epi's mother was pregnant with him, and it was only within the first month I was here that she gave birth. But it was too early, and there were complications. Epi was fine, but now he has asthma and he's smaller than the other children his age. It was a rough time for his parents to see this little baby struggle so much, and I would pray with them every night, standing over Epi's bed. I didn't know much of their language yet, but they took me in as a part of their family, showing the rest of the village that the newcomer could fit in. They were a gift from God.

"After Epi had been born for about four months or so, the first cases of malaria started making their way throughout the village. His parents were some of the first villagers to get sick, and they made me take him away from them to keep him healthy. His father's fever went so high that he slipped into a coma and died within two days, and his mother's fever rose soon after.

"Before she slipped into a coma, she told me that she wanted me to take care of her son. She even had Sowany and the other village elders come to the hut to witness that I was being given the responsibility to take care of Epi. Much of her family had either died or left the tribe, and I was the only one that really knew about Epi's fragile condition.

"I promised I'd take care of him, and when she died, Sowany told me I had a son, and as long as I took care of him and watched over him, I was a part of their tribe. It's a sad story, I know, but if they hadn't died, things would be very different—"

"Ket-si," Epi whispered.

Kathleen looked up as though she had been in a world of her own, her stare following the voice. She saw that Epi had stopped dabbing Ella's head because the exhausted director was sound asleep, her head resting on the dry towel. There was more color in her face, which was a good sign, and her body was completely limp from the hard night's beating.

Epi jumped off the table very quietly, and Kathleen picked him up in her arms, whispering, "Thank you for taking care of her. Let's go outside and eat so that we don't wake her up."

The child nodded and she put him back down to the floor, watching him scamper outside to where some of the other villagers were eating their breakfasts. Kathleen turned back to the sleeping woman, noticing how peaceful she looked when she slept. The burdens of the world didn't seem to show when Ella was asleep; only peace rested on the dormant stranger.

Kathleen started to walk out the door to leave the hut in silence, but she stumbled across a piece of paper on the floor. It looked like a note, and she had to assume it was from Jake because no one else in the tribe knew how to write. She picked it up and unfolded it, reading its contents slowly. Inside it read:

> Jesus tells us in the Bible, "…Love one another. As I have loved you, so you must love one another. By this all men will know that you are my disciples, if you love one another." John 13:34-35.

It continued at the bottom, in nice handwriting: "I read this and thought about what you said. All you have to do is love her, and God will find a way in through that friendship. Jake"

Kathleen refolded the piece of paper and thanked God for such a perfect verse for the day.

God, please give me a warmer heart than usual for Ella. I think she needs all the help she can get. Please work through everyone that she meets, revealing Your magnificent light to her within the next two months.

She felt a sense of peace come over her, and she knew that God would work, like Jake had said the night before, in His own time.

Before she walked out the door, she whispered to the sleeping Ella, "You can trust the people here."

Jake

Jacob Willis sat outside the maintenance shed in a lime-green beach chair that he could put his legs on and stretch out in the sun. He was reading his Bible and saying a morning prayer before work for the day. He thanked God for bringing him to Tanna, and for supplying him with the necessary tools to construct the water tank and shed. His prayers drifted into intercession as he prayed for the Tannese people, Ella, and Kathleen. Then there was the prayer that was for Sowany's heart to be opened to the Holy Spirit.

Jake opened his eyes and leaned against the door to the building, staring at the swaying palm trees. The morning dew had left them shiny, and as the wind hit the fronds, they shimmered, and he saw only a canopy of green sparkles glistening in the sunlight. Still immersed in shadow, the area around the building was cold and gray, but he continued to watch the trees above move around in a chaotic blend of golden yellows and bright greens.

Could life be more beautiful than it is in this moment?

His body was at peace, and he smiled at God, thanking Him for the life that had been mercifully bestowed upon him. Jake felt that he did not deserve to be happy, but he was, and he knew it was by the grace of God that this was so.

Jake had not always been a Christian; as a matter of fact, Christianity was something that he had joined in recent years. He'd known Kathleen in college, and liked her, but never understood why she was so uptight. The two of them had gone to Oregon State together, and Jake had been involved in the stereotypical party life—drinking, smoking, and experimenting with the occasional drug. He had always felt like a good guy, but when he was around Kathleen, his attitude would change. He wanted to show her that he was a good person even though he partied. It was basic knowledge that she was strict about everything in terms of drinking, partying, and boys.

They had both been Anthropology majors, so many of their classes were taken together, and she was always nice to him. He asked her out on several occasions, and the answer was always "no." After a while, he gave up, classifying her as a hard-ass who thought she was better than everyone else. It wasn't until after he found Jesus that Jake realized that that had not been the case at all.

It was Jake's fourth year at Oregon State, and Kathleen was ready to graduate in June. He felt he would be lucky to finish college in four years, especially since Engineering was a second major. The rain seemed to be more depressing that year, and Jake didn't feel motivated to do anything but stay at home and drink. The semester that was supposed to be his last started spiraling downward, and in June, his graduation plans turned to summer school plans, and then fall semester plans.

His parents were good people, and they had paid his tuition the full four years, but when it appeared that Jake would be in school for a fifth year, Jake's dad drove to Oregon from Seattle to see how their son was doing. When Arnold Willis opened the door to his son's apartment, he looked in horror at what was in front of him.

Food and dishes were scattered on the floor, molding from the musty air. There were piles of unclean clothes that had apparently been growing for weeks. It was three in the afternoon, and Jake was passed out on the couch in a puddle of beer left over from the night before.

Arnold Willis' eyes watered from the stench of mold, liquor, and marijuana. He promptly walked over to Jake, pulling him off the couch and onto the floor. The hard fall in the pile of potato chips hardly woke his son up. Instead, Jake rolled over, moaning and gurgling. His father, fuming with anger and disappointment, pulled his son up off the floor by his arms. He dragged him into the bathroom and threw him into the shower, turning the water to a freezing cold setting.

Jake's eyes shot open and he gasped for air. He reached up for the knob in confusion, contemplating as to how he ended up in the bathtub. With a throbbing head and bloodshot eyes, he could hardly function. The real surprise came when he looked up to see a red-faced father staring at him from above.

"Hey, Dad," Jake said, pretending like he had meant to be in the shower. "What's up?"

"You're a mess!" Arnold shouted to his son. The loud voice rang in Jake's head like a gong. "When was the last time you cleaned this place, or yourself? Your mother and I have worked nonstop for four years trying to get you through college, and this is how you repay us? It ends here, Jake. You're on your own. I won't invest my money into a loser."

His father stormed out the door, leaving Jake wet and cold in the bathtub. Jake sat there for a moment, confused by the alteration to his normal day. Did his dad just say he was a loser? His own father?

Jake looked around the bathroom, motionless in the tub. Cigarettes had been pressed into the counter and a pair of woman's underwear hung from the towel rack. There was hair in the shower drain, and Jake noticed for the first time that the tile was lined with green and brown mold.

How did it get like this?

He shivered in the bathtub while cold water droplets still trickled out of the faucet over his head. Anxiety suddenly hit him like a fast-moving truck and he felt lost. Trapped in a cesspool of grime and sin, he stayed in the bathtub for three hours, trying to figure out how life had ended up like this. Tears ran down his face when he looked at the panties.

He couldn't figure out whose they were.

Finally, when it was darker outside and the cold was overbearing, Jake rose from the bathtub and stepped out, stiff from the sitting position. He walked through his apartment in a daze, as though it was a nightmare. How would he pay for his apartment, or his schooling? He knew what rock-bottom felt like, and he wasn't liking it at all. He was twenty-two years old; this wasn't supposed to be happening. Had his father really been serious about not supporting him? Arnold Willis wasn't a sensitive flower. If he said it was over, then it was over.

He sat on the couch in a daze and put his head in his hands.

There was a knock at the door.

Jake listened to it indifferently, wondering who it could be. He decided not to answer it, because he was still damp and his apartment was a dump. He stared at the floor in amazement.

What was he going to do? He had nothing, even in his apartment. For the first time in his life, he felt like a wreck—a lump of crap just sitting in the living room.

The knocking was louder. He heard a woman's voice.

"Jake, I saw your truck outside. I know you're in there."

It was familiar, but he still didn't move. Shame consumed him, and the dark room prevented him from seeing the physical results of his life. This day had been coming; he had seen it a few months before, when his behavior had gone out of control.

A day when a man has to look at himself, inside and out. Re-evaluating his life and actions.

No one ever wanted to have days when the very inner-core of thought and emotion was exposed, and time seemed to have been wasted. He had been so close to graduating, but the life he led had slowed him down significantly. He would still have another year to go if he started getting his classes and schedule in order, but how was he going to pay for it—

"I'm coming in," the girl said.

The door knob turned, and a tall figure stepped into the room. Jake didn't move from his position on the couch, his head still resting in his hands. He tilted it a little to look at the door. It was Kathleen Newman, and even though he was shocked that she, of all people, was there, he did not move.

"Hey, Scout," he said sadly.

She was dressed in an elegant suit and her blonde hair was curled down her back. The contrast of her figure to the rest of the apartment was dramatic, and the look on her face was one of disgust.

"I love what you've done with the place," she said sarcastically. "I haven't seen you in a while. How's it going?"

"How does it look?" he replied. Kathleen was the last person that he wanted to see. She was his friend, and it had been months since he last saw her, but the impression she left on him was one that always made him feel lousy later. And since he was already feeling horrible, the shame was emphasized.

"What are you doing here?" he asked quietly, looking back at the floor.

"I was in town and I wanted to say hi. I assumed you still lived here. What happened to your apartment?"

Jake sighed. He was in the middle of feeling sorry for himself; now was not the time to explain the downfall of his life.

"I don't know," he replied. "I don't know how it got like this."

"Do you want me to help you clean—"

"No!" he erupted. "Can you just leave me alone? My dad was here. He's cutting me off from school. I don't have a job. Please, go away!"

Kathleen stared in disbelief at the tormented boy. He was tall, handsome, and completely beat up. He had done it to himself, and she nodded her head with understanding. That was the last time she would visit college friends. She pulled a piece of paper out of her purse, wrote something on it, and left it on the table by the phone without him noticing.

"Have a good life, Jake." And she walked out the door.

He continued to bury his head in his hands, trying to wipe away the guilt. Now, on top of having no money, no degree, and a trashed apartment, he had just lost a stable friend. He apologized to her in his head, but it didn't help.

Jake stayed in the darkness of his apartment for a week. He unhooked the phone and stayed in bed all day, only moving to get food and go to the bathroom. He hardly changed his clothes. His friends didn't even come by to check on him, putting him into a further state of depression.

One morning, after over a week, he opened his eyes and stared into a bright light. It was early in the morning, and the sun was peeking through a tiny crack in the curtains. Yellow rays hit his whiskered face, and he squinted at the light. It was almost too beautiful to ignore, and it brought peace to his heart for a moment. That moment was just long enough for him to decide that he wanted to go outside.

He crawled out of bed and opened the curtains, and he saw that the trees were a gentle green in the summer's day. On his way into the kitchen to make toast, he caught something out of the corner of his eye. It was a piece of paper by the phone in the living room. He picked it up and squinted at the writing. It was from Kathleen, and it read:

> God never gives us anything we can't handle.
> Meet me at Hope Community Church on Sunday
> at 10:00 am.

Jake rubbed his face.

What day was it?

He looked at his watch and it said Sunday. But she had been here over a week ago. Did it mean today or last Sunday? He decided he'd go anyway, just in case she was there this week, too. He felt like crap and he knew he looked it, but he wanted to apologize for his behavior.

He showed up at the church that morning in wrinkled church clothes, looking for Kathleen. He sat in the back row of the sanctuary, trying to find her, but he never did.

During the sermon, he didn't pay much attention, until the pastor said, "Jesus said, 'Come to me, all you who are weary and burdened, and I will give you rest. Take my yoke upon you and learn from me, for I am gentle and humble in heart, and you will find rest for your souls. For my yoke is easy and my burden is light.'"

Jake's head shot up in attention.

That sounded good.

He tried to listen to the rest of the sermon, carefully attempting to grasp the words that were giving him comfort. After the service, he was so excited, and he shook the pastor's hand with enthusiasm.

"I've never heard anything like that before," Jake said, a big grin lighting up his face.

The pastor gave a warm smile back. "I'm glad you liked it. Are you a guest?"

"Actually, I'm a friend of Kathleen Newman. Do you know where she is?"

"Oh, no. You missed her. She's gone overseas for a year of interning with a Missions organization. You say you're a friend of hers?"

Jake slumped over. She was gone? He nodded at the pastor with sadness. "I used to be a friend, but I think I may have insulted her."

He started to walk away, his depression back on his shoulders.

"Young man? What's your name?" the pastor called to him, distracting him from the anxiety.

"Jake."

"Jake, you know, we're all going to lunch in a few minutes. Would you like to come?"

Jake shrugged his shoulders.

"It'll be on me," the pastor said, and he slapped Jake on the back.

For the next year, Jake kept going to the church to hear the sermons. He made friends, got involved with the college group, and even started teaching guitar to some of the younger members. He had long ago called his parents back for reconciliation, telling them that his partying days were over. They even came down from Seattle one weekend to see his clean apartment and go to church with him.

His grades climbed back up, and his father agreed to finish off the tuition as long as Jake got a job and started taking more responsibility. Jake was so happy when he heard this news, and even happier when he found out that he would be able to graduate the next spring, only a year later than originally planned.

It was never clear to anyone when Jake became a Christian. One day, he just started talking about the grace of God and the gift of Jesus' death on the cross. His heart was consumed by the love of God, and he wanted to tell everyone about how he changed. He had confessed about the drugs, the women, the booze, and he knew that Jesus had forgiven him. He had forgiven him two thousand years ago, on the cross.

After four years of growing, learning, and working, Jake was approached by the pastor about the Missions field.

"You know, missionaries aren't just teachers in the jungle. Many organizations are looking for people like you, Jake. Maintenance men, engineers, anthropologists—you'd be perfect."

Jake prayed about it for six months before finally succumbing to the Holy Spirit and applying. Tribal Missions for the South Pacific branch seemed the neediest, in Jake's opinion, for engineers. He went to their training for a year in Darwin,

Australia, and when it came time to be assigned somewhere, they showed him the little island of Tanna in the South Pacific.

"There is a tribe in North Tanna that has been in dire need of a sanitary water system, among other things," Alice Walker told Jake. "There's a woman living there now who is with our group. She's there learning the language and trying to start a literacy program for the villagers. She's about your age and very independent, so you'll pretty much be on your own out there. This woman's heart is dedicated to the conversion of this people group, but she's very overprotective about who comes to the village."

"I understand how she feels," Jake replied with a sympathetic smile. "I was an Anthropology major. I know about outsiders threatening the culture of a people group, but rest assured, I'm ready for this."

"I've forgotten where you went to school."

"Oregon State."

"That's funny," Alice Walker grinned. "The woman in the tribe went there, too."

Jake's stomach sank. It couldn't be.

"What's her name?" he asked.

"Kathleen Newman."

The jungle birds were crying to each other from within the cluttered nation of trees that surrounded the building. They couldn't be seen, only heard, and it sounded as though they were causing an uproar against each other. No song could be independently heard, but instead every bird cried, trying to scream louder than the others. A gust of wind hit the trees hard, and the birds suddenly rose from the forest, startled by nature's way of mediating the arguments.

Jake opened his eyes and took a deep breath of fresh air. He loved it in this place, where everything that man had worked for meant practically nothing, and the true roots of humanity and instinct came alive. It was a place where a person could find their strengths, and their weaknesses. Ancient methods of agriculture, and raising animals. No television, and no honking horns in rush hour traffic. This was truly one of the remaining places on Earth with primitive lives, and Jake hoped that he would never have to go back to the busy world that he had grown up in.

He heard singing through the small grove of palm trees that separated the building from the rest of the village. Morning devotions were starting and he rose with the Bible in his hand, asking God to prepare his heart for the day.

Life in the Village

There was a fast tapping noise somewhere in the distance, far away from Ella's sleep. It wasn't constant, but it went very fast, and after a while it stopped. Her brain continued to sleep, but then the tapping started again and she was summoned from the dreamless sea of rest that had been consuming her. Her eyes barely fluttered open and she saw the surface of a table.

Where was she?

Her eyes opened wider and she moved her head a little. There was a black, human face staring at her, one that she didn't recognize. Ella didn't move, but continued to look at the stranger while it watched as her eyes got bigger. The tapping was loud now that Ella was awake, and she turned to look behind her. From across the table, the dark stranger spoke.

"Ket-si!"

The tapping stopped and Ella turned around to see that Kathleen was at the desk, her fingers poised at the keys of the typewriter. Ella rubbed her eyes in a daze, trying to remember what day it was; then she remembered the sleepless night before and felt relief that she had gotten sleep.

"What time is it?" she asked groggily.

"I don't know," Kathleen replied. "I'd say it's probably

around noon. You've been asleep for about five hours."

Ella kept her eyes at a squint from the daylight that came in through the window by the desk. Five hours. She felt better than she did that morning, but as her tongue ran across her teeth, she could still taste the bitter remnants of bile left in her mouth from when she had vomited. She turned back to the table and saw that the stranger was still looking at her in amazement. It was a woman, and Ella guessed she was about twenty.

"Hello," Ella said, attempting her first conversation with an indigenous person.

The woman looked at Kathleen and started speaking rapidly in her language.

Kathleen turned from the desk and said, "This is Lauriny. She's married to Saki. She helps me with my work during the day." She turned back around and tapped furiously at the typewriter again.

Ella watched the typewriter and discovered that that was the noise that had woken her up.

"What are you doing?" she asked.

"I'm trying to translate some old tribal stories for the children to practice on. Lauriny helps me with linguistics and story details." She paused. "I'm sorry I woke you up, but I had to start on this. I have three weeks of work to catch up on."

"What exactly is your job here?" Ella asked, yawning.

"I'm a teacher. I am trying to teach everyone how to read."

"Read what? There's nothing out here."

Kathleen stopped typing and faced Ella. "They need to be literate in order to read the Bible. And not just that; they can read and write their legends, traditions, medicinal instructions—the list goes on. A very small percentage of indigenous Tannese people can read and write."

"Is there even a Bible in their language?"

"Only certain parts of the New Testament have been written, and that was in 1990. It's been a long time since more has been attempted."

Ella shrugged her shoulders. She knew nothing about the Bible, or the importance of it. What was another few years if it was not written?

Kathleen continued. "If the people in and around this village learned how to read and write, they could be key players in Bible translation. There are other Mission organizations that specialize in Bible translation, but I'm here to hopefully get them started with the basics. Someday, God will bring someone here to do the really hard work. Translation takes years."

Ella stared at Kathleen in disbelief. Did this lady actually believe that all this would happen? Ella knew a lot of people, probably more than anyone else, and she could bet that no one had ever even heard of Tanna, or Vanuatu.

"No one even knows this place exists. What makes you think anyone cares about these people having a Bible?" Ella asked.

Kathleen broke into a big smile and tilted her head a little.

"God knows they're here. He'll send someone." She continued to type the unfamiliar language on the paper, leaving Ella in confusion at the table.

To each his own, Ella thought. The typing suddenly stopped and Kathleen whipped around in her seat.

"I almost forgot! I'm your new best friend."

"Pardon?" Ella replied, her eyebrows raised.

Kathleen pointed to the corner of the shelter where there was an area shielded by tiny bamboo walls, and dangling from the thatched roof was a portable shower. It looked full and Ella stared at it with her mouth wide open.

She looked back at Kathleen, who said, "That's right. We warmed the water for you a while ago. Enjoy!"

Freshly bathed, and comfortable with the sanitary condition of her body, Ella stepped out of the hut to explore the village. It hadn't been a priority the day before, and wasn't even an option that morning, so she set off toward the other settlements on a mission to deal with these people again. She was only hoping they wouldn't outright shun her for her previous behavior. The afternoon was hot with a cool breeze, the way it had been the previous day, and Ella pulled her sunglasses over her eyes as she started her journey into an ancient world.

The first person she saw on her domestic journey was a familiar face. It was Agmol, her quiet guide from that evening, and he was supporting his weight with a cane. For the first time since she'd met him, she looked at the foot that was injured. It was in a cast and placed in a special walking boot, and Agmol walked very lightly with it, trying not to apply too much pressure to the healing in progress. He saw her and waved while she hesitantly walked over to him.

Agmol was in his early twenties, and it seemed to Ella that he would be very athletic and active if the cast was not hindering his movement. He didn't seem particularly tall or strong, but he looked at Ella with eyes that wanted to learn. And she wanted to learn, too, but the language gap was too grand, and as she went up to attempt a conversation with him, her will was already giving up on the idea that she would find out what had happened to his foot.

Ella pointed to his foot and shrugged her shoulders, and it took him a moment to figure out to what he owed the great honor of being approached by the new guest. Finally, he looked down at his foot and gave a big grin with comprehension. He pointed to a nearby tree and began to shake his arms back and forth like he was tugging furiously at one of the branches. Then, he clapped his hands together like an object hitting the ground. Ella's eyes got big. She understood, or so she thought.

"You fell out of the tree?" she said out loud. Obviously, he didn't understand her, but she motioned her hands in a way so that it looked like she was pointing at a falling object. Agmol nodded with enthusiasm and then shrugged his shoulders with embarrassment. He seemed to like this game, and he motioned for her to follow him.

Ella followed Agmol around the huts in a silently guided tour, watching him point to people and landmarks. She wasn't completely sure what the significance of anything was, but she was ecstatic beyond belief that she had an indigenous friend to show her around.

She thought back to the days when she and John were sought after by thousands of fans at all the red carpet events. Girls cried and reached out to touch her, asking for her autograph. The media would beg for ten minutes with her and try to talk to her. Now, the tables were turned, and she found that it was incredibly ironic for her undivided attention to be given to a crippled Tannese man who didn't have the slightest clue as to who she was. She could visualize the *60 Minutes* cast and crew flying all the way to Tanna and offering the humble tribesman top dollar to get the lowdown on the famous Ella Levene.

Agmol entered a hut that was not too far away from Kathleen's, and Ella followed him in. Inside, there was a woman who was patting a pasty substance into flat shapes, and Ella assumed that it was a bread mix of some kind. Agmol said something to the young woman, and she looked up at Ella in surprise. She rose to her feet and shook Ella's hand with a dainty grasp. Ella gave a grin and shook it back. She didn't know who this woman was, but if it was another friend, so be it.

"Namay," Agmol said to Ella while he pointed at the woman.

Ella did not know if that was her name or a vocabulary word, but her confusion was put to rest when he pointed at Ella and said, "Ella." Then he pointed to the woman, saying, "Namay."

"Hello, Namay," Ella said, trying to cover up her previous ignorance. This was pretty cool. Mingling with the locals. Overcoming linguistic barriers.

Agmol patted Namay on the shoulder and walked out the door again, Ella following close behind. The group of children that had been stalking Ella the day before was waiting for her outside the hut. Agmol shouted something at them, but they followed the duo anyway, observing the intricate moves of the white creature that followed her guide throughout the village. The experience had gone from serene to chaotic within seconds as the young boys fought to walk next to Ella. They stuck their chests out to imitate the perfect posture of the actress, and moved their arms back and forth in a very elegant way. It wasn't for mocking purposes, but to simply try and discover how she could walk on the erratic ground this way.

After perfecting their posture and delicate movements to mimic the amused stranger, they finally figured out why she had had such difficulty on the hike to the gorge: she walked wrong. The older boys nodded their heads in agreement.

Yes, the way she walked was not suitable for the jungle.

They were disappointed that Ket-si would bring a person here who could not even walk decently, so the boys ran off to play, bored now with Agmol's deluxe tour. But the girls in the group stayed and walked alongside Ella, deeply appreciating the posture, and they tried to imitate her out of admiration.

The tour of the settlements came to a close when Agmol turned around the corner of a hut and they were facing Kathleen's little area again, where the large fire pit was. It gave off some smoke as Lauriny boiled water over the top. Kathleen could be seen still typing through the window, and Epi sat on the steps of the doorway, fiddling with some papers that Kathleen had probably given to him.

Ella looked at Agmol and thanked him. He nodded his head like he understood, and walked back to the hut where Namay was probably still working. Ella looked back at the place where Lauriny and Epi were working and snickered a bit. She wasn't sure she had learned anything new on that little tour, but she was happy that it had happened.

Ella's smile faded.

She was happy?

Her heart started pounding faster while she let the news of the year sink in. When was the last time she was happy? The day before was the first time she'd been excited about anything, and now she was happy? What would the next days bring? She stood there for a few minutes, trying to remember when she had felt like this. It had to have been months since she genuinely smiled at something. This made her feel better about everything, and her anxiety temporarily shifted from negative to positive, and for that brief moment, she was glad that she had come to Tanna.

Cultural Anthropology

Kathleen was still working at the typewriter when Ella walked in. Epi and Lauriny were outside by the fire pit, leaving the two women alone in the hut. Ella stood awkwardly by Epi's hammock that was closest to the door. She fingered the frayed edges of its fabric. Kathleen noticed her standing there, so she stopped the typing.

"What's on your mind?" Kathleen asked.

"I was wondering why no other huts have hammocks."

Kathleen smiled and said, "You busted me. I'm guilty of a major crime in the anthropological world. I brought them myself."

Ella looked puzzled so Kathleen continued. "Hammocks are generally found in Latin American indigenous tribes, but I brought mine here six years ago after I had slept on a mat, in the dirt, for a few months. I asked Sowany if it was alright and he didn't really care."

"Then why is it breaking a rule?"

"Anthropologists," Kathleen explained, "enter a culture for studying and observing, trying to keep the culture preserved for as long as possible. Of course, that's practically impossible because whatever culture you assimilate yourself into will eventually be changed anyway. Anthropologists judge missionaries for entering a culture and trying to change its religious beliefs and lifestyles, but lives and traditions are changed even if *they* are here instead of missionaries."

"How so?"

"Well, if a tribesman has never seen clothes in his life, and a western anthropologist, or missionary, comes to the tribe wearing their boots, pants, and shirt, the idea is a new one to the Indian. For example, there was once an anthropologist who went to study a tribe somewhere, and he was homosexual. He brought that lifestyle to the men in the village and changed their sexual preferences. If a missionary brings the Word of God into the tribe, the religious beliefs and animistic traditions are threatened to change, so the table can be turned both ways. Missionaries and secular anthropologists are all guilty of having something to do with change in a culture.

"Even people who are neither can directly affect a culture's belief system. One example of this is Tanna Island's famous for its John Frum Cargo Cult. A big chunk of the population on this island believes that John Frum America will bring lots of gadgets and things to them if they rid the island of Europeans. They believe this because during World War II, when U.S. troops were island-hopping around the Pacific, they landed here and showed their transistor radios and nice uniforms to the indigenous population. The Tannese people even saw that black sailors were in possession of such technology, so they founded a religion based on the belief that if Tanna is rid of all white men, John Frum America will return with all the nice things that were here before."

"If they are trying to get white people off the island," Ella asked, "then why does Sowany let you stay?"

"The cult is not accepted by everyone. As a matter of fact, many people are embarrassed by it. Sowany knows about the cult because he's been to other villages and towns, but this tribe is very animistic, so the cult has not made its way here. He would have no reason to get rid of me."

"And the hammocks?"

"They just assume its how my tribe sleeps."

"Your tribe?"

"Oregon."

"And the religion thing?" Ella asked. "You're trying to get them all to become Christians, so isn't that breaking another rule in anthropology?"

Kathleen smiled. "I got an anthropology degree in college, and made it my foundation for coming here. When I got to the tribe, I used all the knowledge that I could to adjust, learn the language, and fix my life so that it coincided with village life. Their way of life around the village shouldn't have to change when they become Christians. The Tannese who have already become Christians still have ceremonial dances for funerals, weddings, and circumcisions, and they still live in their little huts with no clothes. It's their soul that changes, not their culture, and if for some reason their culture took on more western characteristics as a result of Christianity, then so be it. The value of eternal life with Jesus far outweighs anything that we have here on Earth."

Scout

The second night in the village was not as bad as the first, and Ella got a little more sleep. Then, night after night, sleep became less of an issue, and thinking of sleep turned into sleep. Jungle noises and iguanas no longer plagued the director, and somewhere within the days and weeks that followed her arrival, Ella started smiling more. It was something she noticed at first, and the more she did it, the better her soul felt.

But running through deserts was still something that she did almost every night when her eyes closed and she was surrounded by the suffocating heat. She thought she was finally happy, finally getting to a place in her life that she could function without offending her family, her coworkers, or herself.

Every night when the evening devotions were around the campfire, she listened to the different language. She was almost glad that she couldn't understand what they were saying, but then Kathleen or Jake would translate for her, and her continuing knowledge of the Bible grew as a result. Ella was not looking for God, or the Bible, so the devotions gave her a neutral feeling about the purpose of Kathleen and Jake in this tribe. On one hand, Ella's atheist beliefs caused her to see the missionaries' presence as obsolete. But, then again, everyone that was a Christian was so happy and confident. Even little Epi brought contagious giggles to everyone when a joke was told.

For Ella, life in the tribe was monotonous, but stable. It brought faith in daily activities and a new love for isolation that she had never been able to dream of. Kathleen and Jake seemed to be good friends, despite the occasional agitated looks from Kathleen. Tribesmen like Agmol and Saki brought their wives and children to the nighttime devotionals where love flowed like the heat from the crackling fire. Ella enjoyed this life, and the thought of leaving in a few more weeks saddened her.

Ella was sitting comfortably by the fire in her usually spot, waiting for the evening devotional time to begin. This was her favorite part of the day, not because of the prayer, singing, or studying of the Bible, but rather for observing her new friends while they socialized with each other. A group of about twenty people came to this fire every night to learn about God and tell stories of His blessings upon their children, crops, animals, and the village, but Ella knew the most about the original friends that had greeted her weeks before.

Saki and Lauriny sat across the fire with their two very young children. Saki was one of the fastest and strongest men in the village. He walked with an air of confidence around him, but spoke with the humility of a wise storyteller. His wife, Lauriny, was shy, and careful with her words and movements. Kathleen had given Ella different pieces of Tanna North writing to practice pronunciation on, and Lauriny was always there to help. She was a woman, and a key player in Kathleen's literacy program, so Ella had an immense respect for her.

Sitting next to Saki were Agmol and his wife, Namay. They didn't have any children yet, for reasons everyone in the tribe was curious about. They should have had many by now, but Agmol and Namay were not discouraged. Both believed that

God would give them children when He wanted. Agmol still had his cast, but he continued to wait for the day when it would be time to return to Lenakel for its removal.

Jake was seated next to Agmol's family, holding the guitar that he and Saki shared. He had taught Saki how to play some songs, but tonight, Jake was the worship leader. He strummed quietly at the strings, waiting for Kathleen to come out of the hut so that they could begin.

Ella had been there for three weeks and still couldn't figure out the relationship between Kathleen and Jake. Kathleen could be very cold and bossy with him, but then she would give him warm smiles and kind words when the occasion called for it. It was an odd situation, and Ella hoped that she would get to the bottom of their past.

Someday.

Next to Jake was Epi. He was sitting on a log with his tall friend, staring absently into the fire. Ella loved everything about this little boy: his admiration for both Kathleen and Jake, his silence and his charisma that he offered, and the giving spirit that most children in America had all but lost. There was no whining with this child, and there was no asking him to do anything more than once. He was obedient, but still playful, and Ella found that she couldn't think of words such as these for describing her own son. She decided that that was because she hardly knew her children, but she was sure that if she spent more time with Freddy and Sara, she could find nice descriptions for them, too.

"Scout! Are you coming?" Jake yelled into the hut.

"Just a minute!" Kathleen yelled, heard from within the dark room.

Ella couldn't hold the curiosity any longer, so she asked Jake the question that she was dying to have answered.

"Why does everyone call her 'Scout?'"

Jake's eyes twinkled with pleasure while he heard the question. He turned to the rest of the group, and said something out loud with a big smile on his face.

"She wants to know the story of 'Scout.'"

Everyone started cheering and saying, "Skote! Skote!"

Kathleen came running to the door with a grim expression on her face. She pointed to Jake with a long finger, silently telling him to keep his mouth shut, but Jake returned a little wave to the pointed finger and continued.

"Ella, that is a wonderful question—"

"Jake, *no*," Kathleen said, coming up to his face. Even though she was tall, she looked petite next to him. She looked up at him with forcefulness.

"Remember what I told you about embarrassing stories?"

"Oh, come on, *Scout*," Ella said, trying to get a rise out of the angry blonde. The rest of the group was still cheering, and Epi giggled so hard that he almost fell off the log. Kathleen's face cooled down when she saw her son's giddiness, and she looked Jake deep in the eyes.

"If you tell the 'Scout Story,' then I get to tell them something about you," she finally said.

Jake looked around as though he was hiding something, but then his smile came back and he nodded. Kathleen walked back to the hut, shaking her head, while Jake faced the audience. He rubbed his hands together, smiling at the faces that were lit up with cheerfulness and the light of the fire.

"Okay," he began in English. "So, Kathleen and I were Juniors in college, and during our spring break, we had to go on this anthropological field study down in Central America for a week. There was about ten of us in the group, and we were collecting data from some of the Garífuna villages on the Caribbean coast. It was pretty far out there, and we did a lot of backpacking and camping when we traveled from one village to the next.

"One of the guys in our group was an Anthropology major with a football scholarship. He was big, cocky, and chauvinistic, so you can only imagine the relationship he had with Kathleen. The guy's name was Dudley MacDermott."

Despite Jake's speaking English, the villagers around the campfire erupted in laughter, yelling, "Doodley!" Epi started to giggle uncontrollably while Jake told his story to Ella, making big movements so that the others could follow along.

"Dudley's claim to fame was that he was an Eagle Scout, and that no one knew more about the wilderness and camping than he did. Of course, one person did." Jake pointed to the hut where Kathleen was still doing something inside. "Every time the poor guy lit a fire or bandaged someone's cut, Kathleen would come later and rectify what he had already done. He never figured it out, but everyone else knew, so after a while, Kathleen was nursing all the wounds and digging all the fire pits. Dudley didn't even know how to tie a good knot, but who did a great job at knots?"

Ella pointed to the hut, and Jake nodded.

"That's right."

Everyone was giggling now, trying not to let the laughter out. Kathleen could be heard shouting from inside.

"It's not funny!"

This, of course, made everyone giggle more, but Ella motioned with her hand for Jake to continue.

"One day, Dudley found out that Kathleen was re-bandaging wounds and sparking fires when he wasn't looking. The rest of us thought it was the funniest thing in life that big Dudley was being outdone by Kathleen; but, boy, he got mad. He made a big scene about how he was an Eagle Scout, and if we knew anything, we would go to him if there were problems.

"The teacher got fed up with the competition, so he assigned Dudley and Kathleen to hike to a nearby village for re-collecting data that had been overlooked when we were there before. Dudley pouted, and Kathleen didn't really care—"

"Yes I did!" Kathleen yelled from inside the hut. She came out with two cups of coffee, handed one to Ella, and kept the other for herself. She sat down next to the actress and tried to suppress a smile while Jake continued to tell the story.

"Anyway," Jake said, looking at Kathleen from the corner of his eye, "Dudley and Kathleen set out to this village. Now, no one really knows what happened on the way there, and we'll never know how they got along while observing the people, but it was the trip back that makes the story really interesting. Apparently, Dudley's long, emulous stride down a hill caused him to trip in a small sinkhole. He fell down, sliding in the mud while his foot stayed in the ground. He had broken his ankle.

"Kathleen went to help him, and he was embarrassed, so he yelled at her. But, being the persistent person that she is, Kathleen began to splint it, putting a stick in Dudley's mouth to fight the pain. Then, she lifted him, put his arm over her shoulder, and dragged him for two miles back to our camp. Not even the torrential downpour or unstable, muddy ground could have prevented her from bringing him back safely."

"Don't you think you're exaggerating?" Kathleen asked Jake. Jake hushed her and continued.

"You should have seen it, Ella. We were relaxing at camp, eating soup, when Kathleen comes over the hill, lugging big Dudley with her."

Jake re-enacted the sight, causing everyone to laugh.

"We went running up the hill to help bring Dudley down. The moment they took him off Kathleen's shoulders, she fell down. She was all sweaty and muddy—"

"You don't have to explain every little detail—" Kathleen interrupted.

"But she followed us down the hill with what little strength she had left. Our professor radioed for a car to come and get Dudley. While we were all sitting there, waiting for it to come, Dudley looked at Kathleen with grateful eyes—"

"I can't believe you're telling it like this."

"*Ssshhh!* Dudley looked at Kathleen, put out his hand, and said, 'You saved my life. Put 'er there, Scout.'"

Everyone laughed, including Kathleen. Even Ella was getting a good laugh out of poor Dudley's sentimental attachment to being a boy scout. Epi was hunched over on the ground, holding his stomach from giggling too hard. Jake had told the story several times before, having to explain what boy scouts were, and when everyone understood, they decided Dudley was a fool and Kathleen was strong. Now, every time they heard about Dudley's ignorance, laughter always accompanied the story.

Kathleen wiped a little tear from her eye. "That poor guy. All he wanted was to be like Crocodile Dundee."

Jake was talking through his reminiscent laughter. "But I'll never forget when he thrust his hand out like that. I thought for sure he was going to give you the "Scout's Honor" hand motion."

Ella slowed her laughing down and looked back at Kathleen. "So what's a good story about Jake?"

The laughter came to a stop between the two college buddies, and Jake sat on the log by Epi. The others stopped laughing, too, wondering what Ella had said to halt the joyous moment. All that could be heard now were the crickets and the crackle of the fire.

Kathleen looked around at everyone and translated the question.

"Ella wants to know what my story about Jake will be."

All heads nodded frantically. They wanted to hear it, too. Kathleen had never said anything about him before, so this was a monumental event.

Jake poked at the fire with a stick, his attitude somber now. He was ashamed of the person he was when Kathleen had known him before. He didn't need these people to know what type of person he was in his former life.

"Be gentle," he said under his breath.

Ella looked at him curiously, then glanced back at Kathleen. *That bad, huh?* she thought.

She watched while Kathleen squinted her eyes the way she did when she was deep in thought. Everyone waited for her story about a younger Jake.

Finally, she looked up, and said, "I've got one."

Jake cringed, waiting for his past to reemerge. He knew that Kathleen would rat him out if she had the chance, and now it was here. He thought she would tell them about the time he had drunk-dialed her the night before finals. Or maybe she would mention all the times he asked her out, but she had declined because he wasn't suitable enough. The story he dreaded most was when she had come to see him during his pit of depression and his apartment had looked like Vegas pimps and showgirls had run through. What would she say to get these people to lose respect for him?

"One time," she said in English, "Jake and I were in a study group with about five other anthropology majors. It was the second semester of our senior year, and I got news that I wouldn't be able to graduate in June. I was only a couple of units short of my degree because of a mandatory class I never took during my second year. As it ended up, I didn't need the class after all, but that news didn't come until a few weeks later.

"Anyway, the night I thought that I wouldn't be able to graduate was right before our study group's weekly meeting, so I was pretty upset when we all met at my apartment. The first person to show up was Jake. I knew him as a classmate and nothing more, so when he asked me if I was okay, I pretty much shunned him. I felt bad after that, so I told him that I wouldn't be able to graduate, and he said he was sorry.

"The next week, while I was waiting for everyone to come over for our study group, I noticed that there was a lot of noise outside. So, I went to my window, looked down at the parking lot, and there was Jake with the rest of the group. They were holding bouquets of flowers, and singing "The Wind Beneath My Wings" at the tops of their lungs. Then, one by one, they climbed the stairs and presented the flowers to me. I thanked everyone, and one girl said that it had been Jake's idea to cheer me up. That was when I knew he wasn't only a classmate, but he was my friend, too."

Ella looked at Kathleen with a smile. "What a lovely story."

Jake was frozen with disbelief, staring at Kathleen with big eyes as she translated it to the rest of the group. His heart was beating fast, and he could not believe she had said something nice about him. He finally blinked a couple of times, trying to regain his composure. Maybe she liked him after all.

After Kathleen had retold the story, everyone nodded with smiles while they looked at Jake. Epi put his hand on the tall man's arm with admiration. It was a very nice thing to do, making Kathleen laugh when she was sad. Everyone bit their tongues, though, trying not to suggest marriage. The Tannese sitting at the fire could not figure out why the two of them didn't just marry. They were the same age, they got along okay, and they were both white. A better match would not come again in life.

Even Ella was wondering why neither of them had made a move yet, but then she decided that Kathleen was too hardheaded for marriage. Independence was one of the missionary's strongest characteristics, and Ella could not see Kathleen devoting her life to anyone but her God.

Kathleen carried a tired Epi into the hut to put him to sleep while the others stayed by the fire to sing more songs. His arms swung idly from her shoulders and his head was resting under her neck. She could feel that his breaths were getting deeper, indicating that sleep was near. As she approached the hammock, her arms moved in such a way so that she could gently relax him into the swinging bed. When she put him in, he curled his body into a ball and looked at her, waiting for his goodnight remarks.

Kathleen smiled, leaned over, and whispered, "When the

Lord shows me the stars, I will remember your sparkling eyes. And when He shows me the sun, I will remember your bright smile."

She kissed him on the cheek, and he drifted to sleep with a content expression on his face. Soon, his snoring was the only noise in the hut until there was a voice behind her.

"What do you say to him every night before he goes to sleep?" Ella asked from the lighted doorway. "I always hear the same thing, but I don't know what it means."

"I tell him that God's stars remind me of his eyes, and the sun reminds me of his smile."

Ella grinned. "That's nice."

Kathleen nodded and said, "Are you going to stay up tonight for singing?"

"As usual, I'll pass. Not only do I have an awful voice, but I don't even know what everyone is saying. Besides, I'm exhausted; I was bending over all day helping Namay weave a mat. My back is killing me."

"Okay. Good night."

"Good night."

Kathleen left the hut while Ella climbed into bed, under her mosquito net. The constant movements of the hammock were normal to her now, and she rested her head on the side of it to face the door. The room was silent with the exception of Epi's snoring and the guitar playing outside. Ella's eyes were getting heavy as she watched the fire's light dance through the slits of the palm leaf walls and the doorway. It reminded her of hundreds of people silently dancing in front of a great beam of light, and all she could see were their shadows passing across the openings in the wall. Soon, the singing began, and it seemed as though the fire was now moving and dancing to the music, following the rhythm and charisma of the beat and sound.

She smiled and closed her eyes. For the first time in years, she felt an overwhelming peace come over her, and could not feel her normal burdens turning in her stomach and ringing in her ears. She simply laid in her hammock, watching the orange light through the slits and listening to the beautiful people worship their God. It was such a simple, honest life, one that she had never known, and she closed her eyes to fall asleep to the beautiful music that filled the cool, night air.

Saki was sitting by the fire, strumming a nameless tune on the guitar the way he had done the night Kathleen left for Australia. He loved the time after the devotions when everyone left and he could play Jake's guitar. Lauriny was sitting next to him, waiting for her husband to help her carry their children back to the hut. She knew that this was his most tranquil time of day.

Lauriny looked over to where Kathleen was trying to calm the fire with handfuls of dirt and ash. Then, a shadow caught her eyes, and she saw a dark figure approach the fire from the darkness of the field beyond. It was Jake, returning from his room. He stayed in the shadows next to Kathleen's hut and motioned for the white woman to come to him. Lauriny raised her eyebrows and tried to see what was going on. Kathleen was startled, but she approached him in the shadows. Lauriny squinted at them talking in the dark, watching to see what would unfold.

"Scout, come here!" Jake whispered to Kathleen. She jumped in surprise. She was not expecting him to creep up behind her. He waved his hand for her to come over, and she gave a little laugh while she went to where he was hiding.

"What are you doing?" she asked, half-laughing. Her smile faded when she saw that he was very somber. His eyes were wet, and despite his strong, tall figure, he looked like a lost little boy.

She asked with concern, "What's the matter?"

He looked over to where Lauriny and Saki were watching

from the fire. He knew they couldn't hear or understand him, but he also didn't want them to see his face; they would worry. He looked back at Kathleen and spoke, his voice cracking.

"Why did you tell that story about me?"

Kathleen grinned a little and replied, "It was a good story. Why? Did you want me to tell a different one?"

"No. It's just that—well, you've been trying to get me to leave since I got here. I figured you'd tell a bad story about me to get everyone to hate me."

Her eyes got very deep and she put her hands on her hips.

"You thought I would tell them something bad about you?"

"Well, my college days weren't my best—"

"But I can't believe you would think that I'd tell them all those things. Jake, God has forgiven you. I'm not allowed to dig up skeletons. Do you really think I'm that ruthless?"

Jake didn't answer, but just stared at the ground.

He didn't think that at all. He thought she was the most wonderful person in the world. He didn't think she was ruthless; he thought she was a woman with a hard outer shell. He also thought she was someone who was afraid of love. He didn't tell her this, of course, but he wanted to.

Every day, he wanted to tell her what he thought of her. He would watch her talk to the villagers and laugh. He would see her typing in concentration through the window of her hut. He saw the way everyone in the village, even Sowany, loved her. She was everything he wanted to be, and everything he wanted to be a part of. Almost every night, he sat in bed, wondering how he could tell her. He asked God to soften her heart, and make his stronger.

Tonight was the first time he thought that maybe she appreciated him the way he appreciated her. She had told a story about something he had done that was good and generous. Jake wanted to know why she had told the story because he wanted to know if it was finally time to confess his love.

Kathleen continued to stare at him blankly, trying to read his thoughts. Finally, he responded.

"I don't think you're ruthless."

He walked away, leaving her in the shadows with Lauriny and Saki watching suspiciously from the log. She blinked a few times.

What was that all about?

She turned back to where the Tannese couple was sitting with their sleeping children. They raised their eyebrows and she shrugged at them.

What a weird conversation.

Alone

Ella woke up to Kathleen shaking her.

"Ella! Wake up!"

She opened her eyes and shot up in her hammock, assuming there was something wrong. When she lifted her head, she found that it was completely light out, and she had slept through the night for the first time. There was activity outside where the villagers were usually working at this time of day. Kathleen was standing by the hammock, waiting for a bewildered Ella to get her bearings.

"What is it? What's wrong?" Ella asked, rubbing her eyes.

"Nothing's wrong, it's just that I couldn't wake you up. Did you sleep well?"

"Like a log."

"Good. Listen, I got a radio call from Lenakel. They have the books and school supplies I've been waiting for, but they need me to come and get them today."

Ella looked at her in confusion. She was still trying to wake up and Kathleen was talking really fast. "Okay. So, what's up? You want me to come or something?"

"No, I was wondering if you could stay here with Epi."

Ella was awake now. Of course she'd watch the child, but it

was a surprise to hear Kathleen asking her to watch her son.

She nodded, and said, "Of course. For how long?"

"I don't know. Saki's coming with me, and if we don't get to the trail by dark, we'll camp out in a small settlement near the road, so we may be gone until tomorrow morning. Is that okay?"

Ella nodded again. "I'll take good care of him."

"Great! He's outside by the fire; Saki and I are leaving right now. His asthma medicine is in the gray tackle box where all the First Aid stuff is. Jake should be done working by the river in the afternoon, so he'll make you dinner. Any questions?"

"Nope."

"Super! See you tomorrow!"

Kathleen walked out the door with a small daypack around her shoulder, leaving Ella in the hammock. Ella blinked a few times until she crawled out and stepped onto solid ground. She got dressed quickly and went outside to be with Epi, who was silently playing in his usual place by the steps leading into the hut. He was coloring on a piece of paper, but looked up when she came to sit next to him. He gave her a big smile and continued to draw.

Ella yawned just as Lauriny came up to the hut with her two children. The woman placed them next to Epi and motioned a good morning wave to Ella. Ella exchanged the greeting and they sat in silence while the morning activities started to grow around the village. Plumes of smoke rose sporadically throughout the huts indicating where all the morning fires had been. It was unusually hot this morning, so the gray tint of the village was more muggy than bitter.

Lauriny walked into the hut and started making coffee for Ella, as she knew that the actress would not be able to do it herself. The two small children and Epi played contently beside Ella, and she gave a little smile at the feeling inside her. This was a good place, with good people. She never knew there was such innocence and simplicity in life; she always just assumed that ruthlessness was a necessity for getting ahead in the world. Now, she knew this was not so.

These people were fair, kind, and loving to their families. Children respected their parents, and their parents worked hard every day to provide for the next. There was no planning for life six months ahead of time, and there was no greed for material things. The greatest symbol of pride in the village was whose pig was the biggest.

At parties, the person with the biggest pig got the most respect and village honor. Back home, Ella had three houses, millions of dollars, a room full of awards, and a dozen movies to mark her place in the world, and she had never felt the pride that each Tannese man had when he presented his pig to the village.

A pig.

It put things in perspective, but it still did not make her feel any better.

She came back to reality when Lauriny handed her a cup of coffee. It wasn't the best coffee, but it helped in overcoming the alcohol and nicotine urges. Ella missed all the booze and cigarettes for the mere fact that they kept her mind off of her life. When she was drinking, she was distracted from all the problems with her job, her family, and all the messiness inside her that one would consider a soul. If she felt cognate, that meant she had to deal with all those issues. On Tanna, she could deal with them in a sober fashion, but while being very far away from home. She knew that the first thing she would do when she got back on that plane was to have a good, stiff drink.

Lauriny handed Ella a piece of paper to read for the day, and Ella groaned. Lauriny laughed, but made her read it out loud anyway. Ella saw this as a form of torture; she did not know the correct pronunciations of any of the Tanna North words, and she always felt foolish when she had to read them out loud. She couldn't speak a word of their language, even after three weeks, and the reading was not helping, but Kathleen insisted that Ella get some sort of linguistics lesson while she was there. Ella was sure Kathleen was just trying to humble her, but in the end the actress felt she was rock-hard in the area of pride, and no form of humiliation would ever break her down into believing she was only human.

The heat got worse as the day went on, and at the time when the wind would blow through and cool the region down, it never came. The fields and jungle were giving off a massive amount of heat and humidity that made any work seem like more of a goal than a job. All the children that were usually running around the village playing games were now hunched in the shade of some nearby trees, eating fruit. Normally, they would have run to the gorge to jump in the cold water, but the walk through the trees and up the hill was not a possibility today. It was too much of an effort.

Even Jake came back early from his work site because he was afraid of heat exhaustion. He told Ella and Epi that they could come to the maintenance shed to cool off.

Ella said, "What makes the shed so much cooler than the rest of the village?"

She had seen it hidden behind a grove of palm trees only once, but had never been in. When he took her there, he opened the door, and she felt a cool blast of air from the inside.

The shed was connected to a generator, and had been built with electrical outlets. A fan was turning rapidly in the center of the room and Ella walked in with a dazed look on her face. She could not believe this had been here the entire time.

It was a large, cool room with cement floors and dry wall, like a building found in modern civilization. It had various pieces of equipment and tools stacked at the end of the room, but overall, it was surprisingly neat and tidy. Jake's futon with a blanket was neatly made on the floor, and he had his guitar on a table where there were books and blueprints spread out. The two-way radio was hooked up to the wall, and Epi ran over to play with the knobs.

Jake told him to leave it alone, which Epi did, and Ella continued to stare in amazement.

"Why have I not been brought here yet?"

"I think the scout wanted you to rough it before you knew that I was living in luxury."

"Do you want to trade with me?"

"If you only knew," Jake said under his breath. He'd take Kathleen as a wife and Epi as a son while living in a hot, dirty hut a thousand times before he lived in a cooled shed by himself.

Ella didn't seem to hear his comment because she continued gushing over the modern building. She was surprised by her reaction to the small place. She had not seen a modern building in three weeks, and now that it was before her eyes, she was grateful for it. Even the sight of the futon was bewildering. It was so simple, and yet so complex compared to everything else. The radio crackled, and there was a familiar voice at the other end.

"Jake, come in."

Epi jumped with excitement and looked at Jake with permission. Jake walked to the radio, lifted Epi on the table, pressed the button to talk, and held the mike up to him. The boy shouted into the microphone, speaking in his native language.

"Ket-si! It's me!"

There was a pause for the transmission to get through, and then Kathleen's voice came back on, but this time it was in Tanna North.

"Hello, darling! What are you doing?"

"Me and Ella are here with Jaap where it is cool. The wind machine is getting the heat off."

"Good! Can I talk to Jaap?"

Jake held the microphone to his mouth and said, "It's really hot here. I figured it was time to show Ella the fan."

There was another pause, and Kathleen said, "Saki and I are still here. Bobby won't be back with the truck until later, so we'll stay overnight in Lenakel and come back tomorrow."

"10-4. Do you wanna talk to Epi again?"

"Thank you."

Jake put the hand set back to Epi's smiling face, and the boy said, "Ket-si?"

"Epi, I am going to come back tomorrow. Be good for Ella and Jaap."

"I will." Then, in clear English, Epi said, "I love you."

Ella widened her eyes and looked at Jake who was smiling proudly. Jake said to the actress, "I taught him that."

Kathleen came back on the radio with a voice that cracked with emotion.

"I love you, too."

The radio clicked off and Epi gave Jake a thumbs-up.

Ella was reading a book to Epi in the hammock when he finally fell asleep. He was nuzzled under her neck and started to wheeze. She did not want to move so she sat there for a while. It was dark out, and the heat had gotten thicker. Bugs were buzzing all around the windows, trying to get in to where the light was.

Jake was looking at some blueprints very closely, his nose almost touching the paper. When he and his blueprints were together, nothing could break his concentration. He was trying to figure out how to get the pump flowing that he and Saki had installed. There were going to be three pumps throughout the village. One of them barely worked; the rest were still being tweaked. If only he had the right equipment—

"Jake?"

He looked up and saw Epi asleep on Ella. She pointed down to the boy.

"Can you give me a hand?"

Jake got up and lifted the little body from the movie star. He didn't wake up. Ella crawled out of the hammock and Jake gently placed Epi back in it. They both watched as the child rolled to his side and started to snore.

They smiled at each other and he asked, "Do you want something to eat?"

"No thanks."

"Snooze you lose." He kept eating his rice.

She watched him for a while, and then blurted out, "Why aren't you and Kathleen together?"

He choked on his rice.

"Huh?"

"Why aren't you married, or dating, or something?"

"Oh." He wiped his mouth with his fingers. "She would never get involved with someone like me. I have a past."

"Don't we all?"

"Well, yes, but she's experienced mine firsthand. I doubt she would ever think of falling for me."

"Why not? What happened?"

"Well," Jake said, obviously feeling like an embarrassing story was coming, "the week before she left for Darwin, she came by my place. My dad had just been over and basically cut me off from everything because he saw my lifestyle I had with his money."

"What sort of lifestyle?"

"Let me see. Lots of women, many of whom I can't remember because I was either drunk or stoned when I was with them. My grades were non-existent. I think I had a roommate for a while, but I don't remember that guy coming or going. It was a groggy time."

"And you were friends with Kathleen when all this was going on?"

"It was after she left that I turned the self-destruction knob on full blast. But she had seen it coming, I'm sure. We were just friends when we had all those classes together, and I was starting to get in with the wrong crowd. Anyway, she came to visit me, and I was at the lowest moment I had ever been in my life. I basically yelled at her.

"She left, but she also left a note inviting me to church. After a week of lying in bed like a lump of crap, I got up and found the note. When I went to apologize to her at her church, she was already gone. I kept going after that, and now, seven years later, I'm a Christian."

"How did you know when you became a Christian?" Ella asked, slightly tilting her head.

"I just felt—different. Better, less burdened, happier. Christianity isn't a bad thing, Ella. It doesn't have to be people speaking in tongues or preaching sermons at the tops of their lungs. It's a relationship with Jesus."

"And who's Jesus?"

"He's my Savior."

Ella did not understand, nor did she care to. Christians were weird. It was not as though she regretted coming into the middle of nowhere with one, but she was sure she would be having a better time if she had decided to travel with an anthropologist or archaeologist. But for the time being, Jake and Kathleen seemed to be good and nice people.

"So, this note she left for you," Ella asked. "You think it saved your life?"

"No," he replied, "Jesus saved me. It was Kathleen who pointed the road out. I owe a lot to her, whether she chooses to believe it or not."

Lady Literacy

Math was a difficult concept to grasp, especially since none of the village inhabitants were formally educated. Percentages were something that Kathleen had learned when she was eleven years old, and it was second nature to her. When she saw the statistic that one percent of the Tannese population was literate, she saw a major issue that needed to be addressed. When she would tell Sowany about that one percent, he didn't understand. It was hot air, and an insignificant fact that didn't bring a good hunting season or produce larger yam crops.

Kathleen was sitting cross-legged in Sowany's hut when he rejected her reading classes, again. She was overwhelmingly disappointed, as she had been hoping his heart was finally open to the idea of teaching his village how to read. The sooner they learned to read, the sooner they could learn about the Bible, and one day translate it into their own language. When Kathleen would lay in her hammock at night, she would pray and dream about the day when the New Testament could be written in Tanna North, but it seemed an impossible task whenever Sowany denied her pleas for classes in the village.

Fortunately for Kathleen and the village, nothing was an impossible task unto God.

"Ket-si," Sowany patiently said, his gruff voice raspy and old. "The things that you ask for are not possible. It is a silly trick that you show me when you say things to me while you look at a paper. I believe that you just decide what you want to say, and then say it, pretending to see words."

"I would not deceive you," Kathleen pleaded with him.

"It's no matter," he replied. "I can see that it is a game, and I do not need for people in the village to be playing games all day."

He waved his wrinkled hand at her, dismissing her from his hut. She closed her eyes for a second before she rose and exited the little home. When she walked outside and into the shade of the trees that surrounded his hut, Kathleen clenched her fists and tried not to get upset.

It was another setback, which always led to more development in patience, but she silently told God that she was tired of learning about the virtue of patience. She just wanted Sowany to approve the literacy classes.

While she walked back to her own house, Kathleen mentally vented about everything. Why was she here if the classes would never get approved? How was she going to convince Sowany that reading was real and vital to the salvation of his people? When was she going to get cut a break?

She stopped walking.

Something heavy weighed on her heart while she stood in the middle of someone's garden. She was being selfish in what she was doing, and while she stood there, Kathleen ran the same questions through her head again. They all had to do with her. She crinkled her nose with disgust when she thought of how she'd not even prayed with the hope that the village would somehow be opened up to reading and writing.

As a matter of fact, Kathleen had never tried a new approach. She had been doing the same thing for years, and that was to go to Sowany every few months, ask him for permission to teach classes, then she would get denied, and she would pray for the next few months that God would open his heart. There was never any other action that took place, or goal to set for convincing him. She had simply sat back and not done much.

It was always in God's timing that things happened, but until a person made the decision to step out and float in the ocean, God couldn't steer the boat. When Kathleen thought of this analogy, she stomped her foot on the ground, maddened by her ignorance and irresponsibility. There had to be something that she could do to convince Sowany that reading was important, and real.

"Lord, what should I do?" she asked out loud, and in English, not seeing the little girl playing beside her. The girl looked up at the white lady with confusion, and Kathleen glanced back and gave an embarrassed grin.

She walked back to the house to start getting dinner ready. When she walked in, she was still deep in thought about what could be done to convince Sowany to approve the classes. She had the feeling that his heart was ready, but it was his intellect that was holding him back. If God could just show her some way to—

"How'd it go?" Ella asked from the table.

Kathleen looked up from her deep thoughts and saw Lauriny and Ella sitting at the table with papers in front of them. They looked at her thoughtfully, waiting for an answer that was, hopefully, some good news. Kathleen shook her head with disappointment and Lauriny dropped her shoulders. Ella was sad that it was bad news, but she didn't really care either way, so she continued reading the papers in front of her.

The typewriter needed cleaning, so Kathleen walked over to it. As she did so, she could hear Ella reading slow and sloppily behind her.

"Itama onakotafuaki lanu," Ella read in Tanna North, her British accent making it sound like she was trying to recite a witch's potion. "Timitima ia neai, pah narigam asim…"

Kathleen shot her head around and listened to Ella speaking. When she heard the words, her heart jumped and she started to laugh. Thinking she was laughing at the pronunciation, Ella got defensive.

"Well, I'm not a bloody linguist—" she proclaimed.

Kathleen raised her hands to the sky and shouted, "That's it! 'Our Father who art in Heaven: hallowed be Thy name!'"

Ella looked at her like she'd gone mad, but Kathleen ran to the table and said, "Keep reading!"

"Pah negau raham otuva, pah okatol noam ia nafutani tolkama..." Ella kept reading. She was self conscious, and didn't understand what was happening, but Kathleen shouted again.

"Thy kingdom come, Thy will be done!" she screamed. Lauriny and Ella watched her with wide eyes, and Kathleen started grabbing all the papers on the table.

"Ella, follow me!"

She bolted out the door with all the papers while Ella followed her in a daze. Lauriny was right behind them, curious to know what was going on.

Kathleen and Ella were standing in front of Sowany in his hut. Ella wasn't sure why she was there, but Kathleen had a proud smile on her face. She handed Ella the paper she'd been reading earlier, and spoke to Sowany in his language.

"Sowany, I am here to show you that reading is not a game or a trick. You know that Ella does not speak your language, yet listen to her when she reads."

Kathleen nodded her head to Ella, who started reading the paper again, but this time with nervous, shaky hands.

"Afato nauganien nagitima rauai mine nian arafuin."

Sowany was not initially shocked, but he watched the woman with great intrigue, wondering how she suddenly knew his language, despite her poor accent. He shook his head with doubt and waved his hand.

"You could have taught her what to say," he told Kathleen.

Kathleen smiled, and said, "I thought you might say that. We can write something that I could not have taught her. You tell me something in my ear, I will write it, and Ella will read it back to you."

Sowany looked at her suspiciously, but finally nodded. He leaned close to Kathleen's ear and whispered something. She furiously scribbled the words on a piece of paper, her smile growing larger by the moment. When she was done, she handed the paper to Ella.

"What's going on?" Ella asked while she took the paper.

"Hopefully," Kathleen replied, "a miracle. Just read what's on that paper, okay? And try to pronounce the letters like we've taught you."

Ella nodded and read the paper the best she knew how. When she was done, Sowany's jaw dropped and he looked bewildered. He turned to Kathleen, whose face was more humble and gentle now.

"She stole my words!" Sowany exclaimed, pointing his finger at Ella.

"She read them, Sowany," Kathleen said with a sympathetic tone. She started to write a phrase that took a long time while Sowany looked at Ella's mouth in astonishment. He really thought she had stolen his words. When Kathleen was done writing, she handed the paper to Ella, who rolled her eyes and started reading it.

It translated to: "Sowany, reading is very important. You and your people will learn a lot if you know how to read. There are many words that can teach you new things, but if you cannot understand them when you see them, then you will never know what many things are."

Sowany twisted his mouth a little and thought about the statement for a moment.

He looked at Kathleen, and asked, "What sorts of things can we learn if we read?"

Kathleen wrote an answer on a piece of paper with a prayer in heart. She handed it to Ella, who read, "How to farm, how to prepare for storms, how to heal wounds, and how to follow God."

The old man shook his head like he didn't believe her, but then again, it was possible, especially since Ella had actually told him, not Kathleen. When he thought about this, a new world struck his mind for the first time. If there were things to read that could be useful to his people, then it would be a good idea. Besides, it almost seemed disgraceful for Ella to be able to read their beautiful language when no one else could.

"Fine," Sowany said with indifference. "You may teach my people to read, but it must be at night. I don't want them to be lazy in their work."

It was enough of an answer to send Kathleen on a wild celebration high. She was laughing and shouting, and when the other Christians heard the news, they did the same. Saki, Lauriny, Kathleen, and a few others from the group were jumping in a big circle, laughing and singing praise songs. Jake sat on a log next to Agmol, and Ella asked him what had happened.

"Since her arrival, she's been trying to get Sowany to approve classes," Jake explained. "Now, he has, and the work that she does all day doesn't have to be by herself anymore. She can teach children, adults, elders, and anyone else who wants to learn how to read."

"But Lauriny knows how to read a little," Ella said. "She taught Lauriny. What was stopping her from teaching everyone else?"

"It's not Kathleen's job to change this culture because she thinks it's right or vital. These people have to *want* to read for the right reasons. Unless they see how it's important to them, then teaching them all how to read would be a waste of time and energy. But now, thanks to you, they can see that reading is an asset."

"Thanks to me?" Ella asked.

"Yes," Jake said with a smile. "Do you know what happened in there today, Ella?"

She shook her head.

"God used you, Ella," Jake said. "He used your inability to speak this language. It was a job that none of us would have been able to do. If you hadn't been here, who knows when Sowany would have understood what reading is."

Kathleen waved to them, and Jake stood up and started dancing with the others. Ella sat on the log with a bewildered expression on her face. God had used her? She didn't see it that way, but if that's how they looked at it, it made her feel good. She had never been *used* to do something good before, that she knew of. These people seemed to find the good in everyone, a purpose for every soul.

Ella watched them dance and sing about reading.

Reading.

She had read off a few words and shaken their world within minutes. Was that the way God worked? She shook her head with debate and laughed at how she was starting to believe in God.

Yeah right, she thought. *There's no God. What sort of God would allow me to fall apart, to ditch my family, to watch Tinseltown go straight to hell, and to not try and help me when I need help the most?*

God was something these people had made up because they needed something to blame good and bad things on. Kathleen was an easy person to pick out as being a Christian. Ella thought the woman had probably never seen hard times in her life. Of course it was easy for Kathleen to believe in God—He had probably always been on her side. Jake was a little harder to figure out because he, at least, had a rough time in college—

"Ella!" Kathleen shouted. She waved for the actress to come and celebrate with them, but Ella just shook her head with sad eyes and headed back into the house. Kathleen put her hand down and watched with sadness as the woman rushed into the hut under the late afternoon sun.

"She needs a friend," Jake told Kathleen. "The world that that girl lives in seems so lonely. I think she needs a walk in the woods."

"You know, now that the classes will be taking off, and I'll have tons of work to do, I might take tomorrow off," she said to him.

He looked at her and nodded his head. "Good idea. You two could go on a picnic. You know — girly stuff."

Kathleen nodded, and said, "You're right. I'll kidnap her tomorrow. Maybe she just needs to see things more clearly. Thanks, Jake."

She walked away, leaving him in the jumping crowd of people. He smiled and decided that when someone else was bothering her, she was nice to him.

This was because he was the least of her problems. Spending the day with a spoiled director from Hollywood, who hated to do any sort of hiking or walking, would be just what the doctor ordered if Jake was trying to get on the good side of Kathleen.

Wild Horses

Tanna Island is known for its wild horses, and is perhaps one of the only tropical places in the world where one can go to see them roam free in lush meadows and volcanic landscape. The very essence of the horses on the island represents freedom, and an all but lost journey into the past. This was the day that their spirits would touch another. It was not a mistake that God made such beautiful creatures, nor was it chance that the horses would serve Him that afternoon.

When Ella woke up, it was a cool morning, and the seemingly monotonous village life was beginning for the day. Fires were being started, and children were already communing at the edge of the settlements to begin an unknown and extravagant journey. Most were already awake, but Ella found that her hammock brought peace this day, and its gentle rocking was almost soothing.

Kathleen's hammock was empty, and Ella wondered where she could be. She dismissed the thought, for she had come to the realization that she would never understand that girl. There was no rhyme or reason to the missionary's beliefs, methods, or mannerisms, and it was no wonder why Jake fought for the woman's attention. Kathleen seemed to be on a personal vendetta to ignore his existence entirely. No, Ella was in no mood to understand. For the time being, the cool morning and the swaying hammock were enough.

They were enough.

Ella sat up in surprise, as though someone had fired a gun in the hut. The cool morning air and the hammock were enough? She rubbed her forehead and tried to suppress a grin. Six months previous, two luxury estates and a ten million dollar movie deal had not been nearly enough to feed her pleasures and ambitions. Something was changing, and the irony suddenly turned to fear, and she felt an anxiety attack approaching. Before she could let the fear sink in, Kathleen entered the hut and walked to Ella.

"Are you ready?" Kathleen asked.

"For what?"

"We're going on a journey today. Get your clothes on."

"Do you ever say 'please'?"

"I'll say 'please' when you least expect it. I find it keeps people on their toes."

The path was slippery from the jungle's moisture, and the trees were dripping from the humidity and night's dew. Mosquitoes flew everywhere, searching for a fresh puddle of water to rest upon. It was dark and damp, but Ella knew that the hot sun was somewhere outside the canopy of trees. She could smell the rotten jungle stench that oozed from the plants and dirt.

She had been on this little island for a month now, and had never walked the path that Kathleen was leading them down now. It was odd to Ella that Kathleen had decided to take this journey without Saki or another tribesman; it was just the two women for the first time since her arrival, and Ella found herself trying to think of a good conversation topic. Fortunately for the speechless director, the trail became so uncomfortable in footing and smell that she concentrated all her efforts on walking while breathing through her mouth.

They trekked through the muddy forest for another thirty minutes and, after a while, Ella realized they were hiking around the mountain that the river flowed from. It was the same mountain that the infamous gorge sat at the mouth of, but now they seemed to be on the other side.

A journey indeed.

What was Kathleen thinking by bringing them out here alone?

"Isn't it dangerous for just the two of us to be hiking so far from the village?" Ella asked, finally breaking the silence. "I mean, what if one of us gets hurt or something?"

Kathleen didn't turn around to answer, but continued to concentrate on the downhill slope. "Well, let's just hope that you're the one to get hurt, because I'm the only one who knows the way back."

"I'm serious."

"So am I," Kathleen replied with a little laugh.

Ella decided all attempts of starting a conversation would have to come from her trail mate, because she was tired of hearing sarcasm as an answer to everything. As a matter of fact, the more she thought about it, the more she wondered what they were doing on the excursion alone. Kathleen had never shown much of an interest in Ella as a friend, nor had she made a huge effort to be nice to the star. There were people in the world that would pay a million dollars to have lunch or coffee with Ella, and this egotistical missionary couldn't care less. The question, like the jungle elements, was too much for Ella to bear any longer, and she finally stopped.

"Hold on a second. *Stop.*"

Kathleen stopped and turned around in confusion. She walked to Ella, and as she got closer, it was obvious that the break was well needed for the both of them. Sweat was dripping from the tall woman's forehead. Ella adjusted her small daypack and put her hands on her hips. The jungle was silent except for the heavy breathing from the two women.

"What's wrong?" Kathleen finally asked, licking the salt off her upper lip.

"Kathleen, where are we going?"

"It's a surprise."

"Please, no surprises, just tell me. I'm not a child."

Kathleen smiled, taking a deep breath as though she was re-energizing herself.

"It's a surprise."

"I'm at a loss for words on how you can be a 'child of God' and still be so patronizing. Doesn't it bother you that you have an attitude problem?"

Kathleen continued to smile. "I'm at a loss for words on how you're blaming someone else for having an attitude problem when you have the biggest one in the world."

Ella, offended, dropped her jaw. "I don't have an attitude problem!"

"Yes, you do. And I bet more people like my attitude than they do yours."

At this, Kathleen smugly walked away. She glided with her shoulders back and her head high, like a pre-school child winning a jungle gym war. Ella continued to stand on the path with her mouth wide open.

Was this conversation happening?

Screw manners, the woman had gone too far. Ella stormed to keep up with Kathleen, pointing and talking at the same time.

"For your information, there are people that would kill to spend just a moment with me. I don't see that happening for you. Not to mention that I was raised to be polite and I was sent to the finest boarding school for girls in England, so don't tell me I'm lacking etiquette."

"I didn't say you lacked etiquette. I said you had an attitude problem, but its okay, because I do, too."

"I don't, and if you think you can—"

Wait, did she say "too?" Ella stopped on the path, a little confused. Kathleen also stopped and reproached the dazed actress. The condescending look was gone from her eyes, and she spoke to Ella with the utmost grace and humility.

"I don't need you to tell me that I have an attitude problem, Ella. I don't deny giving rude remarks and sarcasm. I'm a human being, and a very imperfect one at that. It's a good vice, but one that I *do* try to get rid of, believe it or not.

"But there is a reason for the cold exterior, and if you can just handle spending one day with me, then maybe you'll understand. I want to understand the reason for yours, so let's just pretend like we're both on a mission for personal comprehension, okay?"

Ella, surprised by such honesty, shamefully nodded her head. It was almost refreshing to hear someone confess their faults, and Ella found that she wanted to do the same. Something inside her started to beat like a loud drum, and as Kathleen walked away, Ella had the sudden urge to cry and shout everything that was wrong with her. But the moment passed, leaving Ella alone with her thoughts and wishes for someone to tell her that a dying soul was normal in life.

The trek down the path became progressively easier and the dark, muggy jungle eventually transformed into a pleasant stroll through a grove of palm trees. Ferns and tropical flowers graced the wayside of the path and streams of sunlight shone through palm fronds, gently shading the ground as the two women walked. The noises of the dark forest were no longer ominous, but rather joyful, as though a celebration of life was announcing the arrival of strangers in a world unbeknownst to them. Tiny frogs leapt across the trail, leaving little toe prints in the fresh mud. Silent lizards, attempting to blend in, sat on tree trunks and rocks that reflected the sun's heat.

Ella was enchanted by the magic of the place—the cool breeze amidst the shaded overgrowth, exotic birds trumpeting their song in anonymous dwellings within the trees' canopy. She walked softly so as not to disrupt any pattern to the melodious chatter of nature going about its daily business. After a while, she noticed that her steps had gotten slower, and all her attention was on the trees. When she looked back down, Kathleen was well ahead of her, apparently unhindered by the majesty of such an overwhelming grove.

Ella jogged up behind her, and whispered, "Was this what you wanted to show me?"

Kathleen finally looked around and noticed the beauty of the place for the first time.

"Beautiful, isn't it?" she replied. She continued to keep a fast pace, but her words silently broke the serenity. "But, no. We're almost to the meadow."

"What's in the meadow?"

"You'll see."

Ella rolled her eyes with disdain, but continued to enjoy the walk. How could anything destroy such perfect moments?

A long list of things suddenly ran through her head on what would spoil peace, and she found that she was starting to dwell on the negative. But a few moments later, they reached a clearing with tall grass, and Ella's mind was distracted by her overwhelming joy that they had finally reached the mysterious meadow.

Kathleen hunched to the ground and put her finger on her mouth, motioning for Ella to stay silent. She then proceeded to remove the baseball cap that had been keeping the hair out of her face. Ella stayed low, wondering why they were being so quiet and cautious.

What's out there? she wondered.

The crickets and cicadas were buzzing loudly in the tall grass, and it reminded Ella of being on an African safari. All that was missing were the elephants and lions moving around in the grass —

A snorting sound came from the direction of the meadow, causing Ella's eyes to grow big. She poked Kathleen in the shoulder and pointed to the grass. Kathleen nodded like she had heard it the whole time and leaned very close to Ella's ear.

"Be as quiet as possible. We don't want to scare them," then she hunched away, running and ducking.

Scare them? Ella thought.

Whatever "them" might have been, she was sure that scaring them away should be a good thing. Nevertheless, she followed her fearless leader along the grass' perimeter, trying to stay low. It was a struggle to keep her pack steadily on her back, but she wasn't ready to stop and adjust the Velcro straps. She was not ready to make any type of move except for what she saw Kathleen doing.

Kathleen stayed as low as she could, finally turning into the grass. It was not as tall here, and they could see what was around them. Whatever animal had been near them was now long gone, for Ella could only hear the crickets singing in the midday heat.

Ella's pack finally became too much of a bother and she stopped to take it off. After she silently rolled it off her back, she folded the straps over so that the length was shorter. She then clenched the pack between her teeth and let go to test the weight on her jaw. There was only a sandwich and a water bottle in the small bag, so it was light enough to hold in her mouth. When she looked up to continue moving forward, Kathleen had stopped.

The missionary was frozen in her path, and looking in Ella's direction when the snorting and breathing began again. Ella stopped breathing altogether, her pack in her mouth, when she heard a rustling only a few feet from her.

Good god, what is it?!

She looked at Kathleen for support, but the woman was trying not to laugh.

"Don't move," she mouthed to Ella, a huge smile on her face. Ella didn't think this was a funny situation at all. In fact, she was mortified beyond belief, and she couldn't imagine what was threatening as well as funny.

The breathing continued, and the grass began to shift about seven feet from where Ella was crouching. She didn't dare move to look in the direction of the noise so she remained completely still on her hands and knees, watching as Kathleen cupped her hand over her mouth to suppress a giggle.

Ella's teeth started to hurt. She was sure that the weight of the pack was moving her perfectly straight smile out of its place, so in a moment of superstardom weakness, she opened her jaw and released the pack. It hit the ground with a deafening crunch, causing the movement near her to stop for a moment. She looked at Kathleen and bit her lower lip with shame.

Kathleen pointed behind Ella, mouthed, *It's right there*, and put her finger on her lips again.

Ella mouthed, *What is it*, but only got a shaking head from Kathleen. This conversation was obviously not going to take place under the circumstances, so Ella simply waited for the "all-clear." Her muscles were starting to shake from holding her position for so long and she wasn't sure how much longer it would be before she collapsed.

Finally, the grass rustled again, and the sounds wandered deeper into the meadow. Ella looked at Kathleen.

Thumbs-up, let's go.

She put the bag back in her mouth and started crawling again. They continued like this until Kathleen had led them around the outer part of the meadow to the foot of a banyan tree. A large boulder sat in the shade of the big tree's branches, and Kathleen hopped on the rock without hesitation. Ella followed, and when she stood on the rock, she found that they were only staring into branches.

"This isn't much of an improvement," she said to Kathleen. But Kathleen was already climbing the tree, just as casually as she had the day she'd helped Freddy. Ella couldn't believe the strength of this woman, nor did she see how she could do the same without falling back onto the boulder.

Ella whispered, "I can't do this."

"Sure you can. Just put your foot on a steady branch and push up."

Ella looked around like she hadn't quite understood, so Kathleen reached out her hand.

"Put your foot there, now grab my hand. There you go. I won't drop you, just trust me."

"Right," Ella said.

As soon as she had her foot in place, Kathleen pulled her up with great ease, and said, "See? It's easy. Now follow me."

Three branches and five attempts later, Ella reached the limb next to the one Kathleen was sitting on, and said, "Okay. We're here. Now what?"

But Kathleen didn't answer; she smiled at the meadow and pointed. When Ella turned, she was struck with such a view as one she had never dreamed of nor imagined. The two women were high enough in the tree to see through an opening that looked over the meadow.

In the yellow meadow were thirty horses, grazing and exploring the dazzling surroundings. Some laid in the shade of nearby trees that sat at the perimeter of the clearing, while others walked to green patches of fresh grass that had grown from the previous rainstorms. Despite the yellow grass, the surrounding forest was lush and green, making the meadow look like a safe haven for creatures of innocence and fragility.

Beyond the meadow, a long distance away, stood a tall, dark mountain that jetted out of the island like the ruler of a kingdom. Little puffs of smoke grew out of it and floated into the sky. It watched the surrounding jungles and meadows with great responsibility and authority, withstanding the mighty forces of the sun that shone down and the clouds that swirled around its peaks. The mountain demanded respect, and it set the tone for the scene as the horses lived in its presence.

Ella was struck with such a feeling that she had never imagined possible in recent years. The setting was so spectacular, so magnificent, and so surreal that she had to blink several times. Where were they? How had they gotten there? She finally understood what the phrase "breath-taking" meant.

"Every time I come here," Kathleen said, "I wonder how people can't believe in God."

Ella looked down at her hands. Her heart sank into her stomach, and she found that she was also asking herself what would make a place so beautiful if God didn't exist. She felt ashamed that she would allow such a question to enter her mind after thirty-five years.

"Yeah," she replied softly, still looking down at the hands that kept her balanced on the limb.

Kathleen looked over at her and absorbed the woman's reaction.

God, open Ella to Your Spirit. Work inside her heart. Let her see Your beauty and help her to believe that You are a real and glorious God.

Then, she said to Ella, "Can you feel it?"

"What?"

"That feeling. The one that tells you to believe."

"I don't know what you mean." But she did. "All I see is a really pretty view —" more lying " —that is among thousands of pretty views in the world."

The remark was incredible; Ella didn't even believe herself.

Of course there was a God, but who the guy was and why he hated Ella so much was still in question. She continued to look at the horses in the meadow with an overwhelming disbelief.

Trying to quickly change the subject, she said, "So those are the monstrous beasts that we were hiding from?"

Kathleen nodded, and Ella continued.

"Now I know why you were laughing. A horse is not as threatening as a wild animal."

"But these *are* wild, Ella. This island is one of the last places people can go to see wild horses roam free. They just do their thing."

"And the crawling? Why were we ducking through the grass like that?"

"If you scare one, it sets them all running. I didn't think your publicist would appreciate you being stampeded to death."

"I'm sure we would have been fine."

Kathleen smiled, shrugged, and then turned to where the herd was. She let out a loud whistle that echoed from the tree and broke the sound barrier of the meadow. The horses all at once jumped to attention and began moving. The colts stuck to their mothers' sides as the group galloped across the clearing. They turned and ran faster, leaving a giant cloud of dust so thick that Ella could barely make out the grand creatures.

They headed for the tree, and the ground shook violently. Ella leaned over so that she was hugging the tree limb, not trusting her own grip. Kathleen laughed and they watched as the horses galloped beneath them, passed the boulder, and circled the meadow another time before they ended up stopping beneath the tree.

Ella looked down as Kathleen said, "I hope you didn't have any place to be for a while."

The horses enjoyed their time under the women's tree. Kathleen had tried to whistle again, but they didn't budge. She threw sticks down at them, but one horse seemed to think it was just a pest and swatted its rear with its own tail. After ten minutes without a reaction, Kathleen and Ella decided they would just have to wait.

"It's easy to forget that they're wild and they can do whatever they want," Kathleen had said.

Now she was lying on a limb about five feet above Ella, picking at the leaves above her head. Ella rested on the branch below, still thinking about what Kathleen had said about God. She'd remained quiet despite the obstinate horses and the consequential taunting from her trail-buddy.

"How—" she started to say, unintentionally speaking out loud.

"'How' what?"

Ella paused. She wanted to ask, but she was afraid.

Finally, she thought, *What the hell*, and blurted it out.

"How am I supposed to have faith in something I can't see if I don't even have faith in things that I see all the time?"

Kathleen closed her eyes and said a quick prayer. Then she rolled over on her stomach and looked down at the actress, trying to act as though the question was very average.

"What do you mean?"

"I don't have faith in people that work for me. I have no faith in justice or politics. I don't even believe that movies and fame will bring my well-deserved fortune. Why should I have faith in a God that I can't see?"

Please God, give me the words, Kathleen prayed. She opened her mouth to speak, but Ella continued.

"I heard the speech you gave that day in Darwin, when all those students were in there. I was walking down the hall, looking for Alice Walker's office. I heard you mention *The Matrix*, so I stopped."

"You've seen the movie?"

"I love the movie, but I realized that life has never asked which pill I wanted. It simply gave me the one that leaves me in the dark. I live in a world that I don't understand, Kathleen. How am I supposed to understand your world if I've never been able to understand my own? Wouldn't that just leave me searching for everything the rest of my life?"

Kathleen wanted to respond, but she suddenly felt like listening was her role for now. Ella kept talking while Kathleen prayed for her.

"So, I went to Ms. Walker and asked about you. She told me what you did, and I asked to come back with you. But she thinks I'm here for movie research. The truth is that I'm a liar."

Kathleen stared down, still listening intently.

Ella continued.

"I've lied about all of it. I'm not famous anymore. No one wants my picture, or to go see one of my movies. They've heard about who I am, and about my—" she motioned to Kathleen "—attitude problem. The studio has unofficially fired me, and told me to take some time off. Now, I'm hiding in a jungle, trying to figure out what to do when I get back."

Ella hadn't looked up at Kathleen at all, but merely stared out at the view. She didn't cry, nor did she sound like she was going to. After she was done talking, she let out a long sigh that was apparently signifying her relief, but Kathleen could tell that no real burden had been lifted after the woman's confession. She still sat in the tree with the same, blank stare.

Kathleen had become accustomed to that stare. It said nothing and everything simultaneously. Ella's eyes would glance at the world as if she were looking at an object or event, but upon closer observation, one could see that she was actually looking within herself. Her dark, green eyes would become hollow, like a doll sitting at a tea party. All function was there, but any sparkle or glint of hope was absent from the deep stare, and took all effort to pull her from the abyss.

"What do you see?" Kathleen asked.

"Huh?"

"I asked what you see."

"It's a mountain. Yasur volcano, right?"

Kathleen nodded. "What else?"

Ella squinted and shrugged. "The stray horses across the meadow, the fields to the south, more jungle."

"I'm a liar, too," Kathleen blurted out. "I lie all the time. I'm not proud of it, but it's become such habit that I do it and I don't know it. I do tons of things that I shouldn't do. I think things that

I shouldn't think about. Such insights into a person's mind would cause anyone to be physically sick—not just because they've seen into another's psyche, but because they know that they are capable of the same. But I've found forgiveness. There was someone who died for those horrible things that I do and think. It was Jesus Christ."

Ella started shaking her head, trying to stop the conversation. Kathleen continued.

"No, listen to me, Ella. You suffer, and you put yourself through things that are not on human turf. They are battles that can only be fought on a spiritual level, and we're not up to the task when we're alone. Jesus suffered for you, and he defeated evil so that your sins wouldn't keep you from spending eternity with God. It was a gift, not just for your life on Earth, but for eternity, too."

Ella kept shaking her head and waving her hand at Kathleen. "Stop it. I don't believe in any of that."

"Then why are you having such a hard time with it? If it's not real, then why are you struggling to overcome it? You're fighting against something that you don't think exists!"

"Listen! What has it brought you? A life away from normal people, away from civilization. It's even keeping you from loving someone!"

Kathleen was dumbstruck. "I love Jesus. That's all I need."

"You love Jake, too. Doesn't your God encourage loving men on Earth?"

Kathleen lowered herself to the branch next to Ella's. There were tears in her eyes, but she kept a strong figure.

"Don't use that relationship against me. Fortunately for you, Ella, we're the same person. I guess I'm fighting against something I refuse to believe, too. And, like you, I keep it out with bitterness. I shield it and try to prevent any contact with it, because that's safer, right?"

Ella didn't say anything, and Kathleen kept going. Her tears had not fallen, and she seemed to have her composure back, so her voice didn't crack anymore.

"So, I'll make a deal with you. You try not to hide from Jesus, and I'll try not to hide from Jake. Let's see who loses their battle first."

Ella, feeling a little convicted and sharing a new equality with the woman she had once thought to be hypocritical, nodded her head and smiled.

"Deal."

The horses had left, and the afternoon sun was beating down on them. It was much cooler in the shade, so they decided to stay in the tree until the sun passed behind an oncoming storm front to the west. A soft breeze made the leaves bend back and forth, but the limbs didn't budge. They could hear the clopping of the horses' hooves across the meadow. They whinnied and played in the afternoon shadows that were cast over the clearing by the tall canopy trees that lined the edges.

Kathleen had reclaimed her spot on the branch above Ella, and the two women were lounging like monkeys in the tree. No tears had been shed, or tempers flared, so now they were simply enjoying the day.

"What do you miss most about your home?" Ella asked.

"I don't know. Not much. Things are great here."

There was silence below, so Kathleen turned over to see Ella giving her a crooked face.

Kathleen laughed, and said, "Okay. I guess I miss going to the movies."

Ella laughed.

"What?!" Kathleen replied.

"Nothing. It's just funny. You did know that I *live* the movies, right?"

"How could I forget? You know, I don't want to play this game if you're gonna laugh."

"I'm sorry. Please continue."

"As I was saying, I miss going to see movies at the theater. And—I suppose I miss Nestle Crunch bars."

"Good one. Anything else?"

"I never think about it much, but now that you've brought it up—" she smiled "—I miss driving my car, listening to music, drinking coffee at Starbuck's, eating drumsticks at baseball games, and spitting out sunflower seeds.

"I miss how cold Oregon is, I miss the crowds at Disneyland, I would pay any amount of money for a jar of Skippy peanut butter and an Oreo. I wish I had a television to watch the news, and a radio to listen to oldies. I miss having a stove, a refrigerator, a big bed, a pillow, a solid roof, raspberries, roller blades, finger nail polish, hair dryers, Diet Coke, marshmallows, ice cream, and watermelon-flavored Bubbalicious bubble gum."

"But you don't think about it much?"

"Nope, never."

They laughed.

"What about your family?" Ella said, still giggling.

Kathleen shrugged. "I dunno. I guess I miss my dad."

"He's the only family you have?"

"Pretty much. My mother left when I was six."

Ella had stopped laughing. "Where did she go?"

"Who knows? She was a drunk."

Ella's heart sank. She suddenly felt noxious. "I'm sorry."

"Why? It's not your fault."

"I know, but—"

"But nothing. My dad raised me and my brother the best he could, but he was a firefighter, so hours were odd. Most of the time it was just me and my brother, Sam."

Ella nodded slowly. It made sense now. The woman was against all alcohol, was a tomboy, huge athlete, very strong, and not easy to get along with. It made sense that Kathleen would have been brought up in a family of men.

"That's incredible," Ella said, "because you're so maternal by nature. The way you are with Epi and everyone around you is so motherly."

Kathleen laughed.

"That is a purely God-given instinct. I never had any mother-figure in my life to model. Never. I never had someone to hold my hand when I was sick, or tell me about my period. I had to learn things by myself. My dad and brother were never going to tell me how the world worked."

"How old was your brother when your mom left?"

"Eight. Two years older than me."

Ella's breath caught in her throat. That was the same type of family as hers. Sara was six, Freddy was eight, and a husband was trying to get his wife to stay home with their children. It was sickening, and she didn't want to think of how she had wanted to leave her family so many times. It was a revolting realization that a person could leave so easily. She tried to ignore the parallel scenario.

"You don't miss your brother out here?" Ella gulped.

"My brother died when I was fifteen."

Another shock.

"My god. What happened?" Ella asked with concern.

"He was driving home from his girlfriend's house one night, went through an intersection, and a drunk driver ran a red light and t-boned his car."

"Jesus—"

"I certainly hope he's with Jesus. I would give anything to see him again."

Ella had been wrong about Kathleen. She'd thought the woman had been a goody-two-shoes her whole life, being a tight-ass because she was a Christian, not because there was some deep and personal meaning as to why. It was a lesson learned by Ella that it had not been fair to judge a person's life, nor had it been fair for a drunk driver to kill Kathleen's brother, or for her mother to leave the family. It also wouldn't be fair for Ella to give up on her own family.

Kathleen's mother had been weak and stupid, Ella decided. She hadn't gotten the problem fixed, and she'd quit.

Ella wasn't a quitter. She was British.

When they left the tree and headed back into the jungle, the day's humidity had left the path stuffy and damp. For some reason, Kathleen was walking slower than normal, but Ella assumed it was to accommodate the actress' slow pace. When she looked at Kathleen, she noticed that the girl was sweating. Profusely.

"Are you alright?" Ella asked.

"I'm fine," Kathleen replied, trying to watch the trail and wipe her brow with the back of her hand.

Ella shrugged. It was a very humid afternoon, and they had been in the sun all day. All the activity was probably just catching up to her.

That night, Kathleen didn't sing by the fire, and ended up going to bed early. When she crawled into the hammock, Jake walked into the hut in silence.

"What's wrong?" he asked with a serious tone.

"Nothing," she replied while she laid her head back. "We had a long day and I'm really tired."

"Uh-huh," Jake said, not convinced. He moved forward to feel her forehead and check for a fever, but she pushed his hand away.

"I'm fine, I promise," she said casually. He still wasn't convinced, but then Epi and Ella walked in. He decided that if Kathleen was sick, she wouldn't be so stupid as to not mention it.

Being sick in the jungle was a very serious thing, especially since there were so many known, and unknown, tropical diseases. No matter how many vaccinations and medicines missionaries took, it was never enough to prevent that one, previously unknown disease that was carried by a mosquito or fly. A fever may seem like a mild case of the flu, but within a day, a person may end up with cerebral malaria and in a coma. Jake was hoping Kathleen would know when to ask for medicine or a doctor.

After two days of taking it easy, Jake decided that Kathleen had probably been suffering from a fever a few nights before, and had rightfully decided to take care of it. When a group of boys asked her and Ella to go to the gorge, he thought nothing of it.

"I'm never going back there again," Ella said.

Kathleen nodded and said, "I'll go."

"I might come a little bit later," Jake replied, and left to go continue his work in the field next to the shed.

Humility and Submission

Kathleen had always seen herself as strong and independent. The only dependency she felt was on God, and everyone knew it.

No one is perfect, especially Christians, but there are times people feel that life has become so predictable that sin and danger seem unprecedented. People live their lives every day expecting a routine, a similar pattern than the day before, but God is always very quick to prove humanity was meant to be light on its toes, to expect the unexpected. This was the day that Kathleen would finally face that harsh reality—that "missionary" was not synonymous with "monotonous".

It was as though all graceful form was defeated by some cosmic force and for one moment, her athletic figure and keen sense of balance left her. She was merely walking from the gorge. It was a walk she had made hundreds of times in her six years with the tribe. Never had the muddy path, the slippery foliage, or the sharp ledges hindered her trek to watch the children jump from the ledge that Ella had so adamantly refused to conquer.

On this day, the kids had jumped from the top of the gorge, and would make their way back to the village following the river and the lagoon. No one knew why Kathleen hadn't jumped like she normally did, nor did they question her. She hadn't been feeling well the past few days, didn't want to risk submersing herself in the cold water if she *was* getting sick, and for that she would make the downhill journey, through the jungle, by herself.

The clouds were rolling in from the west, and she could hear the distant roar of thunder. Despite its being hidden behind the coming storm, the sun was nearly down, making the path more difficult to see amid the darkening clouds and shaded forest. She picked up the pace, fearful that a downpour would come at any time, putting her in further danger. The trail was slippery from the storm that had come two days before, when they had returned from the horse meadow.

Suddenly, to her right, she heard a loud jungle cry. She didn't have time to think about what animal it was, because when she turned her head sharply, she stepped on a sensitive part of the trail, causing her left foot to push through the mud. This, as a result, caused her to tumble down the hillside through the foliage.

The world spun wildly around her until she was able to at least keep her feet in front of her. It wasn't just the sloping hill that made her crash through at top speed; the mud had formed its own cascade down this portion of the mountain and the more she struggled to stop, the quicker her pace got. It wasn't until she slid over a tiny ledge and her feet hit the ground that she came to a halt, jolting her body forward with her leg still atop where a root had been waiting.

She felt a sharp pain in her ankle and she knew it was sprained.

Badly.

Kathleen Newman didn't move for five minutes. Her body hung precariously downhill while a looped root was all that held her in place. Her foot had found its way into the tiny hole of the big wooden outcrop, and the more she looked at it, the more she wondered how to get it out. The root had obviously been unearthed by the mudslide she had tumbled down, and the tree from which it came was two feet above her. She had slipped right over the small ledge and twisted her foot directly into the root.

A hole-in-one.

She tried to move her leg, attempting to get it out of the hole, but the pain was too great and she let out a small yelp. Slowly, she reached for the vines hanging over the small escarpment. Her foot throbbed as she tried moving her entire body instead of just her foot. The vines held her weight, and after a few minutes of suppressing painful tears, she was able to pull herself against the ledge and observe her surroundings.

The trail, she assumed, was probably about thirty feet up the hill. She couldn't see over the ledge that she was leaning on. Another twenty feet below, she could see the trail that the villagers would sometimes use to take the long way to the lagoon. It was a longer hike to the village on that trail, but it would be easier going down than climbing back up.

Kathleen tried to move her foot sideways one more time, but the pain was excruciating and the swelling made it impossible to pry out. This was when she started to panic.

God, get me out of here.

It was getting darker, and the thunder grew louder. Her heart was pumping at full speed, and she wondered how anyone would find her on the hillside when the rain was pouring. It would be deafening. Would they ever hear her cries?

She forced herself to stop worrying. God hadn't brought her to this lonely island for six years to teach people to read, raise a son, and share the Gospel, only to die of exposure under a muddy escarpment.

No, this isn't going to happen. I have faith in you, Lord!

As she began to sing her favorite worship song, she thought she heard something.

It was whistling from the path above. It sounded familiar. She could barely make out the tune to a DC Talk song from ten years previous, and she knew who it was.

"Jake!"

The whistling stopped.

"Jake, help!" Kathleen shouted again, pushing all she could through a suffering voice. She immediately heard something crash through the foliage above her head, and within a minute, Jake Willis hopped over the ledge next to her. He wore a big grin, and seemed to think this was all a joke.

"What happened?!" he asked with enthusiasm. The smile left his face when he saw the condition of his friend. Kathleen was covered in mud and leaves, and appeared to be pried into the side of the hill with her leg stuck in the ground.

She replied very softly, "Get me out of here, okay?"

"Okay."

Jake knelt down to the big root and observed the situation. He touched Kathleen's ankle and she cringed with pain.

"Sorry."

He ran his fingers over the root, trying to get a feel for how fragile it was. Thunder boomed behind him and he lowered his eyebrows. The situation had just gotten very serious.

As an engineer, he was prone to solving problems. On a normal occasion, he would have relished in something so complicated, but the pain of a fallen comrade wasn't making the incident an enjoyable challenge. He looked at her leg with sympathy and she gave him a sorrowful look. The sparkle that was usually in her eyes was gone, and he could see only agony and worry in her fearful stare.

"Don't worry. We'll figure something out."

She nodded, and lightning struck the air.

Jake looked down at the stubborn root again, and said, "I'm gonna go get a saw. I'll be back in twenty minutes."

Kathleen closed her eyes and nodded again. "Hurry, okay?"

He winked at her, and said, "No problem," and she gave a nervous laugh.

As he left her pressed against the hillside, she stared at the ever-darkening sky. He stopped and knelt down again.

"Maybe we should say a prayer," he said.

"Good thinking."

Jake closed his eyes and held his hand above Kathleen's foot without touching it.

"God, You are a God of miracles. We could really use Your help right now. Please watch over Kathleen, and get us out of here soon. We praise You, and ask that Your hand of protection would cover this situation. In Jesus' name, Amen."

"Amen. Come back soon."

"I promise."

"And have Ella watch Epi."

"Got it."

"And radio the Lenakel base and have them send the doctor."

"Sure thing." He bolted down the hill to the older trail. Kathleen could hear him running until he was too far, and all was silent.

Then, it started to sprinkle.

Jake ran as fast as he could down the muddy trail toward the village. It was an old trail, and the foliage was draped across the dirt so that he could barely see where he was going. He would have to remember to bring a flashlight with him on his return. A flashlight, a saw, and maybe his hatchet, although he didn't want to hack through the root with her leg only inches away. The fronds continued to slash at his pants as he bolted across the flat part of the trail.

After running and sliding down the steepest sections of the old path, he finally burst out into an open field. He recognized it as the clearing next to the maintenance shed. *His* maintenance shed. He ran through the knee-high grass and glanced down at his watch. It had taken him ten minutes to run, downhill, from Kathleen to the village. It would be almost dark by the time he made it back to her.

The thunder in the distance rumbled louder.

Be with us, Lord.

He opened the door to the ever-darkening shed and tried to turn on the light. It didn't work. He slapped his forehead. He hadn't turned on the generator that afternoon because he'd been doing work in the field. No time to turn it on now. He would just get the flashlight.

He walked over to the table and grabbed his Maglite and water bottle. It was full of water, and he figured that having water in the jungle with night coming was never a bad thing. He glanced over at his futon and saw a knapsack in the corner behind it. He rushed over, put the cantina in the bag, and headed deeper into the shed to where his tools were. He turned on the flashlight, as there were no windows in the back of the shed, and began to search for tools he thought would be useful. He grabbed his flimsy hacksaw and, at the last minute, grabbed the hatchet.

Just in case, he thought.

He looked around the room once more. Anything else? His body-length beach chair sat at the edge of the futon, and on top was a bright yellow rain slicker.

Good thinking.

He walked over, picked it up, and headed out the door. He was trying to adjust all of the objects in his arms to fit into the pack when he emerged out of the palm tree grove and into the busy village area. The children had returned from the gorge, and all the fires were emitting sporadic smoke puffs into the air throughout the clearing.

Jake ran to the house, where he knew Ella and Epi would be. As he approached, he saw that Saki and Lauriny were already heading to Kathleen's place for evening worship.

"Saki!" Jake yelled.

Saki turned in surprise as Jake flew past him toward the hut. Saki habitually followed him at full speed, and now there were two men running, although one had no idea why. As they ran, Jake fumbled with his Tannese through heavy breaths.

"Ket-si is hurt. I've got to go help her."

They rushed into the house where Ella and Epi were sitting quietly at the table, coloring with crayons. They both looked up in surprise as Jake dashed into the room. He was talking very fast, obviously more comfortable with his English.

"Ella, you've got to watch Epi. Kathleen has her foot stuck in a tree root up the trail."

"Is she alright?" Ella asked as she rose from her seat.

"I don't know. Her ankle is definitely sprained, along with some scratches and bruises. But it's getting dark real fast out there, and a storm's coming."

Saki chimed in, "Let me come with you, Jaap."

"No, no. You have to run to the road and bring the doctor back—"

Oh no.

He never radioed in for a doctor in Lenakel. There was no time.

"Ella, I need you to radio for the doctor." He quickly gave her the instructions on how to work the CB radio while she nodded her head and bit her lip.

"Are you sure you don't want me to come with you?" she asked.

"No, stay with Epi. And Saki—" he pointed to the native "— Ella will make the call. Go meet the doctor at the road. If we are not back at the shed when you return, we are probably still stuck in the forest. Then we may need help. She's stuck about a hundred paces from the gorge, and ten paces above the old path. Understand?"

Saki nodded.

Before anyone had time to say anything else, Jake was rushing through the door. He made his way to the other path, which would be easier to see, and disappeared into the jungle. Ella ran to the grove of palm trees to make the call while Saki talked to the boy about the situation.

It was dark now, and the sprinkling had turned to rain. Jake pushed himself as hard as he could even though he was out of breath. This jungle seemed stuffier at night, in the rain, during an emergency. He was trying to breathe and also remember where Kathleen was.

After fifteen minutes of running, he came upon the embankment that led to the gorge's edge. He had gone too far. He ran back down the hill, and finally decided to stop and ask for directions.

"Hey, Scout!" His voice barely echoed in the trees and rain, but he got a response somewhere ahead of him.

"Here!" a muffled sound cried.

Kathleen was drenched, bleeding, broken, and freezing cold. She wasn't sure why she was cold since it was about eight-five degrees with no breeze, but none-the-less, she was shivering. It had gotten dark since he'd left, and she was beginning to wonder how he would find her until he'd shouted. She could hear him crashing through the wet foliage above her, a stream of light bouncing through the trees. He hopped down next to her, red and winded.

"Hey," he said. "How's it going?"

"Not good. Get me out of here."

He nodded and reached into his bag. He shoved the slicker into her arms.

"I guess it's too late to keep dry, but here."

"It's okay, I'm freezing."

He looked at her like she was insane. Then, he rubbed his hands on his pants in hopes of drying them a little. He put his hand on her head, and it was hot.

Fever.

He cursed under his breath.

"Excuse me?" Kathleen asked, hearing him swear.

"Old habit, but I think we have another problem on our hands."

"Do I have a fever?" she said, her voice barely keeping calm.

"Cover up, try to get dry. Here's some water to drink." He handed it to her and she took it with shaky hands.

God, we really, really need you right now, he prayed.

He held the flashlight up to the root and examined it. Her ankle had swollen so much that it looked like the wood was pinching her leg in a bear-trap. There would be no attempts to try and pull it out, so he held the saw up to the limb. He gently started a cut in the wood about six inches from her leg. As he got deeper, the strokes became longer and harder. Soon, he heard her whimpering.

"Is that too painful?" he said, looking up at her. She was crying and shaking her head.

"I just want it to be over. Do whatever you can."

Man she's strong, he thought.

He wanted it to be over, too. It was crushing him to see her like this. He looked down at the root again. He would have to saw through it in two places to get it away from her.

The rain fell harder. The jungle was black around them, like being immersed in ink. Lightning struck somewhere close by. Kathleen leaned back against the small ledge. A minute later, a little flow of mud started to fall over the edge, only a foot away from her head.

It was a mudslide, or at least the beginning of one.

She took a moment to stare at it. Jake continued to saw through the heavy wood, not noticing. Her eyes couldn't stop looking at the mud as it flowed smoothly over the side and down the hill. Why was this happening? A broken ankle, a fever, and a night storm weren't enough?

"Jake?"

"What?"

"Can you shine your flashlight up the hill behind me and see if there is more of a mudflow following this one."

He snapped his head up and looked at the small trickle of mud like it was an enemy that had just attacked them. He shined his light up the hill. Kathleen tried to lift herself just enough to see over the edge. The mud was flowing mainly to the right of them, but if enough came down that hill, there would be a problem. She suddenly realized why there was a ledge here in the first place. The entire hillside had an erosion problem.

"Hurry," she managed to say amidst the panic.

"I don't want to hurt you."

"I'd rather suffer through the pain of a swollen ankle than get buried alive, so hurry."

Jake knelt down again to place the saw into the slit that he had almost finished. Upon pushing forward for the first stroke, the blade completely broke free from the metal handle.

"*Dammit!*" he cursed.

She didn't care. She was thinking the same thing.

"Jesus, help us!" he cried, waving the broken hacksaw to the sky.

"Please tell me you have another one."

Jake slouched over, and the water falling on his head dripped down his face and off his nose.

"Okay, here's the deal," he said. She could barely make out his face in the darkness, but she could tell that he was worried. This made her worry even more.

"I have this." He held up the hatchet. "It's not very sharp, and it's gonna hurt real bad."

She shook her head. "I don't think I can handle you hacking away like that."

"Then we have three options. I can use this thing as fast as I can until it gets the job done, or I can go back to the shed and get a bigger, better saw. But it'll probably take me a good forty-five minutes. The mud could be flowing pretty heavily by then."

She shook her head again, obviously not wanting to be left alone. "What's the third option?"

Jake smiled, and said, "We could wait until the rain stops, or until morning, and huddle together for warmth for the next twelve hours, just you and me."

"Hack away, my friend."

"Thatta girl!"

He hit the remaining piece of wood as hard as he could, and she cried out in pain. He didn't stop. It would have to get done quickly or it would never happen. With every blow to the wood, he prayed that God would be with her. He apologized for the cursing, but thanked Him that He had brought him here, to Tanna.

The first slit was made in the wood now, and Jake made a desperate attempt to pull it away, but the root was too thick. He would have to cut through the part on the other side of her foot. He shook his head and asked God for swift, graceful hands. After the first three strikes, though, the mud started to flow more heavily over the edge. It hit Kathleen on the shoulder, and she looked at him with big eyes.

He moved and struck faster, but within seconds the mud was flowing over her head. She tried to lean forward but it pushed her down. She was whipping around under the cascade of mud, trying to find a way out, but she was trapped.

He hit the wood harder.

She was shouting his name from within the mud, but then it got muffled. The dense flow was pouring over her leg and on to his hands. He could barely see where he was cutting anymore. He went faster, knowing that she was drowning inside the flow. Her hands were reaching out to him as it fell harder on top of her, burying her deep into the hillside.

He started to cry when, at the last second, his other hand ripped the wood away, leaving her leg free.

"Now!" he yelled.

He grabbed her by the waist and pulled her to him. The force of her body sent them sliding down the hill together, through the mud and plants. They finally stopped at the trail, but before he had time to react, she was already pushing herself up off him, crawling away on her hands and knees. She was gagging on the path, mud and vomit coming out of her mouth. While she was retching, Jake crawled over and squeezed the mud out of her long pony-tail.

"Water!" she cried.

He looked around and saw that the water bottle had conveniently landed next to them. He forced it into her outstretched hand and she drank it. Then, she spit it back out again, cleaning her mouth of the gritty, red mud. He grabbed her waist and pulled her away from the mudslide while she coughed.

She touched her ankle. It was at an odd, puffy angle. She was sure this was what death felt like—swelling pain, a shaky body, and mud covering your clothes and lining the inside of your mouth and throat. She shook her head and wiped her lips with the back of her hand.

"Ready?" Jake said.

"For what?" she coughed, still wanting to wash more of the dirt from her mouth.

"To go home."

"I don't think I can move."

"You don't have to." He stood and leaned over to pick her up. She pushed him away.

"What are you going to do? Carry me the whole way?"

"Yup."

"You don't think I'm too heavy?"

"'Even faith as small as a mustard seed can move mountains.'"

"We won't make it."

"Yes, we will."

"Whatever." She threw up her hands. She didn't care.

He leaned over again and put his arm under hers.

"Hold onto my neck."

She did, and he put his other arm under her knees. He lifted her easily.

"That's incredible," she said.

"I dig holes for a living. What did you expect?"

They started going, but her legs were sticking straight out and her neck was stiff.

"You know," he said, "it won't kill you to just relax. I promise I won't drop you."

"It's not that. It's just—"

She stopped talking. She felt like a damsel in distress and didn't want to just relax in his arms. That morning she had been an independent, single mother living on an island with a tribe of ni-Vanuatu. Now, she was all of the above, except dependent.

Dependent on Jake.

She cringed, and her ankle was starting to droop. The fever and the fall had caused her whole body to ache. She was covered in mud from head to toe, and inside her mouth, too. Exhaustion swept over her. She relaxed and rested her head under his neck. It didn't matter. She would have to tell him that this was her worst moment, and that this was a once in a lifetime occurrence.

But for now, she would just close her eyes.

Breaking

The rain had gotten lighter, and was gently drumming on the aluminum sighting of the dark shed when Jake entered with the girl. The door flew open, and he frantically searched for a place to put her down without getting everything dirty. They were caked with mud, especially her, and he was out of breath. He looked over at the beach chair and carried her to it. She was completely limp, and had it not been for her deep breaths and occasional coughs, he would have thought that she was dead.

He gently laid her on the lime-green lounge, the clear, plastic material crunching as all her weight was put on it. She rested her head on the back and held onto his arm while he sat down next to her. Her eyes were heavy, and she gave a big sigh of relief to finally be back.

"Are you okay?" he asked.

She sort of laughed with relief but then broke down. Tears began to stream down her face and she put her hand over her eyes, shaking her head.

"No. I'm not okay," she cried. The whimpers turned to sobs, and Jake wasn't quite sure what to do. He decided against hugging her. That could turn weird.

"It's okay now," he said. "You're back. I'm sure they'll have the doctor here any time."

She continued to weep, but then she started to talk in between sobs.

"You tell yourself that you can do it—that you can live in the middle of nowhere by yourself with a different culture. You tell yourself that God will protect you, and that it will be easy. I can't believe I fell down that hill."

Jake stared at her with a frown while she continued to sob.

"It's been six years, you know? I haven't been to the States in seven. I haven't spoken to my dad in eight months. I know that I'm a missionary, and that God is out here with me, but I feel so alone sometimes. And I've never felt more alone than when I was stuck out there tonight."

"But you weren't alone," he reminded her. "I was helping you."

"No, I mean before you came. I was so scared. Then, when you did come, I was so relieved. I just—"

She shook her head and continued to cry. She kept shaking her head.

He looked down at the floor, and said, "You just realized that it's easier to do this whole missionary thing with someone else?"

Kathleen kept her hands over her eyes and nodded, intermittent sobs leaving her mouth.

He thought, *Now's the time. Tell her.*

He shook his head. Never take advantage of vulnerability. This was Kathleen's darkest hour. A guy who she didn't even want to be there, who said "I love you", would not go over well. It would be easier to amputate the leg.

Jake stood, but she continued to hold on to his arm.

"Where are you going?"

"I'm going to turn on the generator."

She still didn't let go of his arm, so he sat back down.

She said, "Can you just wait a few minutes?"

He nodded and looked at the wall, glad to be feeling needed, but also not quite sure what to say. She continued to sniffle and started looking around at the dark room. She was embarrassed for wanting him to stay. The room was stuffy and tense, and neither of them knew what to do until she finally let go of his arm.

They sat in silence for a moment, until Jake spoke.

"Did I ever tell you about the first time I saw you?"

Kathleen sniffled and shook her head.

"It was the first day of our second year at Oregon State," he said, "and while I was walking to my first class, I saw you chasing a guy across campus. He had stolen something from you, I don't know what, but he was running as fast as he could and you were hot on his heels, shouting at him. The poor guy didn't even have a chance with *you* after him.

"Everyone was laughing at him because you were so much faster than he was. I had never seen anything like it. Then, I went to my afternoon class, and you were there. You sat in front of me."

"I remember," she said, slightly grinning. "It was Cultural Anthropology."

"Yeah, and I remember being so impressed. I had been with lots of girls—you know about that—but I had never seen one that was so strong and so intolerant of stupidity.

"You're doing a fine job out here, Kathleen. Whether you feel weak or strong, lonely or scared, you have already done so much in this place. And you haven't quit, or complained, that I know of. Evil tells us that we are doing a bad job, but I want you to know that it's not true. Anything you do for God is a good job."

Kathleen sat there for a moment. She was truly touched, but she was still in a lot of pain. She was also sure that, had he told her that story under normal circumstances, she may have slugged him for being overly sentimental.

"Thanks, Jake. I appreciate that."

He nodded, but began to lean in to her face. For a second, she thought he was going to kiss her, but before she could stop him, he said, "Did you hide Ella's cigarettes in here?"

Kathleen was caught off guard.

"I, uh, think they're in the top drawer of your desk. Why?"

"You have a leech on your neck."

She stiffened up and groaned. He went over to the desk and rummaged around in the drawer until he found them. Then, he opened another drawer and pulled out some matches.

The rain had stopped, and they could hear the symphonic crickets in the field next to the shed. The water dripped from the trees above the shed and rhythmically echoed off the roof. He opened the window above her head and the muggy air drifted in.

The match struck the packet and lit the room for a moment. He put the cigarette in his mouth and lit it. His eyes closed while he inhaled and then blew the smoke out the window.

While he leaned in to her with the burning cigarette, he said, "Who says smoking isn't practical?"

She let out a small laugh and then sniffled. She was suddenly very aware that they were alone together, and it was the sort of situation she'd been dreading since his arrival. Something touched her neck, and she heard a plop on the floor. He had singed the leech off with the cigarette, and was now kicking it to the door.

The door opened, and he kicked it outside. When he shut the door and looked back at her, he said, "All better."

She kept sniffling, but at least she wasn't crying anymore. The leech had taken her mind off the ever-expanding adversities of missionary life.

They stared at each other for a moment, but before one could speak, a stream of light flew past the window. They could hear voices, and they knew that everyone was coming with the doctor.

Jake looked out the window into the palm grove and said, "Here comes the cavalry. I'm gonna turn on the generator."

"Jake—" she started to say.

"If you want to thank me, you can just forget it, Kathleen," he said on his way out. "I'd of done it any day of the week."

He could see her nod in the dark, and he left the room.

The lights turned on just as Epi came storming into the shed. He lunged for his mom, but Jake caught him at the last second and picked him up. The boy struggled, trying to get to Kathleen, but Jake had a firm grip on him and wouldn't let go. He tried to explain to the child that she was hurt, and that it would be best to give the doctor some room. Epi kept trying to get to her, crying.

Finally, Kathleen motioned for Jake to bring him over to her. Jake put the boy down next to the beach chair and continued to hold onto his shoulders while Kathleen spoke to him.

"Epi, I want you to stay with Ella for now. Understand?"

He nodded, and said with a whimper, "Do you hurt?"

"I won't once the doctor fixes me," she replied, trying to force a smile on her face. "Please behave for Jaap and Ella, okay?"

He nodded again, and walked back to where Ella had just entered the room. The dark-haired beauty entered and nearly tripped through the door when she saw the scene. Kathleen was red-faced and covered in mud. Leaves and twigs were stuck to her clothing, and she was resting on a fold-out beach chair that a family would take on a picnic. Her ankle was twisted to one side, puffy and purple.

Jake was as equally pathetic, his hair matted to his forehead with mud and sweat, and his clothes were drenched in water and dirt. He was slouching over like he had just run a marathon—and lost.

Ella continued to glance at the room until her eyes caught something very familiar on the desk.

"Are those my cigarettes?"

A dark-skinned woman entered the shed with Saki. She was obviously of an indigenous ethnicity, but she was dressed for a safari. She was holding a large bag, and Saki carried another similar bag on his back. When the dark woman entered the room, she smiled at Kathleen.

With a slight accent, she said, "Kathleen, this was a call I did not expect to receive."

"Hi, Mikaela. Could you give me a hand with this thing?" Kathleen pointed to her ankle. "I'm ready to amputate."

Mikaela laughed, and said, "Jake tells me you also have a fever, so let's take your temperature and then get you cleaned up. I brought materials for a cast." She turned to Jake, and whispered, "Why don't you take Saki and Epi, and get some other clothes for her. We need to get her changed."

Jake nodded and motioned for Saki to follow him. He picked up Epi, who did not put up a fight this time, and left the shed. Epi waved to his mother on the way out and they left the women to help clean Kathleen.

The two men walked through the palm grove in silence. The jungle around them was alive with insects and animals. The moon was barely breaking through the remainder of the storm clouds, casting a silver shine on everything around them. The wet foliage and grass sparkled dimly, and Jake took in a deep breath of fresh air. It was good to be out of that room.

Saki whispered to Jake in a serious voice. "What will happen to Ket-si?"

"I don't know. It may be a clean enough sprain so that Mikaela can cast it here."

"They won't go back to Lenakel?"

"I doubt it. The hike and the car ride back would probably be more painful than just fixing her leg in the shed."

Saki nodded. This was true.

He had always been on good terms with Kathleen. When she'd arrived six years earlier, Saki had helped her move all of her things into her new hut, which she had designed herself. Some villagers did not like the newcomer. She had brought a hammock, and silly building materials. But he liked her because she tried to get along with everyone, despite many elders opposing her presence.

It had taken many years for the missionary couple that was in the village, before Kathleen, to assimilate into the tribe. When the fever hit the village a year after her arrival, and the white couple left, Saki did not complain. He thought Kathleen was better suited for the lifestyle anyway. It was not as though he had no other lifestyle to compare his to, but it was obvious that the older couple had come from a world with more luxuries. Saki had been to Lenakel and discovered air conditioning.

He figured that the old missionaries had grown up in a home with the air conditioning.

Saki had also known Epi's parents before they died. Epi's parents had loved Kathleen. They took her in and taught her the language. As a result, many of the villagers got to know her, too. The young couple's death had been a tragedy, but Sowany had known that they wanted Epi to be with Kathleen, because the white missionary was physically strong and emotionally gentle. She would take care of the boy, and not deny him his Tannese heritage. Saki knew that she would do well, too.

The trio walked into the dark hut and stood at the entrance for a moment, scratching their heads. What sort of clothes should they pick out? Would they have to get her new underwear, too? Jake gave Saki a puzzled look, but entered the room anyway.

There was a large trunk toward the back of the hut, near the shower, so he decided that that would be a good place to put clothes. He walked over and opened it. Everything was neatly folded, and he shook his head at the organization. He felt funny going through her things, but he would have to be brave and pick something.

There was a set of pajamas that had been casually thrown in, so he grabbed those. He saw some folded underwear, so he grabbed a pair and stuffed it in the pajamas, trying to be as casual as possible. It was like shopping for a gift at the mall; how was he supposed to know what she wanted?

"Do you think they are done yet?" he asked Saki.

Saki shrugged and replied, "How long do you think it will take to clean her up?"

"A couple of days. She was very dirty."

They laughed.

Jake looked over at the shower in the corner. It was empty. He would have to wait until morning to get cleaned up. He knew the girls would probably use all the water in his portable shower near the shed. That was okay, though. He could wait a few more hours.

Mikaela cracked the door open and took the clothes from Jake.

"We are having a slight problem," the doctor told him.

"What's wrong?" he asked.

"I don't have any local anesthetic, but I do have some liquor that will help her. She's refusing to take it, though."

From inside the shed, they could hear Kathleen crying and shouting, like a child having a temper tantrum. It was very uncharacteristic of the woman, and the men stared with disbelief while Mikaela shut the door behind her to get Kathleen changed.

"No! I'm not doing it! There has to be another way!" she yelled.

Mikaela threw up her arms, and said, "You have to try and take it, Kathleen. It will, at the very least, calm you down. We don't need every inhabitant on the island hearing you scream. This is really going to hurt if you don't have some sort of sedation!"

Kathleen puffed her lower lip out and shook her head stubbornly.

Mikaela shouted for the men to enter. Kathleen was dressed now, and the doctor walked to where they were standing by the door.

She whispered, "Her fever is down, but only a little. The only chance at sedation that she might have is if I give her medicine for the fever. It won't do much, but it's something."

Jake asked, "No local anesthesia, no morphine? Nothing?"

"You can write a letter to your Darwin people and tell them we've run out. Anyway, she won't take the stuff, so I guess we are going to try this without the liquor."

Jake nodded and entered the room. Kathleen was clutching the lawn chair with tight fists. She was clean now, and her hair was twisted in a tight, wet braid. She shook her head furiously, trying to suppress more tears.

"I won't take a sip of that stuff. Not ever!"

"Fine, Kathleen. At least take some medicine for the fever, though."

Mikaela handed her the pill and a glass of water, and Kathleen shoved the pill in her mouth and swallowed it, still giving everyone a dirty look. She was being stubborn, and in a few minutes, it would pay.

Ella had been watching the scene silently. She was the only one who knew why Kathleen was having such a hard time with drinking the liquor. The missionary was afraid of the drink. Alcohol had taken two people from her life. Ella knew that a few sips wouldn't hurt her, but she also knew that it was not about the physical effects. Kathleen was having psychological issues with drinking it.

She and Jake walked to Kathleen and each held onto her shoulders. They were pressing her down, and she held each of their hands with a tight grip. The moment Mikaela tried to move the ankle, Kathleen cried in pain. Saki started to pull Epi out the door, but the boy pulled back, watching his mother with wide eyes.

The doctor approached her again, and, again, she cried out in pain.

Jake shook his head, and muttered, "This is ridiculous."

Kathleen shut her mouth and tried to deal with the pain. She was more afraid of it hurting a lot rather than the actual pain it was causing. She knew she just had to calm down, because there was no way she was going to take the alcohol.

No way.

Ella frowned, and suddenly felt compassion for the girl. Kathleen had never had a mother figure in her life, and now would have been the perfect situation to have a mom to hold hands with. Instead, she had a cold-hearted actress and an overprotective man who was smitten with her. For the first time in years, Ella decided to take on the role as care giver, and tried to sooth Kathleen's nerves.

"It's okay," she was telling the missionary. "It'll all be over soon. Then, you can fall asleep, wake up tomorrow, and smile because you made it through all the pain."

Kathleen was nodding and biting her lower lip, trying not to watch as Mikaela came forward to try again. Just as the doctor reached her hand to Kathleen's foot, the girl yelled.

"Stop!" she shouted.

Everyone in the room waited to hear what her new plan was. Would she take the liquor? Everyone wanted to know what she was thinking in these moments of extreme vulnerability.

Kathleen turned to Jake, who was only inches from her face, still holding her down.

"Please pray with me," she asked him, her eyes scanning his face like she was observing him for the first time. He grinned, and she explained, "I can't do this alone. I need God to help me, and I need you to help me, too. Please, just pray with me in English?"

Jake looked at her. She seemed genuine, and he would have prayed with her despite an attitude, but he was glad to know that she needed him on a spiritual level that night, not just a physical one. Jake looked up at Ella and then back at Kathleen. The girl's clean hair was starting to stick to her face again because she was sweating so much. Still, she was beautiful, especially while she looked at him with pleading eyes.

"Of course I'll pray with you," he replied nonchalantly. He looked over at Mikaela, who backed away from the foot, and he closed his eyes. He held his hand out to Kathleen's leg and prayed over it as he had done earlier, when they were in the jungle.

"Heavenly Father," he prayed in English, "You are a good and perfect God. You parted the Red Sea for the Israelites, and Your Son, Jesus, walked on water. Nothing is impossible when You get involved, Lord. I don't know how, but please relieve some of the pain that Kathleen is in. We can't be strong all the time, so we ask that through Your strength, we may combat pain and fear. Be with us in this place, and bless this group of people. Please, please Lord—may You be the only pain reliever that she needs. Amen."

When he opened his eyes, he found that he was looking into Kathleen's grateful stare. She was watching him with deep observation, and when he gave a little smile, she seemed to snap out of it.

"Thanks," she said calmly. "I, uh, feel much better now."

Mikaela moved in and put a gentle grip on the foot. Kathleen clenched her teeth, closed her eyes, and nodded her head. Jake and Ella held on to her hands and pushed her down for impact.

With a horrific popping noise, and Kathleen crying out in pain, the ankle was set, but not without more emotion in the room. Epi clutched at Saki's leg and started to cry. Jake turned his head toward the window with a dizzy feeling. Ella kept soothing a hysterical Kathleen.

"It's over now," she said calmly.

When Jake lifted Kathleen from the chair and put her on the futon, she was almost completely asleep. The fever had wiped her out, the pill had plunged her into drowsiness, and the long night by which she was trapped in the jungle during a rainstorm was finally catching up with her. Needless to say, Kathleen Newman was exhausted, and simply tired of being in pain.

As her head was laid onto the pillow and they covered her with the sheets, Mikaela took one last temperature reading by putting the thermometer in her ear, patiently waiting for the electronic beeping. When it was done, she pulled the device away and saw that the temperature was just above one hundred degrees Fahrenheit.

"She'll be fine," Mikaela whispered to Jake. "But if you guys had been out there for much longer, this fever would be much more serious."

He nodded and kept looking at Kathleen asleep in his futon. Epi crawled next to her, and was also fast asleep within a few moments. Saki came and tapped Jake on the shoulder.

"Jaap," the humble Tannese man said, "I want to stay and pray for Ket-si."

"I do, too," Jake replied.

They all gathered around the sleeping woman and put hands over her, praying for a good recovery and many more blessings to be placed in the village. All were praying in a circle except for one person, and that person could be heard leaving the shed in a hurry, not wanting to be a part of the religious ceremony.

The Goodness

Ella had snagged her cigarettes and was trying to light one behind the shed in the cool, moonlit night. Her hand shook as she put it in her mouth. She had never seen anything like that before. It was a painful scene, both with the ankle and the tearful girl who refused to drink a sip of alcohol.

The cigarette was lit and Ella took a deep breath, inhaling smoke for the first time in a month. It didn't feel as good as she'd hoped, but she could feel her body relax. Everyone was still in the shed, praying over Kathleen who was snoring soundly. After Jake's prayer about miracles and fear, Ella was tired of listening to words being spoken to God. She liked prayers better when they were said in Tanna North. Then, at least, she didn't understand them.

A noise to her right made her jump and she saw Jake walking around the corner to where she was. She threw the cigarette into the ground when he looked at her.

He smiled, and said, "Don't worry, I won't tell her." He was referring to Kathleen.

Ella nodded with pleasure and pulled out another one. She offered one to Jake, and after a short hesitation, he said, "Sure."

Now they were both standing behind the building, smoking cigarettes like fifth-graders hiding on the playground from the teacher.

After a few minutes, Jake said, "It's been three years since I've had one of these."

"Good god. How did you last that long?"

"I've had help from above." He looked up and then waved his hand toward the shed. "After that whole scene in there, I think I'm entitled to just one of these things."

Ella nodded in agreement, her blank stare drifting off into the night. She couldn't get the sound of the popping ankle out of her head.

"How do you people live in such physically painful conditions?" she asked, still staring into the darkness of the palm grove.

Jake smiled, remembering what Kathleen had confessed to him earlier.

"It's a whole lot easier when you have someone with you out here. I've never been out here for an extended period of time by myself. She was living here for four and a half years without an English-speaking soul. And now, after tonight and watching her try and go through all that without a pain killer—" he shook his head "—I've never met anyone who is so strong. Strong in the Lord, strong in herself. Everything."

Ella nodded again and kept smoking her cigarette. Jake started to think out loud.

"I wonder why she wouldn't just take a few sips of alcohol. I mean, I know she's against drunk partiers, but a little bit wouldn't have killed her—"

"Her mother was a drunk," Ella interrupted, still staring into the dark palm grove. She had blurted it out so easily that Jake didn't believe her at first. When that was all she said without flinching, he stared at her.

"You're kidding," he said.

"No, it's true. Her mom was a deserting drunk with no

shame, and I only add the last part in there because I think her mother and I were similar creatures."

Jake blinked, absorbing the news.

"I can't believe she never told me. I mean, I can't imagine what that must have been like."

He looked at his cigarette and shook his head again.

"And I'm out here, going back to my old ways. That won't impress her very much."

He threw the half-smoked cigarette into a puddle and walked away, saying, "Baby-steps, though. I still have a long way to go."

Ella watched him go and then threw her own cigarette into the puddle. Baby steps were always a good thing, even when you weren't looking to impress a mate.

Kathleen's eyes barely opened. Everything was dark and quiet. She thought she was in a cave, but a very comfortable cave. It felt like she was lying on marshmallows, and it was strangely familiar to her. But that couldn't be right; how would she have gotten in a bed of marshmallows?

A bed.

She tried to open her eyes wider. It was hard to see in the dark, but then she became adjusted to the darkness and started to see shapes. Where was she? She thought about the storm. Had it all been a dream? Something heavy weighed her leg down, and she realized that it was a cast.

Nope, not a dream.

After a few moments, she realized that she was on the futon, under the covers, resting comfortably. How did she get there? The last thing she remembered was Jake and Ella holding her down on the green lawn chair. When had that happened? What time was it? Where was everyone now?

Something moved next to her. It was Epi. Her mind started to clear, and she knew that someone had put her in the bed. Epi had probably crawled in next to her. He was wheezing the way he normally did when he slept. The pillow and mattress were apparently just as comfortable for him.

She was almost fully awake now, but her foot throbbed and her body ached. She looked around the room and noticed that there were more people. Saki was lying on the concrete floor in his green cargo pants, sleeping soundly. Ella was sitting upright at the desk, her head resting in her hand. She was leaning on the top of the desk with her elbow, and it seemed as though she was also asleep. Kathleen assumed that the person in the hammock was Mikaela, though it could be Jake. Then she heard a noise near her head. It was a soft noise, like whispering, and she looked back to see Jake sitting against the wall behind her.

Was he praying, or was that just the way he slept? She couldn't be sure, so she took a chance that he might be awake. Without looking at him or even moving her body, she whispered as low as she could so that no one else woke up.

"I know how Dudley felt now. We're going to start calling you 'Scout.'"

The whispering stopped, and there was silence.

"Yeah," he replied in the darkness.

"I'm sorry I lost it tonight."

"You don't need to apologize."

"Yes, I do. I was just being a baby. Thank you for dealing with it."

More silence.

"Your mother was an alcoholic?" he asked.

She paused a moment, and replied, "Yes. She left us when I was six."

"You and your dad?"

"And my brother, but he was killed nine years later by a drunk driver."

Jake did not respond. After another minute, he said, "Why didn't you tell me?"

"It's not something I like to talk about. I don't want to be like my mom, or like the woman who killed Sam. That's why I lost it tonight. I'm sorry."

"You don't deserve that type of pain."

"No one deserves that type of pain."

It was quiet after that, and Kathleen could feel her eyes grow heavy again. Just before she drifted to sleep, she prayed.

Lord, thank You for being there with me tonight. Thank You for good friends that were willing to help me, despite my being stubborn. Help me to forgive my mother, and my brother's killer. And, Lord, please let this cast be water-proof....

She fell asleep.

Love

A few days passed, and the tone between the two missionaries was different. They were almost constantly getting along, and Kathleen didn't seem to always be ignoring him. They would sit next to each other during the worship services and meals, and it was quite obvious that Kathleen was finally starting to let him in. Everyone was happy about it.

Ella was also noticing a change in them, but she was still looking within herself during most days. Something was changing in her, too. She had been feeling it since she had arrived on Tanna. Change was always frightening, but something inside told her that things would be okay when she returned home in three weeks. Somehow, she would try and mend things with her family and job. How she would do that was still in question, because she still woke up every day with the same pain in her heart. She always felt nervous and afraid, and she knew that that would have to change before she returned to the real world where things were much more difficult.

The literacy classes had started and children in the village were showing up at Kathleen's house every night to learn how to read. It was a miracle, and Kathleen praised God in all her prayers. It even looked as though some adults would join the group during nights when there was no work to do. Jake had volunteered some of his time to teaching as well, since his work could also only be done during the day.

The water project was almost done, and Jake was counting down the days for when he would finally be able to give these people clean water.

That day came only a week after Kathleen had sprained her ankle. Jake and Saki were leaning over one of the water pumps in the field by the shed. Agmol had been taken to Lenakel to get his cast taken off. He would not return for two days.

Jake adjusted some of the screws on the pump, then said a quick prayer. Saki nodded his head with affirmation as Jake prayed over the pump, asking God for clean water this day. When he was done, he pumped the lever multiple times, patiently waiting for the water to flow.

After several pumps, a trickle came out of the spigot. Jake and Saki widened their eyes as the trickle turned into a flow. It was clear and fresh. Saki started to laugh and he stuck his hands in it. Jake kept pumping the lever with disbelief. It had taken him a year.

The reality suddenly hit him. He began to shout at the top of his lungs, jumping up and down like a child who had received a race car for his birthday. It started to rain, and that made the men even more joyful. It would fill the tank that Jake had installed.

A teenage boy, running through the field from the river, stopped to see what was happening. They told him to go get everyone and bring them back to see what God had blessed them with. The boy looked at the flow of water coming from the pipe and bolted away, shouting as he ran into the village.

Within minutes, the entire village was dancing and singing in the rain next to the pump. They were dancing in circles and groups, laughing and chanting. They even pulled Ella into the group and she attempted to dance with them. Kathleen was laughing and Jake picked Epi up and put him on his shoulders. The rain fell harder and they continued to have a party in the field.

Kathleen slapped her hand to her cheek and shouted amidst all the noise.

"I'm gonna get the digital camera!"

She pointed to the shed and began to hobble across the field. Her boot was wrapped in a rain slicker fabric, and she had ditched the crutches.

Jake nodded, and Ella slowly made her way through the crowds of people, drenched and laughing.

"Congratulations!"

"Thanks! It took me long enough!" Jake replied.

"I didn't know I would be signing up for such fun when I came here."

"Yeah, *kastom* villages really know how to dance!"

Ella was wiping the hair off her face while the rain continued to pour. Jake was slouching over, trying to hear what she was saying.

"I guess this means the job is done!"

Jake lowered his eyebrows, and shouted, "What?"

"I guess the job is done!"

He stopped smiling and looked at her. Then he looked around at all of the smiling faces, jumping and dancing in the rain.

She was right. Why would they need him here now?

Ella saw the look on his face and patted him on the shoulder.

"I think now's a good time, Jake."

He looked back at her with a confused face.

"What are you talking about?"

"Go and talk to her," she said with a pleasant smile.

They both looked over at the shed where Kathleen had just entered. Jake felt a knot in his stomach. He nodded at the drenched woman and headed for the shed.

Kathleen walked in the room with a big smile on her face. She knew the digital camera was somewhere in there, but she didn't want to waste time looking for it. She wanted to be where the party was.

There was a noise behind her and she turned to see Jake in the doorway. He was drenched, and had a serious expression on his face. She smiled big at him.

"Hey! What are you doing? Why aren't you the happiest guy ever?"

He cleared his throat a little and responded solemnly, "My job is done now."

Her smile faded. She blinked at the floor several times to process the new thought. He continued.

"I should probably go back, now that the job is done."

She didn't answer.

"Unless—" he took a step forward "—I could stay. I could help you out."

It was certainly an idea, but Kathleen started to worry that it would make their relationship even more awkward than it already was.

"I don't know how great of an idea that would be, Jake," she responded, her voice only as loud as a breeze.

He looked down at the ground. Despite his shaky hands and knotted stomach, he decided to tell her. He walked toward her.

"I think you know that I'm in love with you."

Kathleen's breath caught in her chest and she was suddenly very uncomfortable. She crossed her arms and looked at the desk, her eye brows low. He took small steps toward her.

"Everything you do and say makes me want to be with you forever. I love Epi, and I love watching the two of you together. I pray every day that I can be a part of your lives."

She continued to stare at the desk, trying to figure out how to respond. When he got to where he was right in front of her, she looked at him with wet eyes. He took her hands and held them gently.

"Please, tell me you feel the same way."

Kathleen was trying not to cry. She was trying to concentrate on how to hold herself together, from not falling into his arms. Of course she loved him, but an entire lifetime of stubbornness and independence habitually kicked in. She couldn't look at him, and he continued to hold her hands.

She shook her head and her voice cracked with emotion.

"I'm sorry, Jake. I don't feel like that."

It felt like someone had punched him in the stomach. He looked at her with deep, wounded eyes. He blinked and let go of her hands. He slowly moved back, looking for something to fiddle with on the table. Embarrassed and humiliated, he searched for words to pull him out of this new rut.

Anything to hide the pain.

"Oh," he replied while he picked up a rubber band and played with it in his fingers. "I'm sorry."

"Don't be—"

"I just thought, you know—I felt that way, and I—I just thought you should know."

Kathleen nodded with tears in her eyes, arms still folded, looking at the desk.

Jake stood there for a moment before he gave an indignant laugh.

"So, that's it. I'll be out of your hair in two days. I'll leave when they bring Agmol back."

"I think it would be best," she managed to say.

He snapped his head up with tears in his eyes and pointed at her.

"I hope that that stubborn attitude of yours gets broken

someday. I know you don't want things to happen like this."

She said nothing.

"What about Epi?" he asked with a long face.

"You should tell him."

Jake shook his head with a smile, trying to stop the tears.

"Sure, I'll tell him. I'll tell him after I'm done telling myself."

As he walked out the door, he said over his shoulder, "I'm sorry I yelled at you that time you came over to my apartment."

At that, he left the room, leaving Kathleen alone. Alone in the ever-darkening room, damp and crying. She listened to the dancing and singing outside while the rain fell on the roof and left little trails of condensation on the windows.

What had she done? Kathleen put her face in her hand and stood in the lonely room, crying.

The next day was sunny, but not as happy as the previous one. Everyone talked about the new water over their work and play. The children would press the lever down as they ran to and from the river. Saki was able to go out hunting with all the spare time now.

Unfortunately, the two people who should have been happiest were silent. Kathleen worked at her typewriter all day, not saying much to anyone. She had barely slept the night before, and she felt like her heart had fallen into her stomach. After the sleepless night, she had gone to her favorite quiet-time spot by the river and prayed. The prayer left her with a stronger feeling than before, telling her that she had done the wrong thing. The pain of knowing that Jake was going to leave spread through her body like someone had poisoned her blood. It ran through her veins, and struck her directly in the heart.

Ella silently helped Namay with more mat-weaving, occasionally entering Kathleen's hut to grab some food or water. The missionary had been quiet all day, and didn't seem to be seeking advice from anyone, especially Ella. Besides, Ella didn't know what she could say to the woman to make her happy or change her mind. She was also sad that Jake would leave, not just because he was a fun guy, but because it was so obvious that he and Kathleen belonged together.

Jake and Epi were off together, spending time alone. After talking to Sowany, Jake had taken the little boy to the river to tell him what was going on. It would not be an easy conversation, but Epi would have to understand.

The two boys were standing on a flat rock next to the slow moving river. They could barely hear the ripples of water as they skipped stones across its gentle current. Jake threw a flat rock and got ten skips. Epi threw one that Jake had picked out for him, and it splashed into the water, sinking straight to the bottom. Jake laughed, and Epi looked at the water with sad eyes.

"Are you leaving?" he said.

Jake looked down at him and answered, "Yes."

Epi sat on the rock and sniffled. Jake sat down next to him and they listened to the jungle birds crying in the hot afternoon sun. A little ripple of water surged between the rocks, making a serene, gurgling sound. A bright, red bird flew over their heads, but they didn't notice

"Why?" Epi asked, tears now flowing down his face.

"I've given you clean water so that you won't be sick. That was why I came here. Now, I need to go back to *my* village and see who else I can help."

"But we need you here."

"No, you've got Ket-si."

"But she needs you, too."

Jake frowned, and threw a little pebble in the water. "No she doesn't."

"Yes, she does. She just doesn't know it."

Epi kept crying, and Jake put his arm around the little boy. "You know what I need?"

Epi shook his head.

"I need to leave here knowing that you're going to take of her. I need to know that she'll be okay. And I need you to always remember me, and always be happy."

The tiny boy nodded his head and looked at his tall friend.

"I promise, Jaap."

He stood and wrapped his arms around his friend's neck. Jake picked him up and hugged him. The sun continued to hit them on the river bank, and Jake did not put him down for a long time. They stayed in the sun, listening to the river's movements and the jungle birds while they spent what would be their last moments together. Two friends, like father and son.

Change

The day Jake left was different. The air was muggy, there was no breeze, and people seemed agitated. Everyone looked beaten, tired.

Yasur Volcano had been erupting all night. It had blown its fumes and smoke toward the northern part of the island.

Kathleen packed a bag for her and Epi in case they would have to spend the night on the road. It wasn't usually difficult to pack for him since all he ever wore was a grass-skirt or his yellow shorts. She wasn't paying attention to anything she was doing anyway, as Jake's departure was shaking her up.

Every time she saw him, she wanted to run after him and beg him not to go. But pride kept her still, and her only thoughts were at a level that couldn't imagine life without him. She tried to convince herself every moment that it was the right thing by letting him leave, but something kept pulling at her.

Something relentless.

Ella felt funny that day, too, though not for the same reasons as Kathleen. She was edgy and anxious, like she waiting for something to happen. She couldn't put her finger on it.

Epi sat by himself that morning, playing with the sand by the fire pit, not talking to anyone. Kathleen watched him from the doorway of the hut, wondering how long he would be sad for. She did not like to see him so melancholy, nor did she like to feel it herself, but she knew that they would be okay in a couple of weeks.

As good as they had been before Jake had arrived a year earlier.

The four of them came out of the jungle and onto the road by late afternoon. They were all carrying something that belonged to Jake, and when they saw that the jeep had not arrived yet, they put down the bags and sat. Epi was sitting on Jake's lap and Kathleen picked at a blade of grass. Ella sat between the two, looking back and forth, waiting for someone to speak. No one did, and the four sat like that for thirty minutes until the jeep bounced up the road.

The sun was starting to go down, and Jake turned to Kathleen as they stood.

"It'll be dark once you get under way. Will you guys be okay?"

She nodded, and replied, "We'll have Agmol with us. We can just stay the night in the old trading post up the road."

He nodded and turned to Epi, who jumped in his arms.

"Don't go!" the little boy cried.

"I have to. Take care of your mom."

He kissed the boy on the cheek, and Kathleen bit her thumbnail.

Tell him to stay.

Jake walked to Ella and gave her a hug.

"Ella, it was a pleasure getting to know you. You know, you would make a great Christian."

She laughed, and said, "Thanks, but you people seem to be doing fine with the ones you've got."

"Bye."

"Bye. And if you're ever in Hollywood, look me up."

235

"You got it."

Agmol got out of the dirty jeep and limped over to the group without a cast. He winced as he tried to do so, but smiled when he approached Jake.

"So, it is true. You leave us in such a hurry."

"You have good water. You don't need me here anymore."

Agmol looked at Epi and Kathleen, and whispered, "There are people here who need you more than they know, Jaap. I am one of them."

They shook hands, and Jake said, "Be a good warrior for God."

"I will. Goodbye."

They all helped to load up the back of the jeep and Bobby, the young Lenakel boy, said to Jake, "Are you ready?"

"Give me a minute."

Jake looked at Kathleen. She walked to him while everyone else meandered away from the jeep to give them privacy. The sun was almost down, and she squinted at it while it sank over his shoulder. He looked down and smiled.

"So, this is it," he said.

"I guess so."

"Anything you want to tell me before you never see me again?"

Don't go.

"Nope," she replied, her voice almost betraying her pain. He didn't notice.

"Listen," he said, "I know you've played this tough and independent role your whole life, but I know that you love me."

She clenched her teeth and watched the sunset while he continued.

"If you ever need help out here, give me a call, even if it's just something as simple as pulling your foot out of a tree trunk."

Kathleen sighed and gave a nervous laugh.

"I think we've already done that," she said.

"Well, we've had lots of adventures together."

She nodded and he leaned over, kissing her on the cheek. She kept staring at the sun while tears filled her eyes.

"Take care of yourself, okay?" he said.

She nodded and walked away, trying to hide her face.

Bobby and Jake climbed into the jeep and drove off, a trail of dust following the car as it made its way down the road and around a bend. The four people left by the side of the road stood still as the car disappeared.

He'd gone.

Kathleen looked at the trail of dust left behind, and was almost tempted to go running after him, but she knew it was too late. She had stayed strong, proud, and independent, all the things she had always wanted to be. It hadn't been enough. The dreams of who she would become as a lone missionary in the jungle had been achieved, but she suddenly realized that it had never been God's plan for her to be strong or independent. He had her on Tanna Island to be weak, and to rely on Him. He wanted her to break the walls of fear with love, and drop the chains of pain to pursue a life of joy that only He could bring. As a Christian, she had given her life to God, but as a human, she had adopted it as her own.

The breath in her lungs suddenly felt insufficient, and she tried to breath deeper. Fists clenched, she was hyperventilating in the middle of the road.

Ella noticed, walked over, and said to her, "You won."

"Huh?"

With sad eyes, Ella repeated, "You won."

"Won what?"

"The battle. Remember, we'd see who lost their battle first. You against your love for Jake, or me and my relationship with Jesus. Well, you just won."

"Leave me alone, Ella."

Kathleen slowed her breathing back to normal, took Epi by the hand, and began walking to where the old trading post was. Agmol looked at Ella as he followed them. He had a bad limp, but he seemed to be too interested in what had been going on in the village the past few days.

Ella turned around and watched the colors of the sky fade away as night approached. The first stars faded into the purple-blue sky. Wisps of high clouds changed from pink to silver. The moon was rising behind her, and she could hear the rumbling of Yasur in the distance.

As she glanced at the night's first star, she kicked a rock down the road as hard as she could. It wasn't fair for there to be pain, even to people as good as Kathleen and Jake. That's what the world was to her—pain.

Walking to the shack on the road, Ella had no idea that she would remember this night for the rest of her life.

First Faith

The sky was growing darker, but the light hit the desert sand with such a force that it seemed as though an atomic bomb had exploded into oblivion. There was no wind, no animals, and no sign of anything invigorating or cool. The cacti and tumbleweed sat in the dirt, unmoved and monotonous. The landscape was barren, a deserted wasteland that had no end in sight.

Ella Levene's lungs were burning. She felt like she had swallowed a mouthful of the gritty sand. She couldn't stop running. And crying. Sprinting, sobbing, the white light, the dark sky, the heat—

The heat was unbearable.

How would she ever make it? Make it where? She didn't know. Her muscles throbbed and itched.

The sun in the sky got larger, but the sky itself was turning a midnight blue. The high, wispy clouds were moving faster and faster in the sky. Time seemed to be moving rapidly, but she felt as though she was running at a snail's pace, gradually getting slower by the minute.

Before she knew it, the flat desert suddenly dropped off, and she tripped over the edge of a steep hill, tumbling all the way down. The rocks and dirt scraped her clothes and face.

Something kept tugging at her arms, pulling at her as she plummeted toward the approaching base. Just before she smashed to the dirt floor, the tugging in her arms became violent, and she shut her eyes as tight as she could to brace for the impact.

"Ella!"

The actress opened her eyes wide with panic. Kathleen was shouting in her face, shaking her by the arms. That had been what the tugging was. Ella blinked several times, trying to catch her breath. She was sweating, and she felt like she had been holding her breath the entire night.

She tried to look at Kathleen in the dark hut. They had decided not to walk back to the village after nightfall, and had taken shelter at what was once an old trading post amongst the local villages. Now it was empty, and had been abandoned for a long time. There were no lights, and Ella knew that they had forgotten the flashlight, so she tried to let her eyes adjust to the darkness.

Kathleen kept saying, "Get up! Wake Up!"

Ella was dazed. What was the big emergency?

"I'm awake. What is it?" she asked, wiping sweat from her brow.

Kathleen pulled Ella to her feet, nearly ripping the arms out of the older woman's sockets. It was the middle of the night, and the missionary was wide awake. She kept repeating herself, mumbling under her breath.

"I forgot it! I can't believe I forgot it!" she was telling Ella.

Ella didn't understand. "Forgot what?"

"His inhaler!"

Kathleen pointed to the corner of the old shack to where Agmol was hunched over Epi. The boy was wheezing, more severely than he normally did when he slept, but Ella could clearly see that Epi was not asleep. He was watching the two women while Agmol prayed over him, apparently not flustered by the situation at hand.

Ella continued to stare at Epi in disbelief while Kathleen spoke quickly.

"The volcano has been erupting for a while, and we're downwind. The gases are flaring up his asthma. He's having an asthma attack. You have to run back to the village and get his inhaler."

Ella stopped staring at the boy and blinked at Kathleen. Had she heard the woman correctly?

"Sorry?" Ella said, her mouth opening wide with shock.

"You have to run back and get the first aid kit," Kathleen said, her words coming out more slowly the second time. "There's no time to wait. There's only time for you to run and get the inhaler. Agmol and I aren't fast enough because we're injured. It's up to you, Ella."

Now Ella began to panic. She shook her head obstinately.

"I can't," she found herself shouting. "I don't have a flashlight, and I don't know the way."

Her eyes were scanning the room, apparently looking for another person who might be up to the task. Agmol didn't look up from his prayers, and Epi continued to wheeze and watch her with longing eyes. Kathleen looked at Ella's panicked stare and took a deep breath.

She pushed Ella closer to the door while the terrified celebrity continued to stare at the helpless, hyperventilating boy.

"Ella," she said with a hushed, calm tone. "Epi needs you right now. We all need you. Now listen. Run as fast as you can up the trail. When you get to the village, go straight to Saki's hut."

Ella was nodding, but she kept licking her lips and staring off into the corner.

Kathleen continued.

"Communication will be difficult, but try to use names and hand gestures. He knows we're here, so if you just give him the kit, he'll bring it back to us. The inhaler is in the big, gray box that looks like a tackle box. Do you understand?"

She was talking slowly, and Ella nodded.

"Good. Everything we need is in that box, in my hut. Go as fast as you can."

"I don't know the way," Ella said, her words shaky and low.

Kathleen tilted her head a little and smiled. "You do know the way. You know the path to follow. You've just never known to take it before. But God is with you, and He won't let my son die, and He won't let you get lost. Now, go!"

Ella bolted out the door and down the road as quickly as she could. She took deep breaths as she went, trying to keep her breathing in balance with her long strides. She saw the dark opening that led into the jungle and she turned into it.

There was immediate darkness. She could hear her footsteps crunching over the leaves and dirt. As long as she felt that bit of dirt, she knew she was still on the trail. It was so uncomfortable to be running at full speed, in the middle of a dark forest, when she didn't even know where she was going. A cloud cover was blocking any chance of moonlight shining through the trees, but her eyes were starting to adjust a little, so she picked up the pace.

Her breaths were getting heavier, and she suddenly felt as she had only moments before, when she was dreaming. For some reason, her thoughts left the darkness of the forest and started playing with her dream. That same dream she had had for years of running through deserts, crying and choking. This night had been the first time out of all those dreams when she had stopped running and fell down a hill. She wondered why that was.

About ten minutes passed before she slowed her pace a bit, waiting for any indication that the trail would turn. She tried to remember how they had gone that first day, when she had followed the group to the village. They had been strangers, and the village was only an illusion. Now, it was a real place, and one of those people was relying on her to save his life.

The trail started to go uphill more, and she doubted that it had been that steep before. She stopped a moment, but then decided that she would have to keep running. Running and running. It was something she felt she had been doing her whole life.

Running to something.

Running from something.

Which was it?

The forest flattened out a bit, so she sped up. The ground was covered in dark brush, and foliage hit her ankles. She could only barely see the dark line that was the trail—

It stopped.

The trail stopped.

Ella tripped over her feet as she came to a halt. She started to breathe deep and heavy, trying to fight off the panic. She had failed. She didn't know where she was. Tired, and more depressed than she had ever been in her life, Ella leaned over, resting her hands on her knees. She tried to breathe.

She closed her eyes while she caught her breath.

So this was what it all came down to. A sweet, innocent boy's life was in her hands. Despite the circumstances and the immediate action that needed to take place, she couldn't pull through for him. She hadn't paid attention the first day, she had been running too fast this night, and now Epi was going to suffocate in a dark, deserted, moldy hut.

Ella kept hearing Kathleen's voice saying, "You know the way. You know the path to follow. You've just never had to take it before."

What had that meant? It was a comment that had somehow referred to something besides the trail leading back to the village. Ella shook her head and shut her eyes tighter. Her breaths were coming slower now, and she felt a peace rush over her heart and mind.

You know the path to follow.

Ella opened her eyes slowly and stared at the dark ground. There was only one path she had never taken. It was a path she had never wanted to attempt or consider, and even though it wasn't a tangible, dirt path, she decided to try it anyway.

It was only five words long, but for the first time in her life, Ella said a prayer to God.

"Help me," she whispered. "I need You."

Just then, the clouds barely moved and a small amount of moonlight broke through the gray. It slowly drifted through the high tree branches and cast a light on top of her as she crouched over. Something made her glance over and, in the moonlight, she saw a black object. It was sitting still, about twenty feet behind her, and she squinted at it in the darkness. When she saw what it was, she almost fainted.

It was a rock.

It was that damned rock that she had tripped over on the first day. The rock next to all the bugs, on the trail.

The trail!

Ella Levene widened her eyes and darted her head to the sky where the moon had just broken through the trees.

"Thank You!" she screamed at the top of her lungs.

She plunged through the brush and bolted in the direction past the rock. The trail was visible again, and she felt a new passion rise within her. Her heart was beating faster, but not because of the running. She smiled, and pushed herself harder. She started to pray for everything.

Help me run faster.

Show me where to go.

Be with Epi.

Be with Kathleen.

Is the village near?

Ella emerged out of the forest and into the moonlit field used for growing yams. The flimsy bamboo structures could be seen swaying in the cool breeze coming from the south. She raced up the hill, not feeling tired or suffocated. Something was pushing her. She could almost feel someone's hand shoving her up the hill toward the settlements.

Everything was quiet within the area around the huts. It was the middle of the night and everyone was asleep. There wasn't even any residual smoke rising from the fires that had been extinguished that evening.

All was calm; until Ella arrived.

Ella burst into Saki's hut, yelling his name as she let out a breath of air.

"Saki!"

At once, the man was jumping up off the ground and hopping to her in the dark. He was not wearing his usual *namba*, but had on a pair of green cargo pants, assumedly to fight off the night's chill. He stared at her with confused eyes in the dark. Her silhouette was black against the ever-brightening night as the moon continued to break through the clouds.

Ella whispered, "Epi!"

She put her hand in front of her mouth and pretended to be using an inhaler. Then, she pointed to where she had just come from. He stared at her for a second, but then his eyes widened in the dark and she could see that he had understood.

Saki ran toward Kathleen's hut with Ella right behind him. By the time she reached the hut, he was shouting.

"Where is it?!" he cried in Tanna North.

She didn't understand him, but she knew what he was saying. Ella started to touch everything with her hands, knocking stacks of paper over, hitting cups and dishes. He heard her in the dark and started mimicking her on the other side of the room.

When Ella's hand brushed a cold, metal cylinder, she grabbed it, and yelled, "I've got it!"

It was the flashlight. She flicked it on and saw Saki hopping around the room, searching for the gray box that contained Epi's salvation. Ella shined the light everywhere until she saw it sitting on the trunk where Kathleen kept her clothes. Saki noticed it at once, dashed to the back of the room, grabbed it, and ran out the door without the flashlight.

Ella didn't know what to do after that. Should she wait?

"I don't think so," she told herself out loud.

She grabbed a bottle of water sitting on the table and started to head out, but something caught her eye at the last moment. It was Kathleen's Bible, sitting on the desk. Ella looked at it a moment, then walked over and picked it up. They might want it for prayer or something.

She ran after Saki, ignoring her fatigue and shining the light in front of her.

When she ran out of the jungle and onto the road, everything was quiet. Too quiet. Ella huffed and puffed while she jogged up to the little shack where everyone was. As she walked into the dark room, she cast her light on the walls. Everyone was huddled in the corner. She could only see the backs of Agmol and Saki, and they were bending over.

"Is he okay?" Ella gasped when she walked in the room. "Did we make it?"

Saki and Agmol turned to her with glum faces. They didn't speak. Ella's heart fell, and she suspected the worst. Then, she heard Kathleen speak from behind the two natives. She sounded like she was crying.

"Yes, Ella. You made it."

Agmol and Saki stood, and Ella's light touched Kathleen's face. There were tears in her eyes and she was holding Epi. His arms were wrapped around her neck while she rubbed his back. There was no more wheezing.

The two men helped Kathleen stand up with the boy still in her arms. Then, she walked over to Ella, and whispered, "Thank you."

As she walked out the door, Ella looked at Epi's face.

Exhausted, he grinned at her. Ella smiled back, and the moment they left the room, she let out a huge sigh of relief. As they all walked out of the shack to make their way home, Ella glanced at the sky with thankfulness, wondering what had just happened. The world was a little different to her now; as she had once thought that she was all alone and had to be in control, it now seemed as though someone else was taking care of things on Earth.

Saki held Epi while they made their way uphill in the dark. Agmol winced in pain as he walked on his newly un-bandaged foot. Kathleen had an arm around Ella's neck and the actress was trying to help her up the trail.

"I'm making you take your cane with you wherever you go from now on," Ella said, struggling to hold the tall woman upright.

"I didn't think about the uphill climb," Kathleen replied, cringing with some pain.

"How much longer did Epi have before Saki got there?" Ella asked.

"Things were getting pretty serious just before he arrived. You saved Epi's life, you know."

Ella shrugged. She was not sure that *she* had done anything.

Fear

Kathleen unplugged the nebulizer from the wall and looked down at her son. Epi had been sitting upright on her lap to breath from the machine, but now he was leaning on her, falling asleep. They were in the shed—Jake's shed—and it seemed like days ago that Epi had had the emergency.

It had only been hours.

Ella was sitting in the corner in the dark, on the cold, concrete floor. She couldn't sleep.

She watched the pair from the corner of the shed with sympathy. The lights were off, and when she looked out the window, she could see that the stars were beginning to fade away as morning approached. She was suddenly very confused and depressed. It was finally hitting her that she had asked God for help, and He had immediately answered. Fear and embarrassment had kept her from telling Kathleen about what happened in that jungle.

Fear.

Ella was always afraid. Afraid of everything. The most afraid she had ever been in her life was only a couple of hours before when she was all alone in the jungle, thinking that she had let Epi down. She thought he would die.

And worse, she knew that she would have been the one to blame if he had. It was a frightening concept, and she tried not to think about it.

As a matter of fact, Ella found that any thought that entered her mind brought fear. When she thought of her children, she feared that she didn't want to spend time at home and watch them grow, or that she would be like Kathleen's mother and desert them. Or worse, that Freddy and Sara hated her. When she thought of John, she feared that he would leave her. That was an indescribable fear that would bring much pain because she loved him so much. She was afraid of God, Jesus, the island, the jungle, the gorge, and almost anything else. But what could she do about it —

"When God shows me the stars, I'll remember your sparkling eyes. And when He shows me the sun, I'll think of your bright smile," Kathleen said in Tanna North.

Ella glanced at her, knowing what she had said to the sick boy.

The director felt her eyes well up with tears. One of them slowly fell down her face, and it was the first time in years that she was crying. Ella clenched her teeth and wiped the tear away.

So, the famous, cold-hearted Ella Levene is human after all.

This was the moment when she felt more human than ever. All her faults suddenly became very clear to her, and she wanted to pray more. Something stopped her.

It was fear.

At this realization, she lowered her eyebrows with anger and determination. With clenched fists, she stood up and walked out of the shed, leaving Kathleen staring blankly at the door with a sleeping Epi still in her arms.

The Leap

Ella was running as fast and as hard as she could, crying more than she ever had. She could feel the tears streaming down her face as she sobbed, just as she normally did in her dreams. But it wasn't a dream, and it wasn't a desert. She was in the jungle, brushing away palm fronds and bush branches as she ran up the hill. It felt like her dreams, only she was in darkness and a jungle, not a brilliant, hot light in a desert.

The sky above her was turning gray as dawn approached, making it easier to see the trail. Everything about this experience was different from the dream, except for the running and crying. Things were getting brighter and clearer, but the biggest difference was that she was on a mission. As opposed to the confusion of her desert dream, she knew what she was running from, and it was fear. And she knew where she was going—to the gorge.

A small boy was walking down the trail, and she thought it odd for him to be out this early. He waved at her, but she ran past him, not slowing down. He shouted in his language.

"Where are you going?!"

Without realizing that she had understood his native language, she responded in English, with a slight wave, "I have to do it!"

In the next moment, she disappeared up the hill and around

the corner. The young boy shook his head with confusion and headed back to the village, resolving himself to the fact that the newcomer was crazy.

The sky was a dull gray now, the way it had been the first morning she had been there, when she was up all night and had gotten sick. It was different this morning. She had spent five weeks in this place. She had been up all night, but she did not feel sick. She felt alive, and full of adrenaline. It had to be adrenaline.

Ella reached the end of the trail where the embankment could barely be seen. The roots were hanging out of its soil. Another young boy had helped her climb it the first time, but now she would do it herself. Her face was wet with tears, and she knew it was probably dirty, too. She sniffled, rubbed her hands together, and began to make her way up the wall of roots and vines. Clumps of dirt broke off under her feet as she slowly ascended the escarpment. One step at a time and she finally reached the slight overhang. The last three feet, she pulled herself up and over the edge, trying to catch her breath.

She had made it.

There was a palm tree in the ground and she lunged for it. She hugged it while tears fell down her face. She looked at the ledge of the gorge only ten feet away from her. If she went any closer, she would see over the edge, and then she would chicken out. Dirt streaked her cheeks, and she looked at the drop-off with sad, desperate eyes. Then, she cried a prayer in her heart.

I want to trust You, and this is the only way I know how right now. Please don't let me die.

Ella knew that she wouldn't die, because little kids did it all the time, but it didn't make the thought any less transparent.

She closed her eyes, took a deep breath, and ran at full speed to the edge.

She flew into space, trying to keep her feet below her. The ledge was behind her, and then above her, and she had no time to think before she hit the cold water with an abrasive crash. Darkness engulfed her and the icy water made her want to gasp for air. Her legs kicked with all their strength, and, soon, her head was above the surface of the pool.

Ella gasped for air and looked around, shivering. There were stone walls around her, and she knew that she was deep in the gorge. When she turned around, she saw a flat rock at the edge of the pool. She kicked to it and pulled herself out of the water. Her body shook, and puffs of air could be seen leaving her mouth as she breathed. Without getting up, her hands clutched at the rock and pulled her forward like a reptile slithering along the surface.

The adrenaline rush was gone, she was freezing cold, and a night without sleep finally caught up with her. Exhausted and soaking wet, Ella Levene rested her head on the rock and fell into unconsciousness as the gray sky turned to pink. The sun began to rise somewhere to the east.

The sun was rising over the trees and everything began to sparkle in the early morning light as it did at the beginning of each day. A stream of sunshine came in through one of the windows of the shed and hit Kathleen's face.

She had fallen asleep with Epi in her arms, and the sunlight forced her eyes to open. She glanced at the corner and remembered that Ella had left when it was still dark.

Where was she now?

Kathleen placed Epi on the futon and walked to the door. When she opened it, she was greeted with chirping birds and a crisp morning breeze. The sun made everything look beautiful as it reflected the night's dew off the dazzling green leaves of the palm tree grove. A slight mist hovered over the green grass while the yellow light passed through it and melted it away.

A boy walked by the shed, and Kathleen said, "Have you seen Ella this morning?"

He nodded and said, "I saw her running up the path to the gorge."

"Did she say anything to you?"

"Yes, but I did not understand."

Kathleen squinted at him. "Can you try and repeat what she said?"

He blushed, not wanting to blotch the words. Then, he raised his chin, and said, "Aye hobduit."

He looked at his feet, embarrassed. Kathleen tried to figure it out, repeating the words out loud. As she was doing so, Saki came to the shed from the village, rubbing his eyes. He looked at the boy, then Kathleen. She seemed to be making funny noises.

"What are you doing?" he asked her.

"Ella said something to the boy and I can't figure out what it was."

"How can you understand her at all? She speaks very different than you and Jaap."

Kathleen stopped mumbling, and said, "What do you mean?"

"Her words are funnier than yours," Saki said.

Kathleen opened her mouth as a light bulb turned on in her head. Ella had a British accent. What may sound like an "o" was probably an "a."

"I habduit. I have to do it?"

The boy clapped his hands and pointed at her like she had just won a game of charades. Kathleen looked at him curiously.

"Which way did you say she was going?"

"To the gorge."

Kathleen's heart skipped a beat.

Oh God, be with her.

"Saki, please stay with Epi. I need to go to the pool," she said, trying to remain calm. She reached into the shed and pulled out her cane, then hobbled across the field toward the river. After a while, she was gone, and the boy looked at Saki.

"What is happening?" he asked.

Saki shrugged with tired indifference and went in to be with the small child as he slept.

Crossing Over

Ella Levene tumbled down the rocky hill until she came to a stop at the bottom. The sky was not dark anymore, but the sun still shone brightly and it felt like a normal day found in any desert. The dirt felt real, the pain was profuse in her body, and Ella opened her eyes and found that she was still alive despite the treacherous fall. Lying face down in the dirt, she suddenly realized that this was the first time she had been in this desert and had stopped running.

Suddenly, she felt a foot step on her back. Someone was there. After all this time, running through the desert and searching for any living soul, there was a person. But then she heard a rumble and noticed that there were many feet, stomping all around her. When she lifted her head from the dirt, she saw that crowds of people were running down the hill.

She rose to her feet so that they didn't trample her. It was a stampede of people, running down the hill, looking almost as tired and dilapidated as she did. They were in such a hurry.

As she walked to stay moving with the crowd, she noticed that they were people of all different ethnicities and eras. There was a businesswoman with an old blue dress that looked like she was from the 1980's. A man with a white wig looked like he had just fought in the Revolutionary War. A Mexican wearing a sombrero ran with the crowd. A black man with indigenous war paint was running with a spear, apparently from somewhere in Africa.

Ella kept looking around, wondering why no one else seemed to notice the crowd they were running with. After a few minutes of wandering in the middle of the mass of people, she turned her head and saw that there were hundreds of people behind her, all headed in the same direction. Where was everyone going?

They climbed a hill and, all at once, everyone stopped and stared toward the center of the sea of people. They started shouting in their native languages toward the center, and Ella didn't understand why. She walked further into the crowd where everyone seemed to be surrounding something. When it seemed like there were too many people to walk anymore, she tripped over something and fell in the dirt.

When she turned around, she saw a piece of timber lying on the ground. She had tripped over a piece of wood. When she looked beyond the wood, she saw a man lying in the dirt beside it; but he was not shouting at anyone, and he was not running. He was lying there, with blood and open soars covering his body, especially his back. He had a crown of thorns hammered into his head so that they were stuck in his skull. As a whole, he looked like a piece of raw hamburger meat, bloody and grinded to the bone so that he was no longer recognizable as a person.

But it wasn't the blood and torturous wounds that Ella noticed.

It was his eyes.

The man's eyes stared with sadness and cried for mercy. For a moment, he looked at her lying near him, and before she had time to say anything, someone pulled him off the ground with great force. Then, they shoved him onto the piece of wood, and he collapsed on top of it like a rag doll. The person doing the shoving was wearing something that looked, to Ella, like a Roman soldier's uniform.

Ella stared with disbelief as the soldier tied the man's arms to the wood, and held a stake over his hand. With a great blow, the soldier smashed the stake into the man's hand with an iron hammer, the force of the large nail crushing all the bones in the palm. Blood shot out from the wound, but the soldier kept hammering.

Screaming in horror, Ella lunged for the soldier, trying to stop him. No matter what the man on the wood had done, no human deserved that type of torture. She dove on the Roman and pulled at his shoulder. But when the soldier turned to her, she saw that it wasn't a man.

It was a woman.

A woman with beautiful, green eyes, and silky, brown hair. It was Ella.

Ella gasped with disgust as her twin wearing the Roman soldier's uniform snarled and bared her teeth. How was this possible? Ella didn't want this man to die, so why would she be treating him like an animal?

With utter repulsiveness and shame, she fell back from the Roman Ella and watched with nauseating guilt as the soldier turned around and finished the job, nailing the stakes into his hands and feet. It was torture to watch the other stake puncture the second hand, and she couldn't imagine what the man on the wood was feeling.

Why was this other part of her doing this to him?

One of the most disturbing things about the scene was that the surrounding crowd was not doing anything to stop it. In fact, they were shouting at the man on the cross as he lay helpless and bloody on the ground. They cursed him and threw things at him. Ella secretly wanted him to yell something back—a curse, a defensive remark—anything to justify the actions by which he deserved such a ghastly punishment. For such a horrible sentence, she thought, he must have committed a terrible crime. But if he was such a bad person, why didn't he try to fight back, yell at them, or curse at them.

Another soldier came and helped Roman Ella raise the cross.

They stuck it in the ground, and when the cross fell into the hole, the man grunted as the jolt made his nailed appendages move with the stakes. As the second soldier turned to walk away, Ella saw that it was John Tucker, her husband.

He looked angry, and unashamed of what he had just done. Ella cried to him, but he did not look at her. She went to grab him but a rock flew past her head and hit the man on the cross. When she turned toward the crowd, Ella saw that two children had come to the front of the line and had started throwing sharp rocks at him.

It was Freddy and Sara.

They were growling and swearing at the man. Ella started waving her arms at them, trying to get them to stop, but they kept throwing stones. It was all happening so slowly, Ella finally realized. It was like time was moving in slow motion, and she had no control over anything that was taking place. As she looked behind Freddy and Sara, she started seeing familiar faces in the crowd. In fact, everyone in the crowd was now someone she knew.

Actors and actresses that were among the richest and most prestigious in Hollywood, her family, her friends, set designers, costume designers, Alice Walker, Saki, Agmol, and—

Ella stood still and started to cry.

Jake and Epi were in the crowd, too. And with them was Kathleen.

Everyone was shouting, in her direction, at the man that was hanging behind her. When she turned around, she saw that he was slouched over, his breaths heavy and slow. He coughed a little, and she tried to muffle a cry by putting her hand over her mouth.

Why was this happening? This man had done nothing wrong. She had seen it in his eyes. Whips, rocks, and thorns had mutilated his body, but the anger, hatred, and shouts of the people had crushed his very soul. Now he was left to suffer, by himself, with no one around to defend or help him.

Ella kept her hand over her mouth and cried out as she fell to her knees in front of the cross. She had nailed that stake into his hand and stuck him on the cross without remorse or shame.

But she felt ashamed now.

She hadn't wanted to do it, but she had done it. Then again, everyone seemed to be responsible for this man's suffering.

Her face fell in her hands and she cried on her knees. Through the cracks between her fingers, she saw blood drip off the wood and hit the ground, making a tiny stream down the hill. The red stream hit her knee, and she closed her eyes, shouting.

"Oh God!" she cried. "I'm sorry! I'm so sorry!"

She sobbed and cried out to the Lord.

"I didn't know! I didn't know what I was doing! Please, forgive me!"

The second she said it, she felt a cool breeze hit her dirty, sweaty neck. It was the first time any cool breeze had floated over this desert. When she opened her eyes and uncovered her face, she saw that the cross was still in front of her, but the blood was gone. She looked down at her hands and knees, and saw that they weren't dirty anymore. The black clothing that had been suffocating her while she ran in the desert was replaced with a white, cotton dress that barely touched her skin. Her arms and face didn't have any more scratches or bruises from the fall down the hill. The lungs and muscles that had itched and burned were relaxed and unburdened.

When she looked up to see the man on the cross, he was gone. It sat on the hill like a solitary sign that something great had happened. When she turned around, the crowd was gone, too, and the new wind created tiny whirlwinds where they had once been standing.

A hand touched Ella's shoulder, and she turned around as a person spoke.

"Ella?" the person asked. When Ella looked up, she saw Kathleen standing above her. Kathleen was also wearing clean clothes now. She had on a bright, white shirt and light khaki pants. Further behind her, Jake, Epi, the ni-Vanuatu men, and Alice Walker were waiting patiently in a group. Kathleen had a peaceful stare.

"Ella, you can come with us now," Kathleen told her with a

graceful tone that echoed in the air.

Ella looked at the group beyond. Epi smiled, waving at her. She stared in confusion.

"What happened?" she asked. Her nose was congested from crying and her voice echoed, too. "Where did that man go?"

"He went home."

"Where's home?"

"In Heaven," Kathleen said, her eyes soft. She held her hand out to Ella.

Ella grabbed it, and Kathleen gently pulled her to her feet.

"Who was he?" she asked the blonde woman.

"That was Jesus, Ella."

"That was Jesus?" she asked in a soft whisper. "But, I—I nailed those big stakes into his hands. I—I killed him."

"That's right. We all did. But you know what you've done, and you asked for forgiveness. Now, you can spend eternity with Him in Heaven."

"That's all it takes?" Ella asked, looking around at the empty desert. "Ask for forgiveness? That's all I had to do?"

Kathleen smiled, and said, "Yup. But He wants to spend your life on Earth with you. He wants to be a part of every thing that you do. He wants you to help others see Him so that they can spend eternity in Heaven, too."

Ella looked back at where her children had been, and said, "Freddy and Sara were back there. They were throwing rocks at Him. And John was here, too."

"You need to show them the path to take, Ella," Kathleen said. "You know the path to follow. You've just never known to take it before. But don't worry. God will carry you through hard times, and He will give you the words to say. He won't ever leave you or forsake you. Now, let's go." Kathleen pointed to the desert that surrounded them, and continued, "You don't belong in this place anymore."

Commitments

Something was whistling. It was a bird.

Ella barely opened her eyes to see sunlight peeking through the trees on the ledge, fifty feet above her head. She squinted at the light and watched as the wind blew through the branches. The shadows danced across her face. She heard the rustling of the leaves as they moved and hit each other, waltzing in the wind.

Her eyes opened a little more, and she heard the water flowing behind her. It was such a quiet sound, one that she had never noticed before. In fact, every sound was new to her ears. She tried to open her eyes more, and when she did, she noticed that everything looked different. It was peaceful and serene.

Despite the aching in her joints, she rolled over onto her hands and knees, trying to figure out what had just happened. Her clothes were damp, and she remembered that she had jumped into the water. It must have been hours before, because the sun had not risen and she had been soaked. She coughed a little and abruptly remembered her dream.

Still on all fours, she leaned her head down to the rock and started to cry. The guilt was still there, for what she had done to Jesus in her dream. It seemed so real.

That's because it is, something told her.

Ella kept crying, believing the voice. She sat back on her rear and wept on the cool rock for a long time.

Kathleen pushed herself over one rock at a time, trying to hurry up the bank of the river to the pool. She wasn't sure why Ella had decided to jump, but she wanted to make sure everything was okay. As she got closer, she saw that Ella was sitting on the flat rock by the pool, not moving. When she pushed herself over the remaining boulder, Kathleen spoke softly.

"Ella?"

Ella's head turned to face Kathleen, immediately revealing dried streaks of dirt on the woman's face. Kathleen stopped, stunned.

"Have you been crying?!" she asked in amazement.

Ella sniffled, and said, "I think we need to talk."

The two women sat on the flat rock in silence, but the cool water flowed in the river beside them. Kathleen was apprehensive because the fact that Ella was crying came as a great shock. She knew that it was something the woman hadn't done in years, and it must have been either something great or dreadful that could break such a hard heart.

"Ella, why did you jump?" Kathleen asked with concern.

"I've had these dreams for the past few years," Ella began, almost talking into space. "I dream that I'm running in a hot, dry desert. I can't stop running because I don't know if I'm chasing something or running from something—it's always so lonely and confusing. The sky sort of—morphs into shapes and colors that seem to make the sun shine brighter. I cry and cry, choking on my tears. That's the weirdest part about the dream, because I haven't cried in a long time.

"So, last night, when Epi was having his asthma attack, I got lost in the woods. I was so scared, so I prayed. I prayed for the first time in my whole life. And it worked. God showed me the way."

Kathleen stared at Ella with wide eyes.

"I was so scared, and I'm always scared. But God got me through my scariest moment. So, I jumped off the ledge, because you said it was a leap of faith, and I have faith that God will hold my hand again when I'm too afraid to do something on my own—again. I asked you once how I could have faith in something I couldn't see. I think because the ledge was a physical, tangible fear to conquer, I felt like that was the way I needed to overcome all my fears.

"I fell asleep when I got out of the pool, and my desert dream continued. But I wasn't running anymore. Instead, I saw everyone I knew in a crowd, and they were—yelling at Jesus on the cross. You, John, the kids—everyone. I even saw myself nail his hands to the cross. So I sat at the foot of it and apologized.

"I've been living a lie my entire life, following a path that, as I see it now, will lead me to destruction. I can't walk down that path anymore, Kathleen. I want Jesus. I need Him. I want my family to have Him. But there is just something I have to know: you told me in the dream that we all killed Him. What does that mean?"

Kathleen couldn't speak. She was stunned. She mumbled at first, trying to find the words on the spot.

"It, uh—it means that every person that God—ever created is responsible for Jesus' death. Jesus was perfect, yet he died for all of *our* sins so that we could be saved and spend eternity with our Father in Heaven. By admitting that we are sinners, our slate has been cleaned and we're new in Christ."

Ella smiled, and said, "I thought so. So, what do you say you teach me a little more before I go home? I'll need all the help I can get."

Kathleen smirked, and the smirk turned to laughter. Ella started laughing, too, and after a moment, they were laughing with overflowing joy. Their voices echoed off the limestone walls and could be heard far away in the jungle.

The missionary hugged the new Christian, and said, "You're serious? You've accepted Christ?!"

Ella grinned, and said, "I think so. He washed me clean."

Kathleen hugged her again.

"This means you are my new sister in Christ!" she told Ella. "You know, whenever someone becomes a Christian, all the angels in Heaven throw a huge party to celebrate."

"For now, can you just show me how to get back to the village so that I can change my clothes?"

"Of course, I'm sorry," Kathleen said, smiling while she wiped a happy tear from her eye. But before they rose, she said, "Can we pray?"

Ella nodded.

"Dear God," Kathleen said. "You've done it! You have finally reached Ella in a way that none of us could. You mercifully and graciously delivered her from the hands of the enemy. Now, she is permanently written in the Lamb's Book of Life.

"Thank You for not giving up on her, especially after so many people probably have. Thank You for being a kind, loving, and persistent God. And let these remaining weeks with Ella be cause for great learning and celebration. We have a lot of catching up to do! In Your Son's name, Amen."

"Amen," Ella said with a smile.

Transformed

The transformation that a person goes through after they become a Christian is a feeling like no other. Good times are seen as blessings by God, while bad times are considered attacks from the devil, who is perpetually trying to break up relationships with the Heavenly Father. There are emotions that have never been felt, feelings that never existed before, and ideas that pop into a person's mind for the first time in life.

It is an adventure that the secular world is completely unaware of. Like all adventures, it is fascinating and exciting to embark on new areas of life and the human psyche. But with every adventure, there is some sort of danger that makes it exciting—the danger of vulnerability, new beliefs, and the fear of making mistakes.

Ella Levene experienced all of the above, for better and for worse. The events that followed her conversion were normal, frightening, and exhilarating, but she was quarantined on an island in the South Pacific Ocean with a tribe of people who could not verbally influence her, and was also with a woman who was able to help her through the initial shock of becoming a Christian.

What it meant to pray, to worship, to rejoice, to mourn, to keep fighting, to quit, to sing, to cry, to dance, to shout, to listen, to be mindful, to be a teacher, to be a student, to be the lion, to be the lamb, to be the child, the mother, the wife; when to be strong and when to be weak, when to serve and when to be served, when to love (which was always) and when to be loved. The concepts of thinking of others, serving others, and loving others, even if they didn't love in return, were difficult for the actress to understand at first. Though, by the last week of her visit to Tanna, it seemed that her heart had been transformed.

"So, God wants me to love the paparazzi?" she asked one day.

"That's right," Kathleen replied, eating soup and trying to read a book.

"But they have no respect for personal space or privacy."

"Ella," Kathleen said, laughing while she shut her book. "You know how you found yourself at the foot of the cross? Well, what makes you think that you deserve that more than anyone else in the world?"

"You're right," Ella replied, defeated. "But then again, God *has* seen my movies. Maybe He just wants the famous Ella Levene to be a Christian, you know?"

Kathleen threw the book at her and the actress laughed, joking, "Oh, come on, *Scout!* Don't tell me you never saw one of my movies and thought that I would make a really great Christian!"

The missionary smiled, and said, "I'll tell you a secret: you used to be my favorite actress before I left the States."

Ella's jaw dropped and she held her hands high, pressing the fingers of her right hand into her left palm.

"Time out! When were you going to tell me this? When the plane was about to leave Port Vila?"

"Well, I figured your ego was already big enough. I didn't need to tell you that you've been rooming with a fan."

"You're absolutely right," Ella proclaimed, pointing to Kathleen and shoving a cracker into her mouth. "I'm glad you didn't tell me. In fact, I wish you still hadn't. Now would be a good time to practice humility, right?"

Kathleen laughed, and Ella walked over to Epi, who was also giggling. Ella proceeded to dramatically fan her face with a napkin while she pretended to be a damsel in distress. She turned her British accent on at full blast and leaned in toward Epi. The boy was giggling while she seemed to act out a scene from a movie, exaggerating the lines and sending him into a laughing fit.

"We're in London today where the British superstar Ella Levene has proclaimed that she is no longer fit to be an actress. Her head is too big, her ego is too big, and her bum—well, never mind. Oh glorious day! Here's Ella now!"

Ella grabbed a fork on the table and held it up to Epi like a microphone. He looked at it with wide eyes and couldn't stop laughing while she did a mock interview.

"How does it feel to be the worst actor and director in the entertainment industry's history? Good? Bad? Well, join us next time when BBC broadcasts its Ella Levene marathon by which we show the worst movies ever made."

Epi didn't understand what was happening, but he was entertained by the lively Brit. Kathleen had been watching and she casually wiped a tear from her eye after laughing.

"I'm going to miss you," Kathleen said, still laughing.

Ella calmed down and sat back in her chair. She was still smiling, but the comment had obviously made her a little sad.

"I don't know what I'm going to do when I go back," Ella said. She had a grin on her face, but the comment was heart-felt. "What if my family is gone? What if they hate me? Do you think they'll understand that I want to be a better person?"

Kathleen nodded with a smile. "Oh, yeah. Definitely. But Ella, you have to remember that words don't mean anything unless you back them up with actions. We need to show our love for people, not just say it. Your kids and husband will know who you are once they see you in action. Then, maybe you can tell them what's happened."

Ella nodded and watched as Kathleen dropped her head and

stared back down at her soup. Despite the happy times with Ella's new found faith, Kathleen had been quieter and more glum since Jake's departure. It was very apparent that she had not wanted him to go, but had allowed it to happen anyway. Now, Kathleen stared absently into her soup bowl while Ella looked at Epi.

The child had been sad, as well. He was sad for Jake's departure, but he was also sad for his mother. Epi stared back at Ella with a look that said he understood why Kathleen watched her food bowl, perhaps expecting Jake to magically rise out of the porridge and sit beside them at the table. He winked at Ella and then turned to his mother.

"Ket-si, when will Jaap return?"

"Epi, you know that Jaap is not coming back. Why do you keep asking me?"

"Because I do not believe you."

Kathleen shook her head, and Epi spoke again, his little voice soft and meek.

"Would it make you happy if he was here?"

Kathleen smiled at him and said, "Yes, it would. But it's too late, now, so try not to think about it, okay?"

Epi looked at her, his stare a different one. He almost looked mad at her, like she had been the one to scare him off. She took the glance to heart and almost cried when he lifted himself from the chair and silently walked out of the hut, into the hot afternoon sun.

Ella watched him go and turned back to Kathleen, who sighed and hung her head.

"I take it that conversation didn't go well?" Ella asked.

"He misses Jake," Kathleen replied.

"And he's the only one?"

"No, I miss him, too. I've been thinking since he left, though. I shouldn't have turned him down like that. He is such a good man, and it really made a difference to have him here with me. I guess I didn't know what I had until it was gone."

Ella smiled. "And there's that whole thing about you loving him," she said as a joke. She thought it would make Kathleen defensive, but the missionary just nodded her head.

"Yeah, and there's that," she replied nonchalantly.

Ella looked at her like she was crazy.

"So you admit it?!" Ella asked.

"Yeah," Kathleen replied. As the answer left her mouth, the sound of her own falling heart could almost be heard as well.

"Then why didn't you tell him to stay?"

"I don't know," Kathleen replied while she looked down at her hands. "I guess I was just afraid it was too selfish. I didn't want to make a decision that was *that* serious. I mean, he would be my husband, you know? The father of my child, or children. I was afraid that my feelings for him weren't enough justification for me to say, 'Sure, let's try it!' I was so afraid that it wasn't part of God's plan that I totally missed God's words."

Ella watched while Kathleen continued to sulk.

"I believe," Ella said, "that it was you who said that we should forget about letting God down and release that fear, that that fear is from the devil, and it hinders us from actually becoming aware of God's plan for us."

Kathleen smiled while she shook her head. "I knew this would happen at some point. I just didn't think it would be so soon. Ella giving me advice. You're right, though. But it's too late now, Jake's gone, and it seems that I need to listen for God's back-up plan. Many women are single missionaries for their entire lives—I just never really thought that I'd be one of them."

They shrugged at each other, and she asked Ella, "Could you please go find Epi and make sure he doesn't hate me?"

"I know he doesn't hate you, but I'll go find him anyway."

"Thank you," Kathleen said, and Ella walked out the door.

When Ella walked into the cooled shed, she could hear sniffling. She walked in quietly, trying not to startle the little boy while he sat on the floor under the table. He was speaking in his language, but she knew what he was doing. As she approached the table, she saw that he was holding the radio's microphone to his mouth.

"Jaap," Epi cried silently into the microphone. "Jaap, please, this is Epi. Jaap, it would make Ket-si happy if you were here. Please come back!"

Ella looked at the boy with sad eyes. She was only able to understand a couple of words, but the scene itself said everything. The boy missed his friend, and the only father figure in his life. Ella looked at the radio and saw that it was not only set at the wrong frequency, but it was turned off. The boy couldn't be expected to know how a radio worked, but she knew that he was only trying to help his mother.

She squatted down low so that they were almost face to face. He looked at her with tears in his eyes, and a guilty look on his face. She stared at him and gave a sympathetic grin. When she looked at the microphone in his hands, he handed it to her and stared into her eyes longingly.

Ella held the plastic microphone in her hands and looked back at him, wanting to help. There wasn't much she could do. Jake had been gone for two weeks, and could be back in America by now. It would be no use to try and get in touch with him.

Epi finally stopped looking at Ella, sniffled, and stared at the floor. She turned toward the radio and lifted her fingers to change all the switches back to where they were supposed to be.

Anytime

"It has been an interesting couple of months," Sowany, the village chief, told Kathleen. "It seems that once Ella arrived, many things happened. We have classes where you show us to read. Jaap gave us clean water so that we are not sick anymore. You hurt your ankle, marking the first time you have ever needed a doctor for yourself. Epi got very sick, Jaap left us, and now Ella smiles more. What do you think the cause for all this is?"

Kathleen was sitting in his hut on a mat, sharing a cup of Tanna coffee with the old man. She smiled and reflected on his words. It certainly had been an adventure since Ella's arrival, and she was not sure why it had all happened within such a short period of time. Or did she—

"You know," she told him, "that Father God is in charge of all things. He has a grand plan for everyone's life. He gives us many blessings, but I think one of the greatest blessings provided to us is other people.

"It is said that He never gives us anything we cannot handle. When Ella arrived, it made the difficult times more bearable for each of us, because we had each other. And when the good times came, we had each other for support and love. Ella laughs now because she did not have anyone to laugh with before. If she or Jake had not been here when I hurt my leg, it would have made things much more difficult for me. Perhaps if Ella had not been here when Jake left, my loneliness would be more severe. Whatever the reasons are, Ella's visit to this tribe will end up resulting in many wonderful things."

"Like what?" the old man asked, pleased with her answer and curious to hear more from the young woman.

"Well," she continued, "after Ella read to you, you saw that reading was important. Now we will have classes for everyone. And, even though it is a bit selfish, I have found a friend in her, and that is a good and rejuvenating surprise for me."

Sowany smiled and nodded his head.

"Indeed, her presence has brought many good things," he said. "And I am glad you have a friend from *your* village. But when she leaves tomorrow, Ket-si, I want you to know that you have many friends in this village, too. Many other *kastom* villages criticize me for having a missionary, especially a woman, here with us. They believe that you are here to bring new things that will only benefit you and *your* village. But I see that you and Jaap have wanted what is best for me and my people. As long as you are here, you have friends. Ella's departure should not leave you with a great loneliness."

Kathleen was crying softly, but a smile had brightened her face with great honor and pleasure.

"Thank you," she said as a tear rolled down her cheek. "You don't know what that means to me."

He nodded at her, and they sat in a comfortable silence as the sun went down and the hut grew darker. After a few moments, one of Sowany's adolescent sons politely walked in wearing a festive grass skirt and paint on his body.

"Father. Ket-si. The party is starting," he told them.

"Very good," the chief replied, and then turned to Kathleen and said, "This will be a grand feast like no other."

Farewell Feast

It was a form of pride for whoever was throwing a feast to bring his largest, most precious pig to feed everyone. It would be an insult to spare the largest pig and present the village with an average one. At the great feast the night before Ella's departure, Saki's largest pig had been selected to be buried in hot coals and served.

The fires roared in the field, and everyone ate like royalty under the stars in the sky. There was laughter in one group, and a little argument in another. Children were chasing each other in and out of the shadows of people while wild dogs followed them.

Ella sat on a log by the fire, eating her pork and watching everyone in the orange glow of the flames. She felt as though she had been living like this since birth. While she watched the natives preparing for their *nao* dance ceremony, she tried to think about the first days she had spent with this tribe.

The initial days had somehow seemed dirtier, and the people had felt obtrusive and irritating. She had not wanted them to touch her white skin or poke at her face. They had followed her wherever she'd gone, and laughed when she spoke. Now, she saw that her onscreen role had been transformed into a real one. These people didn't have a television or a movie theatre. Their only entertainment was a white, British woman coming to stay with them.

They couldn't be expected to understand what it meant to give someone personal space or privacy. It wouldn't be assumed that they knew about her worldwide fame and fortunes, that she owned more things than any of them could even imagine. The world she was watching while she sat by the fire, the one that danced and sang in the shadows of the flames and by the moonlight, was the world that they understood. It had the basic necessities for a joyful life—love, family, friends, laughter, and God.

The day she had arrived, Ella had thought that fame, fortune, money, and alcohol were the things she needed to live a fulfilling life. Now, she watched with glee as she was reminded that life was about what the natives had. She saw Namay sit faithfully next to her husband, Agmol, who couldn't dance because his foot was still hurting. They didn't speak to one another, but it was only her presence that seemed to remedy his sadness. Saki and two other men were blowing into Yapkisip panpipes, making music for people to start forming into a circle so that the dancing could begin. Kathleen took an infant from Lauriny's arms and held it with a gentle, maternal touch. Epi and a group of children snagged more pork from the platter while an old woman shooed them away.

Ella smiled at the scene, and thanked God for bringing her to this place. At this, she remembered that the biggest difference between this feast and her first days in the village was that she had not been a Christian. She had not seen the blessings, or the simplicity, that the village and the jungle brought. She had been caught up in her own selfish, cruel, cold, and fearful world. She cringed with guilt when she remembered how awful she had acted, but a peace came over her when she visualized her former life being washed clean with the blood of Jesus.

Kathleen had tried to tell her about the good things, but it was true what she had said before: actions speak louder than words.

Ella smiled and nodded while she watched the natives that she knew were Christians. Had it not been for the love and kindness shown by these people, Ella was sure she would have never believed Christianity to be a good and decent faith. It were those thoughtful and selfless actions by these gracious warriors for God that Ella believed had indirectly led her to Christ, and a tear rolled down her cheek as she realized that she owed these simple people more than they would ever know.

Lauriny walked over and sat down next to Ella. Saki's wife had been a good companion over the past two months, and had helped Ella adjust to village life by treating her with friendship and dignity. Ella smiled at the woman whose language she did not understand, and waited as Lauriny tried to communicate.

Kathleen had tried to teach Lauriny some English in the past years, but only one word at a time. It was a poor attempt, but the native woman tried anyway.

"Lif moro?" she asked, a little shy.

"Yes, I leave tomorrow," Ella replied, nodding her head and smiling.

Lauriny pulled out a cloth sack and gave it to Ella.

"Gif frate in sayr. Yu in chone tu."

Ella nodded with patience and said, "Gifts for my family and I. Thank you, Lauriny. I will never forget you."

Lauriny didn't understand the last sentence, but Kathleen came up to them and translated. Lauriny listened, and then nodded to Ella. Kathleen gave the infant back and sat down next to Ella, as well.

"Are you going to miss this? The bugs, the humidity—"

"Yes," Ella interrupted. "None of the bad things would be able to mask how magical this place is. I will never forget these past two months for as long as I live. But you know out of all the fears I have about returning to the real world and reestablishing a relationship with my family, do you know what I fear the most?"

"What?" Kathleen asked with curiosity.

"I fear that I'll forget this place," Ella said, pointing to everyone. "I fear that I will forget the smells and the cool breezes. I'm afraid I'll forget Epi's wheezing when he sleeps, or the sound of your typewriter tapping from the inside of the hut. I'm afraid I'll forget that tingly feeling I have every time we all sit together for evening worship by the fire, when Saki and Agmol have their families, and the other believers in the village laugh with you and joke around. But most of all, I'm afraid that I'm leaving behind a life that I may have been made for, and that this life will continue without me while I go home to one that will now be unfamiliar."

Kathleen smiled, and said, "Those are valid fears, but do you want to hear my opinion?"

Ella nodded.

"Okay," Kathleen said. "First of all, I hate to break it to you, but I don't think you were made for this type of life. You would do well, Ella, but I think God will utilize your beauty and your people skills for somewhere else. Climbing trees and jumping off gorge ledges just doesn't suit you."

They laughed.

"Second, you have been given an incredible opportunity to reach out to a dying community. You will discover when you go home that the life you were living was full of hatred, greed, and heart-ache. Now, you have been given the rare chance to change the system from within. Despite the dry spells you've been having for the past few years, if you do everything with the intention of pleasing God and serving others, I know that that movie talent will be a tool used to make great films. And, even if your films are still bad, at least others may see you as being a person who people want to make a movie with. The reputation you have now—as being the most hated director in Hollywood—can be changed over night as long as you decide to use your powers for good instead of evil. It's up to you."

Ella listened carefully, wanting to absorb the information. She wanted any bit of help she could find before leaving.

Kathleen's words were refreshing, and even though she still had her doubts and worries, she was sure Kathleen was right. No matter what she did, Ella wanted to do it through God so that others could see His love and compassion through her, no matter how difficult it would be to change her cold-hearted ways. She didn't care if it took years, she wanted to walk on to a movie set and shine the light of Jesus in a place that had become one of the darkest industries in the human race's history of dissolved morals.

Departure

Ella shook Agmol's hand with a smile. He had been the one who waited for her at the gorge, when she sat on the ledge until darkness fell. He was the one with the faithful wife and no children. Ella felt sorry for them, because to not have children by the time a couple was in their twenties probably meant something was wrong. He and Namay didn't seem tripped by it.

When she stepped to the side, Saki smiled at her.

"Goodbye, Ella," he said in clear English.

She grinned at him, and replied, "Goodbye, Saki. Take care."

He nodded his head furiously like he understood, but she was sure he didn't. Saki had one of the best hearts, Ella decided. He had four children, had helped Kathleen with anything she asked him for the past six years, and had helped Ella save Epi's life the night of the asthma attack. A servant's heart was not easily found, but Ella had found the perfect one in Saki.

Epi stood awkwardly next to Saki. Kathleen leaned over, and said, "Be good for Saki. I will see you tomorrow."

The little boy nodded and looked at Ella while Kathleen hopped into the jeep. Ella smiled at the little boy who had taught her how to love again. He was so tiny and precious, and she was sure that it would be most difficult to leave him without watching him grow into a little man. Epi frowned while she bent over to face him.

"When God shows me the stars," Epi said in Tanna North, "I will think of your sparkling eyes. And when He shows me the sun, I will remember your bright smile."

A tear rolled down Ella's cheek. She recognized the words that Kathleen spoke to him every night before he went to bed, for comfort and reassurance. Now, he was comforting Ella, reassuring her that someone would be thinking about her, even if it was from very far away.

Ella smiled at him with wet eyes and picked him up to hug him. He wrapped his arms around her neck and didn't say anything else. When he looked at Kathleen who was sitting in the jeep, she winked at him and blew him a kiss. He smiled and winked back.

Ella put him on the ground and gave the three natives one last smile. She climbed into the jeep and, as it drove away, she didn't look back.

Steve Mackenzie and the Cessna had brought the two women to the Port Vila airport where Ella would catch her return flight to Sydney. The airport was bustling with life. People of all different races and languages were rapidly making their way to gates, rental car counters, and customs inspection units. The only stillness in the terminal was Ella and Kathleen, sitting glumly near the departure gate.

Neither had spoken, both had been crying, and now a woman with an Australian accent came on the loudspeaker.

"Flight 582, non-stop to Sydney, will be loading shortly. All first class passengers please have your boarding passes ready."

Ella raised her eyebrows and said, "I guess that's me."

They stood up and started to walk toward the gate. As they

did so, something caught Ella's eye from the side. When she saw what it was, she smiled and waved. Kathleen saw her, turned around, saw nothing, and asked, "Who were you waving at?"

"Oh, there was a kid or something—playing with a toy—I don't know. You know how emotional I've been lately. I would smile and wave at a mailbox if I saw one."

"That's true," Kathleen said.

They walked to the gate and the counter announced that first class passengers would begin boarding. Ella turned around and smiled at Kathleen.

"This is it. It's time," Ella said.

"So it is," Kathleen replied. She pulled a piece of paper out of her pocket and gave it to the actress. "Here's the number of a woman I know in Los Angeles that would be good to talk to if you ever need it. There are also a few church names on there. Remember to start going on Sundays, okay? It's really important to keep in constant fellowship with other Christians, no matter how famous you are."

"Got it," Ella nodded.

"And don't forget to seek the Lord in every decision you make—"

"Right."

"And whenever you feel sad or depressed, it's just the devil trying to get under your skin. Immediately pray."

"Check. Immediately pray," Ella repeated to herself.

"It's also good to read the Bible and sing worship songs."

"But all the songs I know are in Tanna North."

"That's why it's good to go to church," Kathleen said with a smile. She gave Ella a big hug. "I'll be praying for you every day."

"I know. And I'll be praying for you as well. Take care of Epi."

"I will."

They released each other and Ella headed for the gate, trying not to cry.

"Ella?" Kathleen said at the last moment. Ella stopped and turned.

"You've become my best friend," Kathleen said, her voice choking.

Ella raised her chin up high and her eyes welled up with tears. A best friend was something neither of them had expected to gain from this journey. Ella never thought anyone would ever be her friend again, but she knew that Kathleen would always be there for her if she needed it.

"You're mine, too," Ella said, smiling.

Kathleen nodded, and Ella handed the flight worker the ticket and walked through the door to board the airplane.

The airport kept moving. Everyone seemed to be on a mission. People ran back and forth, consumed by their flight schedules and families. Different languages filled the air, making the chaos seem more confusing. Kathleen dropped her shoulders as soon as Ella was gone from sight. She felt very sad all of a sudden.

She closed her eyes for a second to ask God for strength, but she knew that it was appropriate to be sad. A good friend had just left, the man she loved had left weeks earlier, and now she was all alone in the airport terminal. Her heart fell, and she slowly limped back to the terminal's entry.

Her foot hurt a little more for some reason—probably because she finally had the time to think about it. Everyone was moving fast around her and she let her head fall so that she watched the floor as she walked.

Something made her stop.

The motion of the airport was constant, but one person was standing in the middle of the floor, absolutely motionless and facing her. When she looked up, she slapped her hand to her mouth with shock.

Jake Willis stood in the midst of all the moving people that paid no attention. He stared at Kathleen with deep eyes and seemed to be waiting to see what her reaction would be. She just stood there, motionless, her hand covering her mouth.

Without a moment's thought or wonder on how he had known she'd be there, she dropped her hand and briskly limped to where he was standing. She fell into his arms, and he held onto her, surprised. She sank into him and closed her eyes.

"I'm so sorry," she cried while he held her. "I was so scared."

"It's okay," he replied gently. "Many women are often scared away by my handsome features."

She laughed and looked up into his eyes. He kissed her on the forehead and they continued to hold each other in the middle of the busy airplane terminal.

"I'm in love with you," she told him. "I don't know what happens next, but you have to know that I lied when I said I didn't have feelings for you."

"Don't worry, I knew."

"How?" she asked, thinking the reply would be some romantic response about being soul-mates.

"Because when you were sedated from the flu medicine, you told me so."

She smacked him on the chest and they laughed.

"How did you know I was here?" she asked.

"Ella radioed Lenakel last week, and they radioed me here in Port Vila. I was staying with the Mackenzie's to catch some rest before I went back to Darwin."

"I can't believe she didn't say anything," Kathleen said, looking back at the gate.

"She probably thought you wouldn't come if you knew I would be here."

"What makes you think that that would have happened?"

"Apparently, she told Mikaela over the radio, 'Let's not tell Kathleen or else she won't go to the airport with me.'"

"Oh," she said with a laugh. "She was probably right. Surprises are better, anyway."

They started walking to where Steve had the plane, arms around each other. Both were happy and comfortable with each other, obviously not planning on letting the other go any time soon.

"So, what now?" Kathleen asked as they walked out into the hot sun.

"We should probably tell Epi."

"Sure, we'll tell him. But only once we've told ourselves."

"Good plan."

They exited the building together.

Reconcile

When Ella's plane landed in Darwin, it was dark and quiet, just the way she had left it. The air was muggy and hot. As she stepped off the plane, she was expecting to see her family waiting, but she only saw Chester, the limo driver. Her heart fell when she saw him, but she smiled anyway and greeted him.

"Ms. Levene," he said, his raspy old man's voice sounding like he had just walked out of a *Godfather* film. "Please come with me."

They got her luggage and headed to the limo. Ella looked around and noticed that people were staring at her.

Good to be back, she thought.

When Chester opened the door for her to get in, she tossed her luggage in the back seat, and said, "I'm going to ride shotgun tonight, okay Chester?"

He stared at her in shock, and replied, "That's fine, Ms. Levene."

"Ella."

He didn't repeat her first name, but opened the front door for her while he tried to figure out who this new person was. When he got into the driver's seat and started the vehicle, she turned to him and said, "So, how are things?"

"Things?"

"Yes, things. Are John and the kids doing well?"

"Uh, yes, ma'am. They are fine."

She could tell he was uncomfortable talking to her like a normal person, so she decided she would save more shock for later. She nodded with a smile and sat back in her seat while Chester pulled the car away from the curb and headed home.

When Ella opened her front door, the entire mansion was dark and gloomy. This also seemed to be just how she'd left it. The shiny marble floors and crystal vases sitting on tables reminded her of how cold and shallow her life felt when she was here. All the objects in the entry and the living room were of the highest quality, but the knick knacks and antiques that she had once thought would make her life happier were now tangible evidence that they only seemed to make a person feel superficial and disconnected.

Her shoes could be heard hitting the hard floors while she walked in the dark toward John's study. A light shined through the crack at the bottom of the door, so she quietly peeked her head in before she entered.

John Tucker sat in a lounge chair, apparently asleep, while a soccer game played on the big screen TV. It was muted so that the room was silent while shadows and figures lit it in a blue tone. He did not move when she walked in, but she was also being very quiet. She walked over to him and smiled while he slept.

Still handsome, she thought.

Ella leaned over and kissed him on the top of his head. His eyes blinked and he turned to face her. When he saw her smiling at him, he smiled back.

"Hey there, beautiful," he mumbled while he rubbed his eyes. "Is that a smile I see on your face?"

"It sure is," she said. "I'm glad you're here."

"Where else would I be?"

"I don't know. I guess I just thought you would have left, what with me being gone for so long."

John stared at her in the blue light of the television. There was something different about her. She was wearing no make-up, her hair was pulled back in a grungy ponytail, and her clothes were filthy, but she looked happy and calm. He grinned.

"How was the trip?" he asked.

"Life-changing," she replied. Her eyes started to fill with tears. When this happened, he sat up straight and laughed.

"Are you *crying*?!" he asked.

She smiled and nodded. It was ironic how Kathleen had had the same reaction.

"It's a little something I picked up in the jungle," she said. "You see, I have these—" she pointed to her tears "—and I have this now—" she pointed to her smile.

"I love both of them," he said with charm.

She smiled, but then started to cry. She fell beside him in the seat and hugged him. He had to blink a few times, but he held on to her while he listened to her quiet sobs.

"John, I'm so sorry," she told him. "I've been so cruel for so long. I don't want to be like that ever again. No more booze, no more cigarettes, and no more long periods of time when I'm away from you and the kids. I know it's hard to believe, but I just want to show you that I've changed, and that I'm here for good. Just don't leave me!"

He smiled while she cried, and rubbed her back.

"Sweetie," he said, "I'm not going anywhere. For better or for worse, remember?"

She smiled while more tears fell, thanking God for her husband's faithfulness while he consoled her.

The door opened, and Ella quietly walked in to the pink and purple room where her daughter slept. Sara was twisted in her sheets, snoring loudly. The moment Ella saw her, she almost doubled over from the knots in her stomach.

This was her daughter, the one and only Sara Tucker that she had given birth to. It seemed too pathetic to be realizing how precious her child was six years after her birth. When Ella walked over to Sara's bed, she held her hand over her mouth to suppress a cry.

It was how old Kathleen had been when her mother had left her. Ella looked at her little girl sleeping, and tried imagining a scenario where she was coming in to say goodbye to this little creature rather than greeting her after so long. It was a sickening thought, and Ella asked for God's love while she untangled her daughter's sheets.

"Mommy?" Sara said, barely waking up from her sleep.

"Hello, darling. You don't have to wake up. You can keep sleeping."

"Will I see you in the morning?" Sara asked, her little voice drifting back to sleep.

"Yes, my love," Ella said with a wide smile. "I'll be here when you get up in the morning."

Sara fell back to sleep, and would probably not remember that Ella had even come home by the time she came down for breakfast. Ella leaned in and kissed her baby girl, gently covering her neck with the sheets she had just unraveled.

Ella walked down the hall and entered Freddy's room. There were dinosaurs on the floor and glow-in-the-dark stars on the ceiling. Freddy was sleeping peacefully in his *Star Wars* pajamas with a teddy bear tucked under his chin. When the light from the hall entered the room, it shined in his eyes and he woke up.

"Hey, buddy," Ella whispered. He didn't respond, but looked at her with sleepy, sad eyes.

"Hello," he said.

"How are you?"

Freddy shrugged.

Ella's head sagged a little. She remembered the last time he had seen her. He had asked why she hated him, and then called her by her first name. It was obvious that he had not forgotten that day. Ella tried to keep the smile on her face while she thought of how to console her eight-year old son. She went and sat down next to him on the bed.

"I missed you," she said.

"You did?"

"Yes. I thought about you every day."

"Really?" Freddy said, a little more interested in his mother now.

"Really," she told him. She was starting to cry a little, but she kept her composure and stroked some of the loose hair from his forehead.

"I know I've been a bad mum, darling. I've actually been mean to a lot of people, but I shouldn't have been like that to you."

He stared at her while she spoke. He loved having her there, fussing over him like she was. It was the sort of thing he had always wanted.

"But," she continued, "things are going to be different now. I know it will be hard to think so, but I want you to know that I'm going to try and stay home more. Maybe we can all go on a vacation somewhere or something."

"Can we go to Sea World?" he asked enthusiastically.

She laughed and said, "We can try and do that."

He took the hand that was brushing his hair and interlocked his fingers with hers.

"I love you, Mommy," he said.

"I love you, too, sweet boy," she said as she scooped him up and held him in her lap. He put his head on her shoulder while she rubbed his back. Slowly, he fell back to sleep.

The most amazing thing about holding her son after so long was that he was so big. She couldn't believe how old he was. It seemed like yesterday that she was changing his diapers, and now he was a young man at the age of eight. He was still a little boy, but she decided while she was holding her son that she wouldn't take advantage of her children anymore. The fear of watching her children grow up and experience life was gone, and she wanted to be with them for everything from that point forward.

At that moment, it was suddenly very clear to her how truly substantial God's love was. She had never been very caring or maternal, and now she felt more like a mother than ever before, but as a result of God's love flowing through her. She couldn't do it on her own before, but by His love, she knew that her children would always have what they really needed.

It was just the same way as it had been with Kathleen. The missionary had never had a mother, and yet she was such a wonderful one. It was God's grace that poured through people, and now that Ella was a believer, she understood the matrix analogy that Kathleen had explained to the students at the headquarters. She remembered the conversation she had had in the tree on the day of the wild horses.

She, like many other people in the world, claimed that they couldn't believe in something that they didn't see. Now that Ella was a Christian, she saw how false and ignorant that statement had been. Since her conversion, she had begun to see God everywhere. He was in nature, in people, in emotion, in love, and in that very room. Just because she couldn't see it before didn't mean that it didn't exist. She had been too consumed by her own life to open her eyes to what God was really doing with the world.

He had given her a palpable, visible love for her children when she came home. It wouldn't have existed had she not asked for it, or allowed it to flow through her. She apologized to God for all the years she had ignored Him and refused to hear His voice, but she also praised Him for the moment she was in. Sitting on her son's bed, and holding him while he slept, was a greater feeling than she had ever imagined, and Ella Levene knew that after that moment, anything else was possible. Anything could happen, and God could enable all things through people and events if they simply allowed Him to.

Footprints

Ella's feet sunk into the sand as she walked on it. When she looked at her bare feet, she wondered why she was back in the desert. Her attitude changed when she looked around her. It was a beach, and a beautiful one at that.

The water was so blue that it sparkled like a diamond in the mild sunlight. Little fish jumped out of the water, their bodies changing colors while they leapt through the light and back down into the depths of the ocean. All around her, colorful birds flew and danced in the cool, salty breeze that came from the crystal waters.

It was a wonderful feeling to be here. She stood with tranquility and patience, not wanting to disrupt any part of this dream. When the wind blew against her face, she could hear heavenly music in the breeze. It made her smile wide, showing her perfect, white teeth.

When she turned around to look at where she had just come, she noticed that beside her footprints were another set of prints. When she looked around, she didn't see anyone, but when she looked down at her feet, the other set of prints seemed to stop where she was standing. It was as though an invisible man was standing next to her.

She started to walk, and watched with delight as the second set of prints magically appeared next to hers while she took steps. Someone was with her, walking next to her, and she continued to stroll down the beach with the footprints while the cool breeze hit her face.

When Ella woke up, the wind was making the curtains to the balcony dance in the shadow of the moonlight. She was in her room, in Darwin, and her husband was snoring softly next to her.

The room was dark, but the moonlight gave it a soft, comfortable feeling, and she felt calmed by its presence. It was the same moonlight that had led her to the trail the night she first prayed, and it was the same light that had lit the field in the jungle on the clearest, cool nights on Tanna.

As she slid out of bed, she grabbed the silk robe that sat on the chair beside the night stand. John was snoring loudly, and she smiled at him while she wrapped herself in the robe and grabbed a blanket at the foot of the bed. She walked out to the balcony and took in a deep breath of fresh air.

There was a lounge chair out there, and under normal circumstances she would have avoided the dirty thing, but she had changed. She sat down on the musty cushions and wrapped the blanket around her while she looked at the stars in the sky. The ocean was lapping against the shore, and the crickets were singing their song under the bright sky.

"Can you hear it?" she whispered while she closed her eyes. "It's the sound of beauty."

A star fell somewhere to her right, and she smiled wide at how God had answered back.

"I don't quite know how to do this prayer thing properly," she said at the volume of a hushed breeze, "but I wanted to say thank You. Thank You for not forgetting about me, and for taking care of my family all these years that I've been away.

They need You, too. I guess we can work on that together.

"I just wanted to ask permission to continue to do movies. If You have people in there already, I understand; and if You think it may hurt my relationship with You, I understand that, too. It's just that—I think I could do a good job representing You, and sharing Your love with the lost. Those people are so burdened, and I don't think they realize how much they need You. I mean, look at me. It took getting me out in the middle of a jungle, on an island, for my ears to hear Your voice. People in Hollywood don't get an opportunity like that, so all I'm asking is for You to use me however You see fit, even if it means me bringing that jungle to them. I may be a world-renowned actress and director of blockbuster movies, but I am eternally, first and foremost, Your servant. I'll take that title over any others.

"So, You don't have to take me up on this suggestion, but just know that I think I could do a good job in the movie industry. And if John becomes a Christian, I'm sure he would do a great job writing. But we'll leave that for Your timing, not mine."

The sky remained silent, although she half-expected it to nod or talk back. The only affirmation she felt was a peace that, two months earlier, would have been a myth that she could only dream of. It was the type of peace that allowed her to sit still, in the silence and the dark, and count the many blessings that God had given her.

2½ years later...

"I really need you to pull these words from your heart," Ella Levene told the young actress. The girl was biting her lip and listening carefully to her director's instructions. They had been trying to film the same scene all afternoon, and the feel of it was still off. It was one of the most dramatic parts of the movie, and Ella wasn't catching the vibe that she felt was needed for the scene to be as great as it should be.

"Some scenes are easier to pretend that you're sad than others," Ella continued with a patient tone, "but this has to be right. This scene is vital to your character, and I know that you can nail this. It's Friday, we're all exhausted, but we've got to get it right. We owe it to the essence of this film to get the scene perfect."

The actress nodded her head and walked away, trying to force tears to her eyes before Ella yelled for the cameras to begin rolling. Acting was not the easiest job when everyone wanted to go home and the lead actress wasn't able to shed a tear for her most dramatic lines. Ella understood the pressure placed on the girl, so she tried to soothe things over with everyone else.

Ella nodded to the cinematographer, affirming that this time would be the last. She had become the muse by which the set's tone was based. If she was happy, everyone was happy, and if she was upset, the crew humbly wondered what they had done wrong.

Since her mysterious trip to a secret island in the South Pacific, everyone discussed, it was known that Ella Levene had changed. She didn't yell at people, her temper was far less severe, and the way she treated the cast and crew was with the utmost respect and understanding. The woman had been out of the spotlight for three years, and had shockingly re-emerged from the grave one day and directed a movie that was now up for an Academy Award. No one understood where she had come from, or what had been holding her back, but now everyone felt it a privilege to be working with her.

After the young actress was done with her scene, Ella yelled "Cut" and applauded. Everyone followed her cue and clapped for the girl who had just masterfully acted out a very definitive scene from their movie.

Ella yelled, "Okay everyone, I'll see you all on Tuesday! Have a great weekend!"

The crew applauded with smiles and Ella started to pack up her things as fast as she could. One of the producers walked over to her while she hurried, and looked at her with an amused grin.

"Are we in a hurry?" the producer asked.

"Well, Oscar weekend is never easy, Harold," she replied while she snatched her water bottle and briefcase. "These awards ceremonies are always easier when you're not nominated for something."

"I think that there may be plenty of other directors who would kill to be in your shoes on Sunday night," he said with a smirk.

She stopped packing and calmed herself.

"You're right," Ella said, taking a deep breath. "I really am thankful to be nominated, but the next couple of days are going to be insane. I've got friends flying in tonight, tomorrow we fit one of them for a dress, and then Sunday is the Oscar's. I haven't even cleaned the house yet."

"Aren't you rich enough to hire someone to do that? Besides, isn't it your jungle pal that is coming to visit? I'm sure she'll just be impressed with the couch, Ella."

She laughed, looked at her watch, and smiled at him.

"I need to go!"

Ella ran out the door waving to everyone while they all told her "Good luck." She bolted to the end of the hall and saw her husband waiting for her at the door to the parking lot. He was smiling and holding the door open for her.

"We're late," John said while she ran toward him.

"I know. I'm sorry," she said, and kissed him on the cheek while they both left the building and headed for the car.

"What time are they supposed to be here?" he asked her while they climbed into the limo.

"I think around six."

"It's four-thirty, Ella."

"It's okay, we'll be fine," she told him with a self-assuring tone. She was fiddling with her fingers anxiously and humming an oldies tune. John smiled at her because she was obviously nervous.

"Are you excited to see them?" he asked her, already knowing the answer.

"Of course, darling. It's just that—" she paused.

"Just what?"

"I need so much time to prepare for their arrival, but I want them to be here right now."

John reached over and held her hand. She smiled at him and tried to relax. The limo drove down the street toward Beverly Hills and Ella was more than anxious by the time the security gate to their home opened and the car drove in.

Freddy Tucker was playing basketball in the driveway when they pulled up. He waved to them as they got out of the limo. Ella kissed him on the top of the head.

"How's the jump shot, kid?" she asked.

"Going good," he replied. He was eleven now, and had

grown much taller. The dinosaur shirt was gone, and now he was wearing a blue, button-up polo shirt and khakis, trying to shoot hoops and not get dirty.

"When are they going to get here?" Freddy asked his mother.

"In God's timing," she replied. He gave her a look and she laughed.

"Okay, okay, one more hour."

Freddy smiled while John took the ball from him and began to play.

"No, no, no!" Ella said, trying to interrupt the game. "Little boys can stay out here and play, but old men need to help their wives clean the house."

"Sorry, kid," John said, tossing the ball back to his son. Freddy laughed at his mother's "old man joke" and kept playing while the couple went inside.

The house was large, but not obscenely grand. It was two stories, painted yellow and white, and had shutters on the windows. Jasmine bushes were woven in trellises that climbed to the roof from the base of the house. Large maple trees and aspens shielded the house from nosy neighbors and tourists while a beautiful ivy fence surrounded the grounds.

When Ella and John walked inside, they could hear Sara singing in the kitchen. Linda, the housekeeper, waved when they walked in. They made their way to their singing daughter. Sara's Spring Choral Pageant was in one week, and she had been singing like mad, all day and every day.

When they walked into the kitchen, they saw her coloring a picture on the kitchen table while she sang very loudly. When Ella cleared her throat, Sara looked up and smiled.

"Mommy! I drew a picture for Kathleen! Do you think she'll like it?"

Ella looked down at the picture and saw a drawing of what appeared to be a monkey.

"I know that she will love it," Ella told Sara. Sara was almost nine, and was growing into a beautiful girl, just as her mother had been. Everyone was worried about when Sara reached puberty, though, because it was very obvious that she would be breaking many hearts with her beauty and flirtatious behavior.

"Do you think she'll remember me?" Sara asked.

"I don't think a missionary could ever forget the person that called them a 'monkey-lady,' sweetheart."

"Jeez, mom," Sara said, rolling her eyes. "I was only a baby. And besides, she *was* climbing a tree."

Epi stared out the window of the limo. He looked at all the auto malls and billboards as the car took them from the airport toward Beverly Hills. He was mesmerized by the four-lane highway and how the traffic didn't seem to move. He wondered how all the cars were still able to fit on the road when *everyone* was driving.

Kathleen fiddled with the vent in the ceiling above her head, trying to get the air flow to hit her in the face. She was sweating, but it wasn't because the day was hot.

"You'd think with all the money they put into these limos," she said, "they could at least have a super flow of air for women in their third trimester."

Jake smiled at her from the side, and said, "I don't know how many women that are eight and a half months pregnant usually ride in these smaller limos. They probably put the ones that are your size in those new, SUV limos."

She smiled, casually smacked him on the shoulder, and looked across the car at Epi.

"Epi, what do you see?" Kathleen asked in English.

"Lots of cars," he replied. "When do we get there?"

"Pretty soon, kiddo," Jake replied. "Are you excited?"

"I want to talk to Ella in my English," he told his parents.

"She'll be very impressed," Kathleen said to him, smiling.

The limo left the freeway and headed toward the residential neighborhoods. While the trio in the car looked at the large mansions and palm tree lined streets, Kathleen was suddenly very excited. She rested her arms on her big belly and fiddled with the ring on her left hand.

"This is so cool," Jake exclaimed while they drove. "I get to meet John Tucker and Ella's up for an Academy Award. This weekend is going to be awesome!"

"Yes, and they'll both get to meet me," Kathleen said.

Jake raised his eyebrows at her with confusion, and she said, "I'm Mrs. Jake Willis now. That's pretty cool, too, don't you think?"

"Indeed, I do," he said with a smile. He gave her a quick kiss on the lips and then turned back to watch the famous, rich people drive their cars and walk their dogs. She shook her head at the two boys looking out the window while she said a quick prayer for a good, blessed weekend.

"Look at you!" Ella screamed as Kathleen walked in the door. "You're so big! When are you due?"

"Another two weeks," Kathleen said with exhaustion. They hugged each other, and Ella whispered in her ear.

"I knew you'd end up with him."

"Thanks to you!" Kathleen exclaimed with a laugh.

The two families faced each other for the first time, and Ella turned to John. She pointed at the Willis family, and said, "John, it is my pleasure to introduce Kathleen, Jake, and their little boy, Epi."

John gave Kathleen a big hug and said, "So, this is the famous Kathleen of the jungle—the one my wife owes her Christianity to."

"I'm not the one to blame," Kathleen said, blushing. "If anyone is to blame, it's Epi. He was the one who forced her to run through that jungle."

Epi shyly clutched on to Kathleen's leg, trying to hide from the strangers. He was nervous, and wanted to talk to them, but was too embarrassed.

Ella knelt down, and said, "Hi, Epi. I hear you speak English, now."

Epi nodded.

"You look very handsome in those new clothes."

He smiled at her and emerged from behind Kathleen, giving Ella a monstrous hug. Ella laughed, and he said, "I didn't save you! You saved me!"

Ella opened her mouth at Kathleen and Jake, and they both nodded with approval at the boy's clear English. Jake walked to Ella and gave her a hug, too.

"Hi, Jake," she said. "This is my husband, John."

"He needs no introduction," Jake said, shaking his hand. "I'm a huge fan."

John shook his head, and said, "No, I am. You and your wife were all Ella talked about for months after her trip."

"It was certainly an adventure none of us would ever forget," Jake replied.

Ella chimed in, "Yes! And how is the ankle, Kathleen?"

"Besides swollen from retaining too much water, its fine," Kathleen blushed.

After everyone was done greeting one another, Epi ran off with Freddy and Sara, Jake and John went in the backyard to look at a broken water fountain, and Kathleen and Ella went to the living room. Kathleen plopped on the couch, let out a big sigh, and leaned back, putting her feet on the stool. Ella sat in a big chair across from her and watched while the pregnant woman closed her eyes and tried to relax.

"I can't believe how —*pregnant* you are," she told Kathleen.

Kathleen laughed, and replied, "My dad thought the same thing."

"So you all went to Oregon before flying down here?" Ella asked.

"And Seattle, too, to see Jake's parents. We weren't able to have a real wedding, with family and everything, so they threw a reception for us. It was pretty funny to be celebrating a wedding so many years later, especially since the bride is ready to pop."

"I can see how that would be weird," Ella said with a giggle.

They sat in silence a moment, not quite sure what else to say. It was funny to be in a developed place with the other, since they had only experienced their friendship in the middle of nowhere. It wasn't an awkward silence, and they both contentedly watched their husbands fiddling with some pipes coming out of the ground in the back yard.

"I think," Ella began, "that John is taking advantage of Jake's engineering skills. He hasn't said anything about that silly fountain for months, and now all of a sudden it's important."

"I think it's just a guy thing," Kathleen said. "Like, male bonding or something. If there's something to fix, they can work together to fix it."

"It'll probably end up worse than when they started."

"You're probably right."

They laughed.

"Ella, how have things been for you?" Kathleen asked, changing the topic.

Ella took a moment and reflected on the last two and a half years. Things had certainly changed, but for the better. After the arrival to Darwin, Ella shared her testimony with her family and started going to church. Had they not been so shocked by her transformation, John and the kids would not have been so open to her new-found faith. They had their wife and mother back, so any religion that was responsible for such a change couldn't be bad.

They decided to sell the Darwin home, move back to Los Angeles permanently, and buy a smaller house to live in. Ella had suggested that all the vacation homes, large mansions, and gaudy possessions wouldn't help them unite as a family, and the others didn't argue with her. They had been in their quaint, yellow house for two years, the children started going to a real school, and the butlers and nannies had been fired. The ornate lifestyle Ella had seemed to punish them with for so long was replaced with something more fulfilling and meaningful.

The home they lived in, no matter where it was located, was finally filled with love. There were fights, disagreements, and hard times like any other home, but it was finally founded with a deep understanding that God would weave all of His wonderful characteristics into their lives if they simply allowed Him to.

The month Ella returned home, she came across a script written by an unknown screenplay writer. It was a drama, and was considered by Ira Manning, the studio's head, to be a difficult movie for the newly-transformed Ella to undertake. But Ella, still fierce in her attitude and persistent in her heart, insisted that she was up to the task.

Now, after two and a half years, the Academy had nominated her for her directorial skills, and the movie itself was nominated for many other awards. She blamed its success on God, and on the tools he had used — the Willis family from Tanna, Vanuatu.

She had written a letter to Kathleen many months before, anticipating that the Academy would nominate the film, and asked her and Jake to bring Epi to Hollywood and attend the ceremony. It was the least she could do for her friends, and she wanted the whole world to know the reason she had changed. It had been because of love, trials, friendship, and most importantly, Jesus.

Ella smiled at Kathleen, thinking of all that had happened within the time since they had separated.

How have things been, Kathleen had asked.

"Things have been great," Ella replied, with the most peaceful of tones in her voice.

Kathleen nodded with gratefulness.

The sun was going down, and it lit the Hollywood streets with a dim glow while cars and people made their way to the red carpet events. Limos lined the entrance to the Academy Awards ceremony, and the most luxurious of its members stepped out of their cars to face the camera flashes and fans' screams. Entertainment's elite from film to fashion to music stood in line to walk through the security gate before entering the courtyard where reporters and journalists were waiting with questions. Fans held t-shirts, hats, and books out to be signed by the celebrities.

A black limo pulled up to the curb, and everyone waited to see who would step out. The camera flashes started to whiz away in a frenzy as Ella Levene and John Tucker stepped out of the vehicle, holding hands and smiling. She was wearing a luxurious black gown that was high on the neck, low on the back, and flowed down to her feet. At the bottom were delicate ruffles that danced around her expensive, black shoes. She looked more beautiful than ever, particularly because her face possessed a true, honest smile.

John smiled shyly at the photographers, still flustered by the attention after so many years, but since the couple had already been to many awards ceremonies that season, he seemed to finally be getting the hang of it. They waved to everyone when they entered the courtyard and slowly made their way from one reporter to the next, answering the same questions at every station.

"Ella, how does it feel to finally be back at the top of Hollywood's 'A' list?"

"How do you feel about your first nomination as a director?"

"Is it true that you spent time in a monastery a couple of years ago?"

"How is it to be one of the most sought after directors in the business right now?"

Ella responded to the last one, "Well, the key words in that question are 'right now.' I'm so happy to be back in the game after so long, and even though this may be just another fifteen minutes of fame for me, I'm going to try and enjoy every second."

"Thank you, and good luck," the reporter said with a smile.

"Thanks," Ella said, and they made their way into the grand building to be seated for the ceremony.

On their way in, they saw Kathleen and Jake standing near the entrance to the auditorium, waiting awkwardly. They weren't quite sure how to deal with all the excitement. Ella waved and approached them.

"Are you excited?" Ella asked them as she walked up in her elegant gown.

"I was just going to ask you the same thing," Kathleen replied. She was wearing a royal blue maternity gown that Ella had bought for her the day before. The designer had come to their home, fitted Kathleen, widened his eyes, and written down the measurements while he shook his head.

"This is so cool!" Jake exclaimed to Ella. "I think I just made eye-contact with Sean Connery, but I'm not sure. He may have been looking for the bathroom that was behind me."

"Now listen," Kathleen said seriously to Ella, ignoring Jake's school-boy excitement. "No matter what happens tonight, I just want you to know how much it means to us that we were invited—"

"There's George Clooney!" Jake waved.

"And despite the outcome of tonight," Kathleen continued, nudging Jake in the ribs with her elbow, "you have really made a good name for yourself, and I know that you truly do have a gift, Ella."

Ella nodded with a glamorous smile. "I wouldn't rather have anyone else here with me tonight besides you two."

The women hugged, and Jake turned back to the group, finally including himself in their sentimental moment. They all looked at his white face and serious glance, thinking he was going to say something profound to Ella.

In a low, humorless voice, he said, "Catherine Zeta-Jones is standing right behind me. Nobody move."

Ella and John laughed while Kathleen shook her head at him with disapproval.

After six original song performances, a dozen awards presentations, a tribute to an actor that had passed away, and two bathroom trips, Kathleen thought her ankles were going to swell out of her shoes. The baby had been kicking for the past hour and a half, and despite the glorious night and incredible experience it all was, she was ready for Ella's category to be announced. She was thankful that they had at least been given an aisle seat so that she could get up as much as she pleased. She figured that Ella had had something to do with it.

Jake didn't seem phased by the long show. Then again, he didn't have a child doing gymnastics in his stomach, or a bladder the size of a chipmunk's. Every time someone would win an Oscar, he would whistle like a baseball fan, whether he had ever heard of the winner or not. After the first five, Kathleen figured he would become bored with it, but he seemed to still be having the time of his life.

"And now presenting the award for Best Director..." the announcer's voice boomed to the audience. He introduced someone that Kathleen was sure she was supposed to know, but didn't. She blamed it on the day job.

"Thank God," she whispered out loud, to no one in particular.

Jake turned to her, and said, "That miserable, huh?"

"I just want her to win already. Then I can go back to the house and get into my sweat pants."

He smiled at her while she faced the stage and bit her lip with anxiety.

"This is it," John said while he squeezed Ella's hand.

Ella didn't seem nervous. In fact, she appeared to be perfectly calm, and for a moment, John thought he would have to remind her that it was her category. He held her hand and didn't feel her fidgeting or shaking, and he knew that she would be at peace with whatever the outcome of the whole circus was.

The presenter was a male director who Ella had actually made a movie with in the days when she was a young actress. She knew that if she won, it would be an honor to receive the award from him, but Ella's mind was not on winning. She seemed to be in a tranquil zone that no one could touch. To the common observer, it looked like she was unimpressed and unaffected by the approaching announcement for Best Director. Inside, she was trying to remain calm.

Her heart was pounding, and the only thought that was able to rest in her head was, *Don't trip when you go up.*

The male director listed off each of the film names with their respective directors, one at a time, and Ella's name was read last.

"Ella Levene, for her work on the dramatic story of a boy whose mother leaves him to pursue a life in Las Vegas, in *Dangerous Intentions*," the director said. Everyone applauded, and she could hear Jake and Kathleen somewhere behind her, shouting with enthusiasm at her name.

So, this was the moment of truth that she had heard about her whole life, the moment when something big happens and its importance defines who the person is by what they had done. Ella had worked on *Dangerous Intentions* for two years, and its production all came down to this moment; an envelope would decide her fate, or so it seemed, and before she could convince herself otherwise, the presenter opened the envelope, looked at it with a smile, and said, "And the winner is… Ella Levene."

It is said that when someone wins an Oscar, all mental and physical capabilities slow down, and the only thing the winner can do is walk up to the podium and accept their award. When Ella heard her name, she shut her eyes and tried to comprehend what had just happened.

The first thought that entered her mind was, *No one likes me, why would they pick me?*

"You did it!" John was shouting, but it sounded like a voice echoing from another world. She heard a loud noise around her, and she assumed it was the applause, but it added to the confusion along with everyone patting her on the back and hugging her.

As Ella Levene slowly made her way to the stage, she saw familiar faces that she instinctively gave hugs to and smiled at. The loud noise kept ringing in her ears and she wasn't sure how she was reacting to the honor of it all. Out of all the times she had been drunk and in front of people at parties or on the set, she didn't feel more vulnerable than how she felt walking up to that stage. A million thoughts raced through her mind, though she had no physical control over any of them.

It's too hard to walk in these shoes.

Is my make-up smudged?

Does my hair still have its curl?

Where do I go?

All these people are clapping for me.

I just won.

Ella walked up the steps and was suddenly by herself on the stage, the loud noise now in front of her. The lights were shining down on her, and she was surprised by how hot they were on her face.

When she approached her former director, he handed her the golden Oscar, gave her a kiss on the cheek, and said in her ear, "Congratulations! They're eating out of the palm of your hand. The only really important job right now is to keep breathing."

Ella nodded with a smile and walked to the microphone. Everyone was clapping, but as soon as she opened her mouth to speak, the applause stopped and everyone sat down.

"Um," she mustered out nervously. She wanted to say so much, and thank so many people. The little statuette was heavy in her hands and she looked down at it like it was a stranger in her arms.

"I—I can't thank you enough for this incredible honor," she finally said, but all words after that left her head, and she was dumbstruck.

Lord, please use me as a tool in this place, she found herself praying.

A peaceful calm suddenly came over her and she looked at the audience for the first time. She smiled when she caught sight of Jake and Kathleen about twenty rows back, waving at her with beaming grins on their faces. She was happy they were there.

"There are so many people to thank for making this happen, but I really just want to thank everyone for not killing me during those years that I was so cold and empty."

A few people laughed, understanding because they had been the victims of her abuse.

"But," Ella continued while she stared down at the statuette, "there's only one person really responsible for this award and this movie, and that's God. He saved my life, He can save yours, too, and after so many years of waiting to hold this award in my hands, I can see that it doesn't change who I am. I thank you all for this incredible honor, but the greatest reward out of all this is knowing that I didn't actually need this little gold statue to see how wonderful life is and to understand what talents are actually working with me in this business. Have a wonderful evening, good night, and God bless."

She raised her statue in the air and everyone clapped while she left the stage. Some were clapping for the sentimental speech while others clapped with respect, not really appreciating anything she had just said. Most people were simply glad that she hadn't preached a fire and brimstone sermon, but either way, the woman had deserved her award, and whoever she chose to thank after winning an Oscar was her business.

Kathleen and Jake stood to their feet as she left the stage, clapping and shouting with pleasure. When they sat down, the couple next to them stared in shock at the two loud fans.

Jake saw that they were staring, and said, "We know Ella— personally."

"Whatever," the man said.

"Seriously," Jake said, but Kathleen put a gentle hand on his arm and shook her head, as if to say, *Don't argue with them. It's not worth it.*

Backstage, everyone congratulated Ella while she smiled brightly and thanked them with sincerity. She seemed genuinely happy, and anyone who had known her before, or had heard about how she used to be, nodded with approval while she walked to the room where there were journalists waiting to interview her.

A little platform was waiting with a microphone and she stepped up to it, holding her Oscar and laughing with bliss. The reporters began to fire away at her with questions.

"Ms. Levene," one woman said, "congratulations on your win. Why didn't you give a stereotypical speech by which you thank your family and people that work with you?"

Ella laughed, and said, "Well, I didn't realize my mind would go blank when I was up there, but I know that my husband understands how grateful I am to him, and he knows that I don't need to tell the whole world that I love him. For everyone else, I guess I'll just have to add their names to interviews during the next week."

"Ella," a man shouted from the back, "why did you pick this particular script when you knew it was a risk? It was the writer's first screenplay, you had a reputation for failing at dramas, and your record as a director up to that point was horrible—"

"Whoa! Slow down!" Ella waved at him with a laugh. Everyone else laughed, too, because the reporter was mercilessly grilling her at the peak of her euphoria. "First of all, thank you for the support—" Everyone laughed. "—and second, I was a different person when I got my hands on this script. My views about life had changed, my attitude was more positive, and I had decided to start putting my faith in God rather than myself. All the other movies I had directed up to that point were coming from hot air. As soon as I read the script for *Dangerous Intentions*, I knew that it had the potential to be a great film, so I decided to take a leap of faith and do it."

"What brought about the change, Ella?" a female reporter chimed in. The room went silent except for the clicking noise the cameras made. They waited for an answer.

"It was Jesus," Ella said with a smile. The room stirred a little, but she continued, "I know, it seems like a holy-roller remark, and I never thought that I would be one of those people to admit it, but every ounce of happiness within me should be blamed on Him. I stayed in an indigenous tribe with a missionary for two months a few years ago, my eyes were opened, and now I see that everything before I became a Christian was harder, and I don't know how I did it. It was a life that suffocated me, and pulled every ounce of energy from my emotional and physical body. It was like—"

Ella looked at her Oscar with a pause. It all became very clear after so many years, and she was finally able to understand what the dreams had been trying to tell her.

"Life before Jesus," she continued, "was like—running through deserts."

"Deserts?" a reporter asked, not understanding the analogy.

Ella glanced at her with a blank stare and said, "Yes, deserts. Hot, suffocating, sweltering deserts. Everything before I met the Lord was like running for my life through a terrible, endless desert, with no end in sight." She looked back down at her

Oscar, and smiled. "But I don't have to live that life ever again, and I blame it on God. And you should, too."

It had started raining while they were in the auditorium. When they all climbed into the limo, water dripped from the roof of the car and splashed onto the carpeted floor of the vehicle. Ella tried to cover her head to protect her hair-do, but Kathleen ignored the falling water and ended up drenched as she sat back in her seat.

The limo drove away from the auditorium and made its journey back to John and Ella's house, where the children were probably asleep in their beds. Even though the building had been packed with people, and Wilshire Boulevard was occasionally jammed with traffic, the streets were surprisingly empty. The green and red intersection lights reflected off the wet ground as the rain fell, making the streets look like a wild Christmas celebration.

The four occupants of the limo sat in silence, watching the streets and the rain bands as they lined the glass windows. John and Ella sat on one side of the limo with Jake and Kathleen facing them. None of them spoke, as the night had been very eventful and the adrenaline rush had finally subsided.

Kathleen sighed, and without turning away from the rainy window, said, "You know, I used to want to be an actress."

Ella replied, also staring out the window, "Well, you would have been horrible at it."

Jake and John turned to Ella with a smile, thinking she had cracked a joke, but her face remained serious. She continued to look outside at the rain. Kathleen looked across at her with an amused face and Ella turned to the pending group.

"Well," she finally explained, "you have to be a certain type of person in this business. John and I both know that you can't go through this industry and expect to become famous without compromising some sort of morals or promises you've made to yourself. I can't imagine *you* ever compromising anything having to do with morals or faith, Kathleen. You'd never make it in this business. I'm sorry, but in the same way I'm not made for the jungle, you were not made for Hollywood living."

Jake and John smiled with amusement, and Kathleen stared at the Oscar winner.

"You've done okay, though," she told Ella while nodding her head to the statuette in the seat.

"Yes, but it took a lot of yielding to get here—too many scars and hurts have come with this award, and if it were all I had to show for making it through, I'd be in big trouble."

"What else do you have to show?" John asked her.

Ella turned to him and smiled. "Well, besides the Oscar, my pain has brought me happiness. And strength, too. It's brought me my faith, my religion, and it gave me my family back. I wouldn't recommend having the scars that I possess, but I wouldn't trade them for anything. They are the things that have taught me how to be better."

Everyone nodded in agreement and Kathleen replied, "Well put."

The car continued to drive down the street in the rain, and the group silently rode with it, not talking anymore. After all, it had been a long night, and they were tired.

Conclusion

The clatter of pots and pans hitting the kitchen floor was what woke Ella up. When she opened her eyes, the bedroom was bright, but she could hear the rain outside her window and remembered how it had stormed the night before. The clock said nine, and she got out of bed and went to see what all the commotion was downstairs.

It was the morning after the Academy Awards, and she smiled when she remembered how much fun it had been. Her smile grew bigger when she remembered that the award hadn't met the expectations she'd had. They hadn't even come close to the award she had received after she'd accepted Christ. Even though the whole world knew that now, Ella was still glad she used the opportunity to tell a tiny bit of her story—the amazing Tanna trip a couple of years earlier.

When she walked by Freddy's room, the three children were playing with toys and giggling. Ella was glad that Epi was making friends with her two children; it added to the overwhelming joy of having her good friends there to visit. She walked down the stairs to the kitchen with the laughter of the children behind her.

Jake and John were standing in the kitchen, drinking cups of coffee and talking. They were still in their pajamas, but had obviously been awake for quite awhile. Jake smiled at Ella when she walked in, and John said, "There's the Best Director! Is it as fun the morning after?"

"Even more so," she smiled, and pecked her husband on the cheek with a kiss. She grabbed a cup of coffee and looked around the kitchen, searching for Kathleen.

"She's in that funky, glass room that you guys have," Jake said, reading Ella's thoughts.

"I'd like to think of it as a solarium," she smugly responded.

"Well, either way, it's a funky, glass room," Jake said in return. "She was up a lot of the night. The baby is kicking hard these days."

"It wants to come out," she told him.

Just then, Freddy bolted down the stairs in a frenzy.

"Mom! Sara just kissed Epi!" he tattled.

Ella's eyes widened with shock and she almost spit out her coffee.

"What?!" she laughed, wiping her mouth.

John shook his head, and said to Ella, "She's eight and it's already starting. I'll take care of this, hon."

"I'll join you," Jake chimed in, following John up the stairs. "You can have the 'Don't Kiss Boys' talk, and I'll give the 'Don't Kiss Back' speech. It'll be fun."

They left Ella in the kitchen, but she promptly headed to the notorious, glass room. It had been built to extend off the living room and into the backyard. There were padded lawn chairs in it, and it was a nice place to relax. When she walked in, she saw Kathleen lounging in one of the chairs, apparently sleeping.

When Ella laid down in the lawn chair next to her, propping her legs up and breathing a deep sigh, Kathleen opened her eyes and smiled.

"Hi," she said sleepily.

"Good morning. How'd you sleep last night?" Ella asked.

Kathleen shrugged her shoulders. She was lying on her side with a pillow under her big stomach. She wasn't moving, and her eyes were bloodshot. It looked like it had been a hard night.

"I didn't sleep that much," she replied, her voice sounding like she was a bit congested. "Not only is this guy kicking, but he's kicking my bladder. I was up at every hour. I kept waking Jake up, so at about five this morning I just decided to lay down in here."

"You said 'he.' Do you know it's going to be a boy?"

"Yeah, that's what the doctor in Seattle told us."

Ella laughed. "A family of boys. You poor thing. Have you picked out a name?"

"Yes. We're going to name him Samuel. Samuel Jacob."

Ella gave a sympathetic grin, and asked, "After your brother?"

Kathleen gave a slight smile, and then said, "I have a favor to ask."

"Anything," Ella said.

"You can decline if it'll be a huge inconvenience, but I was wondering if we could stay with you until the baby comes, and then Jake and I will travel back to Seattle to be with his parents until it's old enough to go back to Tanna. I just don't know if I'll be able to fly back to Washington this week. I'm really dragging."

Ella was honored. "Of course you can stay. I'll be on the set most of the days, but I'm sure you guys will be able to find things to do. And we'll make sure Cedar Sinai gives you the best room after you've delivered."

Kathleen smiled again, adding, "That'll be a sight for sore eyes. Me—in labor."

"Yeah," Ella agreed. "You thought that the sprained ankle was painful. Just make sure you don't forget to ask for the epidural."

"Got it," Kathleen replied.

She closed her eyes again and listened to the rain hit the glass room. It hit the ceiling above them and Ella could see the drops run across the glass walls to the base where a tiny puddle was forming in the back yard. It was a gentle rain, and it made her a little tired, too.

Just before Ella thought she might want to also take a snooze, Kathleen opened her eyes again, and said, "I never expected it to be like this."

"For what to be like this?"

"Life," Kathleen responded, looking out at the yard in the rain. "I mean, I know that there is a plan for us all, but I never thought that I would've ended up here. If you'd told me in college that in ten years I'd be a missionary on an island in Vanuatu, with an eight-year-old Tannese son, married to Jake Willis, pregnant, and staying at Ella Levene's house so that I could go to the Academy Awards, I would have thought it'd make a good story for a book. It just doesn't seem fair to have this many blessings."

"I think most people have that many blessings," Ella responded. "They just don't see them as blessings. I didn't realize what I had until I became a Christian. I saw that I had things—material possessions, a family, a great career—but they weren't considered blessings until I felt the love that Jesus gives."

Kathleen asked, "When did you know it was real? When you saw the rock in the jungle?"

"Yes, that was when I knew *God* was real, but I didn't know everything would be okay until after I jumped off the cliff, at the gorge. After I had that dream about Jesus, I woke up and wondered if it had been real. When I got an answer back, I knew that things were different.

"My whole life, I've lived in the dark, by myself. I thought that everything was up to me, and that whatever happened in my life would lead to me consoling myself, and trying to figure things out alone. After I had that last dream where I was in the desert, and it lead to Jesus, I finally heard a voice that told me that I wasn't alone. Everything I am, and everything I know tells me that that voice was real, and that Jesus is the Way, the Truth, and the Life, and that's because I never heard anything before I met Him. I was empty, and searching, and afraid.

"The day I met Jesus was the day that all the puzzle pieces of my life were finally put together, and I could see why things had happened to me. There is a reason for everything, and I know that now. It became real when I was crying at the gorge after I'd thought there were no more tears left in me. It was real when I saw how He'd chosen the perfect time for me to find Him, while I was out there with you. It was real when I felt like coming back here, and sharing that same love with my family—a love that I never imagined I'd be able to give.

"We're both sitting in this place, Kathleen, where the rain is hitting the roof, and our husbands are upstairs talking to our children. I have the benefit of knowing that we will all be in Heaven together someday, and that until then, I have good friends in you three. I know that you never would have expected to be where you are now, but I can honestly say that my situation is much more extreme. I'm alive, I'm sober, and I can't wait to go to my daughter's Spring Pageant this Friday. I think that the lesson we've both been taught through all this is that it's impossible to predict the future, and every time we try, something else will change. I'm just glad that my future is in the Lord's hands, because then I know that no matter what happens, everything will be all right."

Printed in the United States
35096LVS00004B/49-258

9 781413 766202